Indentured Hearts

HANNAH MEREDITH

SPS

Singing Spring Press

This is a work of fiction. All names, characters, and incidents are the product of the author's imagination. Any resemblance to actual occurrences or persons, living or dead, is coincidental. Historical events and personages are fictionalized.

INDENTURED HEARTS

ISBN: 978-0-9895641-4-4 (Print)
ISBN: 978-0-9895641-5-1 (E-book)

Published by Singing Spring Press

For Barbara
I got lucky with the
genetic lottery.
If you weren't my sister,
you'd be my friend.

Prologue

London
June 1755

L ady Cassandra Spathe braced her hands against the desk and lowered her head between her outstretched arms. The sour taste of nausea pooled at the back of her tongue. Swallowing hard, she straightened and turned to face her father.

"I'll not have him," she said.

"Oh, you'll have him." Edward Spathe, Earl of Chelle, calmly adjusted the lace at his cuffs. "The marriage contracts are signed. Lord Tilton will take you without a dowry and he'll pay off the loans on Mount Clare, so you will most definitely have him. I didn't spend a fortune outfitting you in finery to see you marry one of those feckless younger sons who've been buzzing around you. None of them have a pence in their pocket, while Tilton most definitely does. You knew your duty before we came to town. Agreed to it, as I recall. The season is over. So now you can make good on your agreement."

"Baron Tilton is a pig." Cassy hugged herself as if warding off a chill. "He makes my skin crawl."

Her father's smile was not kind. "I've no doubt he'll make you crawl, but the overly high opinion you have of your own worth could stand some lowering. I shouldn't have left you to be raised by your Aunt Amelia. Your mother's family has long thought they were too good for the rest of us."

"You left me with my mother's kin because I didn't cost you anything while I was there." Anger at the injustices in her life curled within her. "But then I grew up, and you decided I could be an asset instead of a liability."

"And I can dispose of my assets as I see fit. You'll marry Lord Tilton. The man's come to call and I've given him permission to woo you. Whether the wooing is gentle or rough is up to you, but you will agree to be his wife. That's the end of it. I'm off to my club."

Her father swiveled on his heel and exited before she could say more. Lord Tilton's bulk immediately filled the doorframe. With an oily smile, he closed the door, locked it, and slipped the key into his pocket. Turning to where Cassy stood frozen across the room, he said, "Hello, my dear Lady Cassandra. I understand you're not enthusiastic about our nuptials. I'm here to convince you otherwise."

"I will not marry you." Her voice was more breathless than she would have liked, but the words still rang with conviction.

"Of course you will." His smile pulled up the corners of his thick lips, but the expression didn't reach his dark eyes. They remained as flat and opaque as those of a dead fish. "I've paid a great deal to have you grace my arm and my bed. The first will give me status, and the second," he shrugged, "well, I've wanted to tup you since I first saw you, but your father wouldn't let you go for anything less than a ring."

"How noble of my father."

"Sarcasm is not wit," he said with the gravity of a tutor. "Say yes and we will be married in July with all the pomp you young girls love."

"The answer is no!"

Cassy wouldn't have believed a man of Lord Tilton's girth could move so fast. In the blink of an eye, he was right in front of her, crowding her back against the desk. How had she let herself get trapped in this manner? Stupid, stupid. She raised her hands and pushed against his chest. Heavens, the man had breasts. Her hands popped back as if she'd touched a boiling pot. An odor of stale sweat and unclean linen swirled around him.

"There are two ways to tame a fractious horse," he said, leaning into her. "With soft words or with spurs. I've personally always favored the spurs."

He grabbed the neckline of her dress, jerking it forward and down. The tight stitches she herself had sewn held and she was pulled against him. Then there was a ripping sound; she was able to put some space between them, only to be horrified when he squeezed one of her now exposed breasts.

She hit him, the slap loud in the small room. And then she screamed, a shrill and piercing sound, an echo of the fear coursing through her.

She never imagined he would hit her back. Not even her useless father had ever raised a hand to her. The fisted blow therefore came as a surprise, knocking her head back, catching her tongue between her teeth and filling her mouth with blood.

For a moment nothing was in focus. She floated in a gray space, without concern or direction. When clarity returned, she was splayed across her father's desk, the various items that littered the top now scattered around her or stabbing her in the back. Tilton had both of her hands gathered into one of his, with her arms stretched above her head. Her lower body was trapped against the desk by his bulk. He ground his pelvis against her.

She tried to scream again and Tilton stuffed her own lace neckerchief into her open mouth. She gagged and whipped her head from side to side, but he continued to push in more material. He outweighed her by more than ten stone and no amount of wiggling or bucking could dislodge him.

"The servants have been dismissed, but persistent caterwauling might bring someone to pound on the door," Tilton said almost conversationally. The wig he wore was crooked. He would have looked amusing had he not been so horrifying. "Too bad. It's such a waste of your lovely mouth. But it does give me some idea of how you'll look when I teach you to suck my cock." He smiled and for once his eyes did not look dead.

"For now, your pretty tits are begging for my attention." He laughed and lowered his lips to one of her breasts. His mouth was wet and hot and horrible, but there seemed to be no way to escape it. He suckled her, his teeth nipping at her sensitive tip. "Ah, see how your nipple has tightened. You like this, don't you Cassy girl? I'd guessed you'd like a hard ride."

He transferred his attention to her other breast, sucking and smacking his lips like a pig at a trough. Cassy thrashed about, making muted keening noises. With his free hand, he pulled up the bottom of her skirts and soft-hooped petticoat. He inserted a knee between hers and with a grunt forced them apart until both his legs stood between hers. She felt his hand on her bare thigh and struggled harder. This was a nightmare beyond all imagining.

He moved his hand to the junction of her thighs, squeezing and stroking her. Never had anyone touched her there. She fought for breath, her tears causing her nose to fill, the material obstructing her mouth. She would die. She was sure of it.

Tilton leaned forward and again sucked one of her breasts into his mouth. He released her imprisoned hands and painfully squeezed the other nipple tightly between his soft, damp fingers.

Cassy frantically tried to push him away. One of her questing hands closed on the ivory handle of her father's quill knife. She stabbed at his head, feeling the small blade slide though his wig and go into his scalp. Tilton jerked his head up and she stabbed again, hitting his eyebrow. As if in a dream, she watched the blade slide down and sink into his left eye.

Tilton uttered a strange, high-pitched shriek, fell back onto his rear, and then flopped prone on the floor. Cassy scrambled off the desk, jerking the fabric from her mouth just in time to empty the contents of her stomach onto the rug. When she stopped retching, she looked at Lord Tilton. He lay where he'd fallen, his arms and legs jerking convulsively. The knife protruded from an oozing socket. His other eye was rolled up into his head. His mouth continued to move in a disjointed sucking motion.

Dear God, she'd killed him. She'd killed a peer in her father's study. Panic beat through her, burning like a swallow of scalding tea. She grasped the edges of her ruined gown and dashed to the door. Locked. She returned to Tilton's stilling body and gingerly reached into his coat pocket to retrieve the key. When she was again at the door, her hands shook so badly that she had trouble finding the keyhole. Once the door was open, she dashed into the hall. As Tilton had said, it was vacant of the usual footmen and staff.

Cassy sprinted up the two flights of stairs to her bedchamber. Her only thought was to reach this illusion of safety. She staggered through the door at the same time Peg, her maid, walked in from the dressing room.

Peg dropped the gown she was holding and hurried toward Cassy. "Oh, milady, what has happened?" She enfolded Cassy in her warm embrace and all the horror of the last half hour burst out in great, hiccupping sobs.

"I killed him," Cassy gasped into Peg's soft shoulder.

"Killed who?"

"Lord Tilton. He attacked me, ripping my dress, and, and..." Sobs again shook her.

"Oh, my dear. We need to get one of the footmen to run for the magistrate. Where's your father? The butler?"

Peg loosened her hold on Cassy as if she intended to move to the door. "No," Cassy yelled, clutching her maid tightly. "The servants aren't about. They were dismissed by Father. He intended this to happen. He insisted I marry Lord Tilton."

"Merciful God, do not say such!" Peg hugged her again.

"It's true and I killed him. I killed a peer and if the magistrate comes, I'll hang." Cassy was suddenly the one to break free. She hurried toward the dressing room, the torn edges of her bodice flapping. Sweet heavens, she could be executed. The necessity to hide, to flee, burned through her.

"I have to change clothes. I have to leave."

Peg caught hold of her and forced her into her dressing chair. "Sit. Be calm. Think." Peg sounded like she always did, issuing orders and pulling Cassy back from whatever cliff she was about to leap from. How could Peg sound so normal when the entire world had gone mad? Her maid had been providing sympathy and advice since Cassy was a young girl. Peg was the closest thing to a mother Cassy knew.

"Are you sure he's dead?"

"He was twitching, but I'd put a knife through his eye."

"That'd do it. And you're right. We need to leave." Peg released Cassy's arms and moved back toward the dressing room.

"*I* need to leave," Cassy said.

"It will have to be both of us and you know it," Peg said. "Where did you think to go? Your Aunt Amelia's?"

"Heavens, no!" Her father had been right when he said her mother's family had always felt superior to any of the Spathes, and that included Cassy. Growing up under Aunt Amelia's thumb had not been pleasant. Her aunt would probably turn Cassy over to the authorities just to prove that corruption was rampant in the Spathe line.

"I suspected not," Peg said. "Then where?"

Far, far away, Cassy thought, and the word "America" burst out almost without thought. "Massachusetts, in the American colonies. Lieutenant Michaels is now stationed in Boston. He'll know how to help us make a new life there."

She remembered Gilbert Michaels with affection. He'd been dashing in his uniform, a slender blade of a man with curly blond hair and an infectious smile. He'd kissed her in

Templeton's summerhouse, a soft meeting of lips, nothing like this recent abomination. Cassy shivered.

Peg gave her a considering look. "That's not an altogether bad idea. I thought Lieutenant Michaels seemed to be a fine man."

"But we have no way to pay for a long sea voyage." Cassy gritted her teeth. Money. It always came back to the lack of money. "All my jewelry is paste, except for Mother's locket, and I don't think it would bring enough to pay for two passages. If we had time to sell the clothes we've remade..."

"We haven't the time," Peg said. "But there's a way to do this. Cook's sister got free passage to America by selling her labor for the period of time that would cover the expense of the journey."

Pieces seemed to be falling into place and hope shown through the darkness. "When we get to America, we'll contact Lieutenant Michaels and he'll pay the ship's fee. I'm sure he will. We can pay him back a little at a time." Cassy wasn't sure exactly how she'd accomplish this. Spathes seemed more adept at losing money than making it, but she was confident she could do something. At the worst, she could be a companion or a governess. It didn't sound like much of a life, but how long could it take to pay back the price of their passage?

"Where do these special ships leave from?" Cassy asked.

"Bristol. At least, Cook's sister left from there."

Relief weakened her knees. Bristol was doable. Cassy was sure there were a couple of her mother's silver forks her father hadn't sold. She'd use them to pay their way to Bristol and she'd escape the hangman's noose. She'd be free, truly free, for the first time in her life.

Then all was motion and hurry. When she and Peg slipped out of the back of the house clutching their valises, Cassy felt almost happy. She was taking her life into her own hands. Adventure waited. Even with the horror she'd experienced, everything would turn out fine. Nothing bad would ever happen to her again.

Chapter One

York, Virginia
August 1755

$\mathcal{T}$ he women pushed and shoved as they shuffled along the ship's passageway. Some laughed and joked, but the majority were silent. The hideous voyage was finally over. The unknown lay beyond the bright square of light coming through the hatch.

Lady Cassandra Spathe was one of the silent ones. She held herself upright only by force of will. Dear God, could she finally be done with this nightmare? As she stepped onto the deck of the *Agatha Jane*, the sun blinded her. She unconsciously put a hand on the woman in front of her, following wherever she led.

"Women to the right," a crewman yelled at the group emerging from the hold. "Form a single line." A hand roughly grasped Cassy's arm and shoved her back a few steps. She retained her balance only with difficulty. "Single line, ya stupid jade."

The deck burned her bare feet, but she resisted the urge to move them around, not wanting to draw the crewman's attention again. The past six weeks had taught her the wisdom of remaining as invisible as possible. She wiped her watering eyes and squinted around her.

The refuse from the holds had assembled on the deck. The men formed a line directly across from the women. Some stood proudly. Some appeared as beaten as Cassy felt. She had always thought of herself as a daring risk-taker. Now she was defeated.

She took a deep breath of untainted air. It smelled of salt and fish and rotting seaweed. After the stench of the dank hold where eighteen unwashed women had been closely confined for nearly two months, no perfume had ever been more alluring.

"Not a very promising-looking group this time." A bewigged man walked the deck with Captain Haslett, surveying the men and women assembled. The man, evidently one of the planters come to buy laborers, was a prancing peacock in a bright blue suit with ruffles at his neck. The gold top of his walking stick flashed in the sun.

"It was a hard voyage, Sir Peyton," Captain Haslett said. "We lost eight of them, one free-willer and seven convicts."

"Cuts into your profits when that happens, doesn't it?" The planter sounded pleased with this misfortune. "And the prices you've got on them—ridiculous."

"Fair prices," the captain said. "I've some skilled workers and strong men in this group."

The planter made a derisive grunt. "You've got convicts and the desperate scum of London. No need to try to make clods of earth sound like jewels."

He strolled along the line of men, asking a few of the larger laborers to step forward. Then he walked by the women. He stopped next to Cassy, but he was interested in the big gap-toothed whore standing to her left. Tess. One of the bigger bullies in the women's hold. Cassy was sure Tess had her wide feet stuffed into Cassy's missing shoes. She hoped they pinched.

The planter picked up the piece of parchment hanging on a cord around Tess's neck. In the process, he rubbed his knuckles over the woman's ample breasts. Tess grinned widely.

"Cook?" he asked, fondling the parchment and what it rested on.

Cassy had a similar tag attached. Unlike most of the women, however, Cassy had been able to read hers. It said, *Cassy Spade, seamstress. Four years. Nine pounds.*

"I cook plain, but fast." The big woman rubbed against the planter's hand like a cat looking for food.

"Step forward," he said and continued on down the line. Tess turned back and gave Cassy a satisfied smirk.

Other prospective buyers looking for indentured servants crossed the gangplank and wandered the deck. One woman professed to be looking for a lady's maid and loudly proclaimed the entire group unsuitable. Had the heat not bludgeoned away the last of Cassy's reserves, she could have applied for that position, but she stood mute, swaying on her feet.

When she and Peg had blithely signed their articles of indenture, they'd been asked for a skill to make their labor more saleable. Peg had said she was a lady's maid, since that was what she was. Cassy, realizing that dancing, riding, and conversation weren't what was desired, had said she was a seamstress. Since her father had provided only the most basic wardrobe, she and Peg had haunted the secondhand stores, remaking fancy gowns so not even their previous owners could recognize them when Cassy wore them. If there was one thing Cassy could do, it was sew.

An ever-present, dull pain of loss pierced her. How hopeful she and Peg had been at the beginning of this cursed voyage. The trip to Bristol had been uneventful, and there was no indication of pursuit. Their escape to the American colonies was going to be successful. They didn't even have to pay for their passage. And once they'd arrived in America, she'd contact the charming Lieutenant Michaels, he'd pay off their indenture, and life would be rosy.

Nothing in her nineteen years as Lady Cassandra Spathe had prepared her for the reality. Once the hatch had closed, she and Peg had been imprisoned with the dregs of the London stews. Over half of the women were being transported for theft. The rest seemed to be prostitutes going to the New World in search of either new customers or a better life. Fights frequently broke out, filled with hair-pulling, scratching, and shrieking. She and Peg tried to stay away from the rest, a task made easier by Cassy's persistent seasickness. No one wanted to be near Cassy when she might spew at any moment.

Mal de mer had felled her before land was out of sight. Many others were similarly afflicted, but most recovered. Cassy never really had. Peg had taken care of her, as she always had. Then some illness had struck Peg, and in a matter of days, a horrific fever had burned her life away.

Watching the body of her friend, her only stability in a chaotic life, slide into the water had left Cassy without hope. She'd retreated to her narrow bunk and prayed that death would also take her.

Now, bereft and abandoned, Cassy couldn't even attract someone to buy her labor. The lady once compared to a Dresden figurine in London ballrooms had fallen very low indeed.

Her semi-comatose musings were interrupted by Captain Haslett's loud call. "Mr. Anders. I've been expecting you." He raised a hand in greeting to a man coming up the gangplank.

The new arrival crossed the deck and pumped Captain Haslett's hand. Haslett greeted him more as a friend than as a customer. Anders, the captain had called him. He looked different from the other planters, bigger, harder. He wore his own coffee-colored hair clubbed back, emphasizing the sharp jut of his nose.

"I've kept the men I thought you'd want below decks. I'll have them brought up," the captain said. He turned and nodded to one of the waiting seamen.

Mr. Anders raised a skeptical eyebrow. "You kept them below because you figured they'd cause trouble otherwise."

Haslett shrugged and grinned, but he made no reply. The sound of clanking chains brought both men's eyes to four transported prisoners being herded onto the deck. They were large men, now uniformly thin, their loose clothing indicating that all had previously carried more bulk. "Fourteen years indenture each, compliments of His Majesty's government," Haslett said, "and for you, bargain priced."

The newcomer nodded and left the captain to walk to where the convicts stood. He carried on a low-voiced conversation with the men, then returned to the captain. "Ten pounds each," he said.

"Bloody hell, Anders, it's fourteen years' labor. That's good for at least twelve a piece."

"Ten, and I'm overpaying at that," Anders said. "We both know you save the most dangerous convicts for me. They're all bound to either run or cause trouble once they get their strength back. If you sold them to any of your other buyers, they'd be clamoring for their money back the next time you docked here in York. Take the ten."

"Done," the captain said, again grasping Anders' hand. "Now, do you have any particular skills you're needing? I've still got a mason left."

Anders shook his head, grinning as if he'd heard the captain's sales pitch a dozen times.

Haslett threw a hand in Cassy's general direction. "How about a seamstress? I've a fine seamstress, a free-willer, who's going begging. I can make you a good price."

Anders smile widened. "Actually, I might be able to use a seamstress. Mavis has been complaining that I keep adding crew for her to clothe and she doesn't have enough help."

The two men approached and stared at Cassy in silence. She wanted to grab the big man's hands and beg, *Please, please*, but the words stuck in her dry mouth. She'd do almost anything to avoid going back in the hold and traveling on to another port.

"Not much to her," Anders finally said. He stood directly in front of Cassy, catching her in his shadow, allowing her to look up into his dark, shrewd eyes.

"Well, she puked her way across the Atlantic. We had rough weather and a hold full of poor sailors." Haslett's voice came from the brightness behind Mr. Anders.

"You sew well, girl?" The man towered over her.

Cassy managed to croak out, "Yes, sir. I can cut patterns as well."

"Let me see your hands."

Cassy extended her hands and watched them disappear into the man's much larger ones. He rubbed his thumbs along her palms and the sides of her fingers, a surprisingly sensual movement. "You don't have calluses from working a needle. If you've been sewing, it hasn't been often." He suddenly grabbed her chin and turned her head from side to side. "You some man's discarded dolly-mop? You're not breeding, are you? That'll cause you to lose your meals."

Anger spiked, overcoming her debilitating lethargy and stiffening her spine. Cassy forgot who she was, or, at least, who she had recently become. How dare this colonial oaf speak to Lady Cassandra Spathe in such a manner? She glared into the man's eyes. "My fancy work is exceptional. My seams are invisible and tight. I don't need bought patterns to put together the most elaborate designs. And I assure you that I have never been any man's mistress, so there is no fear of my 'breeding,' as you so vulgarly put it."

The big man glared back at her and Cassy felt panic curl in her gut. Dear Lord, she'd destroyed her chance to get off this cursed ship, to breathe untainted air and eat something other than hard biscuits and stale water. She'd just compounded the biggest error she'd ever made, and it could be the death of her.

Then Anders threw back his head and laughed. The sound rolled over her like distant thunder, surprising the gulls that were perched in the rigging and sending them shrieking into the air. Still grinning, he said, "I'll take her for four pounds, and that's only because I think she has enough spirit to not up and die on me. From the way she looks, I wasn't sure she'd live to make it to the Bloomery, and from the way she smells, I thought she might already be rotting."

Anders laughed again, leaving Cassy to stare down at her bare feet, chagrinned. He was right. The odor of her unwashed body had intensified as she stood and sweated in the sweltering heat. A strong, feral smell wafted up from the neck of her filthy dress.

And then she smiled. The foolish man had asked if she were a discarded mistress. What a laughable question. If she'd been willing to sell herself, albeit in marriage, she wouldn't be here. She had no mirror, but she could imagine how she looked. Her dress hung from a skeletal frame; the neckline, once supported by breasts poets had lauded, now sagged. Her fair hair fell in a greasy mass down her back. What man would want her for a mistress? She couldn't even compete with the common trollops who had made up the bulk of this shipment of indentured women.

"Come along, girl," Mr. Anders said, giving her a slight push in the back to propel her toward the gangway. She'd been sold, or at least four years of her labor had been sold, and she'd missed the eventual price. Cassy had never imagined her worth could be measured in just a few pounds. Lord Tilton had offered her father a fortune by comparison. But then, Lord Tilton had paid a great deal more than money. The ivory handle of the knife protruding from his ruined eye returned vividly to her mind. She shuddered, then drew back her shoulders and stepped forward.

The lowering sun had baked the deck to an inferno. Cassy tried to hop from foot to foot as she made her way across the planking, sucking in her breath to keep from crying out.

"Bloody hell," Anders said, picking her up like a child, cradling her against his chest and carrying her with his long-legged stride off the ship and down the pier to a waiting wagon. Her face pressed into his neck, which smelled of clean linen and warm male. Cassy inhaled deeply, becoming almost lightheaded from the wonderful, nearly forgotten fragrance.

She was unceremoniously plopped onto the bench seat at the front of a wagon. The four convicts clambered into the rear. The men were a silent presence at her back. The only sound was the click and scrape of their shackles on the wagon bed.

Mr. Anders mounted a rangy bay while a small-boned, elfin-looking man in a ridiculously large hat swung onto the bench next to her and gathered up the reins. The wagon wandered through a bustling area of wharves and warehouses, then climbed a bluff to the main street of a substantial English-looking village. Well-kept homes were scattered among taverns and shops. The streets were crowded with late afternoon traffic. Many people stopped to stare as the wagon passed. Cassy hoped the gawkers were most interested in the convicts who crouched in the back.

Mr. Anders wove his way through the throng ahead of them. He rode competently, but without the grace he'd exhibited when walking. Nonetheless, he was soon lost from sight.

As they left the town of York, the road narrowed to a single track hedged in by towering trees. The air cooled and the smell of the sea was replaced by the haunting fragrance of the pines. Slanting rays of sunshine came and went on the road in front of them. Cassy found her head nodding toward her chest.

The loud voice of the driver pulled her back from the edge of sleep. "You in the back," the elfin man said in a remarkably low-pitched voice, "give thanks to God that yer goin' to Anders' Bloomery instead of sweatin' yer life away ina tobaccy field. But know that iffen you misbehave, you'll get sold off quicker 'n grease goes through a goose."

He swiveled to look at her. "An you miz, you mus' be one of those stupid free-willers, so what're you supposed to do?"

Cassy agreed that signing an indenture contract of her own free will had indeed been stupid, but felt no need to comment on that. "I sew," she simply said.

"That's good news." The little man nodded happily. "Maybe you ken make me some breeches that ain't so big. Mavis thinks we're all one size. I'm Hats, by the way." He pointed to the oversized tricorn sitting on his head and smiled, showing surprisingly fine, white teeth.

"Call me Cassy," she said.

"Cassy." He nodded again and then, turning his attention back to his horses, he ignored her. She had no idea how to continue a conversation with such a person. Remarking on his ability to handle the team seemed inappropriate for someone in her present station. A myriad of questions about where they were going surged through her mind, but she couldn't figure how to ask them. Cassy fell as silent as the sullen men in the rear.

Finally, they turned through a set of elaborate stone gateposts. "Anders' Bloomery," Hats announced, throwing his arm wide like a showman.

All Cassy could see were cleared fields and stands of tall pines. "Do you grow flowers here?" It seemed like an odd type of enterprise, but she really knew nothing about the colonies. It wasn't until they were well on their way that she'd discovered the *Agatha Jane* wasn't headed anywhere near the Massachusetts Colony, which was as distant from Virginia as the wilds of Scotland were from London.

"Flowers? Why'd we grow flowers?" Hats' face expressed his confusion.

"Well, you called it a bloomery and I thought—I'm not sure what I thought, but flowers seemed logical."

The little man began laughing. He'd mutter "flowers" occasionally and the word would set him off again. Finally he straightened, wiping his watering eyes. "A bloomery's an iron works. Mr. Anders is one of the biggest iron smelters in the colonies. We got huge furnaces. We got water-powered bellows. We're even puttin' together a new kinda furnace. We make iron blooms, but we ain't got no flowers."

"Oh, I see," Cassy said, even though she didn't. She'd never considered that anyone would actually *make* iron.

They continued to follow a well-tended lane past a wide assortment of buildings. Hats stopped in front of a large, open-sided barn. A strong, metallic tang lay heavy on the air.

"This is the forge and where ya git off, gents," Hats called to the men in the back. The convicts hesitated, swiveling their heads from side to side in confusion.

"We're to be blacksmiths, then?" one of the men asked.

"Somethen like that. But first I figerd you'd want them shackles off. Jus go through the door and it'll happen."

Looking disoriented, the men got out and shuffled their way to the door.

"Shouldn't someone watch them?" Cassy asked. There must have been some reason these men were restrained.

The little man clucked to the horses and got them moving again. "Where they gonna go with all that iron on?" Then he chuckled. "Besides, someone is watchin 'em. Anders don't pay good money for workers to let 'em walk off into the woods. The boss is fair, but he ain't no charity. You work yer time with a good will and yer freedom dues'll include fifty acres like it ought. Anders don't cheat. That acreage'll give most a decent start. Iffen you don't want the land, you can sell it and start whatever business you fancy."

He pivoted to look her directly in the face. "What business do you dream of, Cassy?"

Good heavens, she'd never dreamed of any business. No Spathe had ever fallen into trade. Maybe that was one of the reasons she'd ended up here. "A dress shop," she said, hoping that sounded realistic.

"Good choice. You could end up one of the richest women in York."

During their conversation, they'd driven behind a large, white clapboard house. It stood in the middle of a swath of lawn, but it looked forlorn and unfinished without any trees or gardens around it. They stopped in front of a small building made from the same white clapboard. "This here's where you get off," Hats said.

Instead of offering to help her down, he yelled loudly, "Mavis? Gotcha a new one."

A portly woman with wildly curling gray hair popped out of a smaller dwelling attached to the big house and hurried toward them. As she drew near, she eyed Cassy with distaste. "What in the world is Jase thinking?" she asked the driver, who did nothing more than shrug his shoulders.

"Well, get down, girl," she said. "Why ever you're here, the first thing is to get you washed. I don't want any bilge scum or fleas in my house."

She frowned as Cassy climbed awkwardly from the wagon. "What's she supposed to do?" she asked the driver.

"Seamstress."

Mavis's face relaxed into what was almost a smile. "Seamstress. If she don't keel over where she stands, she might be useful. She got any belongings?"

Hats again just shrugged.

"I had luggage." Cassy suddenly remembered the hastily packed bag she'd brought with her to the ship. Any thought of it had disappeared in the chaos of the voyage. Its loss now pierced her.

"Well, you don't have it now. We'll have to find something of the other girls for you to wear until you can make something up. These rags you've got on are good only for burning." She started to walk away. "Well, come on."

Cassy followed her into a washhouse where two large wash vats sat on the flagged floor. The room smelled of harsh soap and cleanliness. The odor was wonderful.

"You're lucky. The girls washed some of the men's clothes today and we still have hot water. Shuck out of those clothes and we'll get one of these vats filled enough for a good bath." Mavis walked back to the door and yelled, "Ellie, Bess."

Cassy thought of the silent footman in her father's home. Here, the method of communication was bellowing. She was definitely a long way from civilization.

"Come on, girl," Mavis said. "Get those clothes off before the fleas on them over-run the place. But give me your sale tag so I can enter you in the Bloomery's books." She held out her hand.

Cassy slipped the thong over her head and gave the piece of parchment to Mavis. "Cassy Spade," Mavis read, then looked up quickly, eyes wide. "Sweet Jesus, please tell me Jase didn't pay nine pounds."

"He offered four." Cassy's hands trembled as she worked the laces at the front of her dress. She'd always bathed with a maid in attendance, but this was different. This was a common washhouse with the late afternoon sun slanting through the windows and the door open to all. As if her thoughts had conjured them, two women walked in, one angular and rawboned, the other round and cherubic.

"Ellie," Mavis said, pointing to the taller of the two, "and Bess," she pointed to the rounder one, "meet Cassy. Cassy is in great need of a bath. She's also a seamstress."

The last word brought grins from both women and they hurried to draw water from a big iron pot on the hearth. "Does this mean I can stop sticking needles in my fingers and pretending to sew?" Bess asked.

"Yes, that's what it means," Mavis said. "And I'm assuming you want her cleaned up some before she shares one of your beds."

Both of the women began filling a tub with diligence, smiling all the while. Cassy slowly slipped off her dress, embarrassed that she wasn't wearing stays. Her stays had been removed during her illness and had disappeared along with her shoes. No one seemed to notice. She finally stood in her shift and watched the water level in the vat increase.

Mavis peered over the side of the tub. "That looks like enough. She's a scrawny little thing." Turning to Cassy, she said, "Get rid of that rag and get in."

Hiding her embarrassment, Cassy pulled her shift over her head.

"Is she really a seamstress?" Bess asked.

"Yes." Cassy and Mavis answered simultaneously.

"Then she deserves something special." Bess crumbled something over the washtub and the air was filled with the scent of lavender.

Cassy stepped over the edge and folded herself into the tub. The warm water lapping around her was heavenly.

"Do you want to soak for a while?" Mavis asked.

"Yes," Cassy croaked. Her eyes were already closing. Behind her heavy lids, life continued on as it had always been. She would meet a handsome man at the upcoming ball and he'd love her and marry her and they'd have a houseful of children and she'd never be alone again and…

"Wash your hair before you leave," Mavis said, interrupting Cassy's pleasant dream. Then she and the two women walked to the door.

"My God, you can count her ribs, and her bubbles are smaller than mine," Ellie said in a loud whisper as they left.

Cassy didn't care what they said about her. Fragrant steam rose around her face and her sore muscles relaxed in the warm water. She'd lost something of herself in these past miserable months, but in this place, she might find that integral part again. With luck, she had come to journey's end. Maybe here she could be safe.

Chapter Two

*J*ason Anders sipped the Madeira and tried to convince himself he liked the cloying taste of this sweet wine.

"With a bit more practice, you can drink the proper liquor without grimacing." Mavis gave a deep, throaty laugh, as thick and sweet as molasses. For a brief moment, Jason could see the beauty that had captivated most of London three decades earlier. Now the hair that peeked from her mobcap was liberally sprinkled with white and the shape of her chin was lost in soft roundness, but the sparkling eyes and the contagious laugh were still there.

"You're sure this is all that I'll be offered? I see you're sensibly drinking rum."

"Madeira is what you should *ask* for. It's what gentlemen drink. If you're going to play at being a gentleman, then Madeira it is. Old women are allowed to drink whatever they want." The throaty laugh again circled the room like smoke on a damp day.

"I bow to your greater knowledge," Jason said, confident the information was correct. In her youth, Mavis had been an actress, and she'd known a number of true gentlemen intimately. Before time had completely diminished her demand, she'd immigrated to Virginia with her savings in hand and had started her own enterprise in York, The Blue Heron, which catered to the sexual desires of the colonial version of gentlemen.

It had been a lucky day when he'd managed to convince Mavis to sell The Blue Heron and come work for him. He'd hired her as his housekeeper and etiquette instructor. Fortunately, Mavis had come at a price he could afford, since he held Hats' indenture papers. What the large, former madam and the tiny ex-jockey did in the privacy of her room was not something Jason wanted to contemplate, but he knew he'd hold Hats to every day of his indenture since it also kept Mavis here.

"Of course, I should also point out that a *gentleman* wouldn't strip down and offer indentured convicts an opportunity to take pokes at him."

Jason gingerly touched the bruise on his left cheek. "It shows, does it?"

"Yes, it shows. It shows you're still a ruffian and no amount of my tutoring is going to change your basic character."

"Ah, Mavis, there are just some things men have to do that are incomprehensible to women. New men are always angry. They've been convicted of some minor crime, clapped in irons, thrown in the bowels of a ship that takes them away from everything they know, and then sold like slaves on the deck of that same ship. They're bewildered and frightened, and for a man, that adds up to being angry.

"Transported convicts want to strike out. They need to hit something. I just make myself a target. These men have this one chance to act on their anger and then they have to buckle under and do everything they're told. If they don't, I'll sell their contract away, and most of them quickly figure out that if this happens, they'll wish like hell they were back here."

"But it's not often that one gets to you." Mavis sounded almost pleased.

Jason grinned ruefully. "That was Tom. I misjudged his reach."

"But you put him down?"

"Oh, yes. I put him down hard. His face will not be pretty for a while. But I think I removed some of the stupidity from the lot of them."

"Is this what you wished someone had done for you?" Mavis asked, then blanched, realizing she'd overstepped her bounds when he leveled a stare at her.

"There is no wishing about the past," he said. "All wishes have to be aimed toward the future, and even then, I doubt they do much good."

"And that scrap of a girl you sent me. What are your wishes for her future?"

"She's a seamstress."

"So her tag said."

Jason rubbed the wine glass across his forehead. He wished for a better breeze to eddy through the open windows, but the night remained sultry and still. More proof that wishing never did much good. "I thought you'd be happy to get someone to help you."

"And I will be happy, especially if she can actually sew. The other girls are willing to treat her like a princess if she can take over making the foundry workers' trousers. They really hate that rough material. And it would be even more helpful if those trousers didn't have to be replaced so often."

Jason laughed and unconsciously took a sip of the Madeira in his hand. It was still horrible. "Mavis, making iron is a sweaty, dirty business. Sparks and hot metal don't always land on the leather aprons. I don't want the workers running around in rags. These men have sold their labor but not themselves. They deserve the dignity decent clothing can give them."

"Well, you sure give them a lot of trousers."

"And this is why I thought you'd be pleased I found you someone who can sew."

Mavis shook her head. "Let us pray the new girl actually can. Right now, she's starved and lethargic, but there's something about her that doesn't say 'seamstress' to me. Put some weight on her and I think she'll have decent bubbies. Now her hair's washed, it's the color of ripe wheat. The bone structure of her face suggests true beauty." She gave Jason a sharp-eyed look. "You noticed this about our new seamstress, didn't you?"

There was no need to lie. Mavis would see through any prevarication. "Yes, I noticed." But he wished he hadn't. When he'd taken the woman's face in his hand and seen her clear, blue eyes, something long coiled within him seemed to loosen. He liked women in all their guises, but never before had a pair of eyes had this effect on him.

"Then why in the hell did you buy her contract, Jase? You always told me you'd never use an indentured servant in a carnal way, and, up to now, I've believed you."

Jason's anger rose, but he tamped it down. Mavis had reason to be suspicious. He, too, had had his doubts about the woman's skills, but when she'd come back at him, spitting and showing sharp, little claws like a half-drowned kitten, he couldn't leave her there on the deck for someone else to misuse.

"Did you speak with her?" he asked calmly.

"Not much more than 'yes' and 'no' and then she was asleep on a pallet. Why?"

"She speaks with an upper-class accent, and she was most irritated when I took her for, well, something less. Spoke like she was the lady of the manor and I was some under-footman. But she swears she can sew well, and I believe her."

Jason took another sip of the Madeira, schooling his face to avoid a reaction. "I figure she was a lady's maid who got sacked for theft of a hair ribbon or some such nonsense. Without references, no one would employ her. Like most of the poor idiots who voluntarily sign indenture contracts, she probably thought she could come to the New World and be a new person, start over and build something. So, I'm willing to give her a chance."

Mavis shook her head. "Are you starting to go soft?"

"Hardly. I think the girl has skills we can use. You and I imitate high-class speech, but, at times, it's still obviously an imitation. I think she can teach me better speech patterns. She's probably spent most of her time in big houses and estates and can help us decorate the house." Jason knew he had to move cautiously here, since Mavis had been responsible for the furnishings and drapes in the study where they sat. He thought it looked good, but had gotten a few hints that Mavis's taste might be a bit flamboyant.

"And let's be honest," he continued, "fancy sewing is not your forte. I'm thinking that I might want something fancy." He at least hoped the young woman would know how to design cuffs that stayed where they were supposed to. He was tired of always pulling them down to cover the scars left by the shackles.

Mavis suddenly looked serious. "Jase, is all this really necessary—the house, the speech, the clothes? Your friends like you as you are. And as for the rest of 'em…"

"Yes, it's necessary. No one is going to have confidence in me unless I seem worthy. I have to prove I'm as good as any of them."

"No, you have to prove you're better than Sir Peyton Hyde," Mavis said.

Jason laughed. "I've always been better than that bag of shit, but I want him to know it. I want to prick his overblown pride and laugh in his face when I beat him."

At one time, Jason had dreamed of physically beating Sir Peyton, had salved his own wounds by imagining the man bruised and bleeding under his fists. Recently, it seemed Sir Peyton was trying to provoke him to do just that. But maturity had shown Jason he could cause Sir Peyton the greatest pain by taking away his position in society, by diminishing his importance.

This was the goal toward which he'd worked the last ten years, and he'd do whatever it took to accomplish it, even learn to like this vile Madeira. He took another sip.

"If you have nothing else for me to do this evening," Mavis said, rising from the settee, "then I'm for bed."

"No, there's nothing pressing. Just keep me abreast on how the new girl is working out. She's called, eh—"

"Cassy," Mavis supplied.

"Right, Cassy. Let me know if she can sew. And try to find out what her background is. If she can give me and this place some extra polish, it would be a good thing."

"So, you'll not be seeking her out?"

"No more than any of the other girls. They're your department."

"Good." Mavis turned and walked away, her steps silent on the Turkish rug. At the door she paused. "You know, Jase, Cassy might have been a rich man's mistress. I know what attracts noblemen, and once she gets over the effects of the voyage here, she'll be stunning. If she decides to improve on her position here at the Bloomery, shall we say, how are you going to handle it?"

"Bloody hell, Mavis, you're my housekeeper, not my mother. I don't need you minding my moral virtue. I never noticed you turning away my money when you still owned The Blue Heron. And what this new woman does on her own time is no business of mine. If using her body for recreation or profit eliminated a woman from working here, this would be an all-male establishment."

"I was more concerned about your principles than with your virtue," Mavis said sharply and left the room like a ship under full sail.

Jason got up from his chair and placed his wine glass on the ornate tray covered with cavorting cupids. Like many of the pieces Mavis had chosen, the tray didn't seem quite appropriate for a gentleman's study.

Mavis was a good friend, but she hadn't the right to question him about the new girl. Of course, he'd noticed the beauty hiding under that dull exterior. Anyone looking closely couldn't miss it. But that didn't mean he had any plans for Cassy other than having her sew.

He picked up a decanter and poured rum into a clean glass. Bringing it to his lips, the taste exploded on his tongue. God, yes! This was what liquor was supposed to taste like. Sometimes becoming genteel seemed like more trouble than it was worth.

But a pretense to gentility was what he needed to get the votes to defeat Sir Peyton Hyde in the next election for the House of Burgesses. And he *would* defeat the bastard. Finally and completely, he would vanquish Sir Peyton. For himself, for Kate.

Kate, with the crooked smile and trembling hands. Kate, laid across the table in the dairy, her skirts bunched up, exposing pale, stick-thin legs, blood streaking her thighs. And Sir Peyton pumping himself into her as she whimpered.

He'd attacked the man with all the fury lodged in his fifteen-year-old heart. Emotion alone should have carried the day. He was tall and wiry, but he hadn't the mass to prevail over a grown man, especially a grown man with the power to order others to restrain him. It was the first of many times Sir Peyton had whipped him bloody. But this time sat most heavily on Jason's heart. He'd been unable to rise from his pallet when they found Kate hanging from the beam and buried her in unhallowed ground.

Yes, for both himself and Kate, he would beat the son of a bitch. He was no longer a young, hapless boy from the stews of London. He was a man of property. He *would* be elected to the House of Burgesses and then bankrupt the man. He'd have his revenge.

And so he'd drink the damned Madeira and pretend he liked it. But not tonight. He took another swallow of rum.

Chapter Three

"*I* swear. His prick's as wide as the handle on an ax. There's no way I'm riding that thing two nights in a row." Bess's voice echoed in the dark room.

Ellie poked her head over the edge of the bed and looked down at Cassy in the trundle. "The size of the handle on a ladle, more'n likely," she said. This was followed by a muffled "umph" and then, "No need ta kick me, Bess."

"No need for ya to make fun of my man," Bess replied.

"Well, ya gotta admit he's a bit of a runt."

"Not in the area that counts."

Ellie and Bess could go on like this for hours, poking and prodding at each other, but never really drawing blood. On more than one night, Cassy had fallen asleep with their bickering acting as a lullaby.

Not that she'd get much sleep tonight. It was just too hot. She lay in the trundle bed in a pool of her own sweat. She wished she could throw off the sheet, but she'd quickly learned this made her a feast for the insects that whined and buzzed around her head. Virginia must be the buggiest place on Earth, and at least half of the insect population had found its way into this room.

"Bess thinks Tim would be a good match for ya," Ellie said, her head again popping over the side of the mattress. "He's only got two more years on his contract."

"I don't know him," Cassy said. The two women she shared the room with were constantly trying to get her to join them on their late night forays to the men's area.

"A course ya don't know him. That's why we've been tellin' ya about him." Bess's head also appeared.

"I'm sorry. I haven't been attending," Cassy admitted.

"*She hasn't been attending*," Bess said, her diction a good imitation of Cassy's. Both of the women on the main bed laughed. "Oh, flower girl, you kill me when you talk."

Flower girl! Since her arrival, she'd been teased about her initial blunder in thinking a bloomery had something to do with flowers. There were no secrets in this place and gossip flew on swift wings. Of course, the other servants had known she was different the first time she'd opened her mouth, but they accepted her as long as she did her job. And since Cassy took over duties that no one else wanted, everyone treated her well.

She'd had to come up with some story to explain how she'd ended up in Virginia. She wasn't about to tell the truth. There were undoubtedly other murderers in the motley collection of people who lived at the Bloomery, but none of them admitted it, and Cassy wasn't going to either. She certainly wasn't going to admit to being Lady Cassandra Spathe, since there were few plausible reasons for her abandoning her privileged life.

Instead of the truth, she'd offered the other women a tale of a governess, the well-educated daughter of a parson, who'd been attacked by her students' father and subsequently dismissed. The attack lay close enough to the facts to give her story the feeling of truth. She couldn't go into the attack in detail—the fear still curled around her when she thought of it—but the other women recognized the horror of the situation without explanation. They'd readily accepted her story, since they already believed the wealthy always took advantage of the poor.

"So, iffen you want to know about Tim," Ellie said. "He's middle height, with a nice smile and gingery hair."

"But not carroty," inserted Bess.

"Yeah, not carroty. But he does have freckles, but that's mostly cause he's been fellin' trees for the charcoalers and's been outside all summer."

"An speakin' of tree cuttin', were you there when Mr. Anders was showin' the new men how ta make the best cuts ta bring a tree down fast?" Bess asked.

"Oh, yeah." Ellie exhaled on the last word and the two women laughed.

"Now that's why havin' to stay inside and sew is so bad, Cassy. Ya miss the good shows. Mr. Anders comes up and strips down to his shirtsleeves, all those big muscles bunchin' under that sweat-tight shirt, and whack, he takes about half the tree trunk off in one swing."

"Doncha wish he'd take his shirt off like the rest of the men?" Ellie asked.

"Dear Lord, yes. He was so sweated yesterday, it almost made no difference. Ya could see every muscle that fine bull has. Even his breeches was glued to his thighs. I swear ya could see a huge bulge where his prick was."

"Now I'da believed ya, Bess, iffen you'd said Mr. Anders was thick as an ax handle. An he's probly about as long."

There was a moment of what seemed to be reverent silence from the top of the bed.

"The man what diddled you, Cass, did he have a stretcher or a twig?" Bess asked.

"I, eh, have no basis for comparison." That, at least, was the truth. Cassy hadn't even realized men's parts came in different sizes until she'd moved in with Bess and Ellie two weeks ago. Lord Tilton hadn't gotten that far, something for which she praised God daily. She was unable to understand the other women's preoccupation with sexual matters, but she was receiving an education, even if many of their descriptions failed to make sense.

"Bess, it's not nice to ask such things."

"I'd ask you."

"That's different. We know how to play the game. Cassy here didn't have a choice. She didn't enjoy it like we do." Ellie's head reappeared. "That's right, ain't it?"

"Why, eh, yes." Cassy was sure she didn't like it. Hands and mouth on her naked body, poking and probing into her. The smell. The disgusting sounds as Tilton grunted and sucked on her. Cassy shivered in the heat.

But there must be something enjoyable about swiving or Ellie and Bess wouldn't sneak out so many nights. And they weren't alone. Nine women slept in three small rooms above the kitchen and on some nights, Cassy suspected she was the only resident. The attraction remained a mystery.

A woman's indenture period could be lengthened to cover loss of labor if she became pregnant, so there was a good deal of discussion about avoiding this condition as well. Most agreed with Ellie's blunt assessment. "Jus tell him to pull the damned thing out afore it spits or ya'll chop it off." Perhaps Tilton's eye had not been the best place to use the knife.

Mavis should have more carefully monitored her charges' nighttime activities, but Mavis was evidently busy entertaining in her private room in the basement of the big house. The women often reported passing her lover, Hats, as they wandered in opposite directions.

"Well, Cassy'd get to enjoy it iffen she met up with Tim. I mean, once ya broke the eggs, ya might as well make a cake," Bess said.

"Damn these bugs," cut in Ellie's voice. "I need some sleep."

There was much shuffling around on the bed, the straw mattress groaning and snapping, and then all was silence save the occasional hum of an insect next to Cassy's ear.

Cassy also tried to go to sleep, but she found herself heated inside as well as out. The women's talk of sex often left her restless and with a tight feeling down between her legs. Deep inside was hidden the fear that Tilton had been right when he said she liked what he did to her. She'd hated it. She was sure.

But on more than one occasion, she'd awakened from a doze to discover her hand between her thighs. Lord Tilton had been far from her thoughts when this happened, however. Instead, she remembered the feeling of Mr. Anders' arms around her as he carried her from the ship, the smell of fresh linen, his dark, knowing eyes. Cassy didn't understand the connection and wasn't sure she wanted to.

Mr. Anders—Jase, as Mavis sometimes accidentally called him—was the only person at the Bloomery that gossip couldn't explain. Everyone knew pieces about him, but those pieces didn't add up to a whole. Understanding Jason Anders stayed tantalizingly out of Cassy's grasp.

She knew he'd come to Virginia as an indentured servant and that he'd been little more than a boy at the time. Some said he'd been a transported convict. Others said not. But either way, Anders was a shining example of how those who were indentured could pull themselves up.

Rich. Everyone agreed Mr. Anders was rich. He owned huge tracts of land along the river, stretching north and west from the town of York. He filled ships bound for England with his iron blooms. He'd recently built the big house and was setting himself up as a gentleman.

Most of this was probably true, but anything about his personal life remained only rumor. It was said he visited a brothel in York called The Blue Heron with regularity. That was where he'd met Mavis and lured her away to work for him. But at no time had his name been linked to any of the Bloomery women who went sporting at night.

Cassy saw him only as a distant figure, coming or going from the house. But she found she looked for him. In the darkness of her sleepless nights, she remembered the massive solidness of the man who had handled her with the ease of a doll. Something about him called to her.

She flipped over on her side, trying to get comfortable, looking for a cooler section of sheet on her small bed. She kept her hand away from the juncture of her legs. She would not go there. She'd think about—what? Her mind was blank.

Ah, she'd think about the dashing Lieutenant Michaels. He'd looked so handsome in his regimentals. He'd been so kind. Yes, she'd think about him. But no visual image of the slender, blond man came. She couldn't recall his face.

Instead, all she could see were dark eyes, a sharp beak of a nose, and coffee-colored hair.

"Hell and damnation," she muttered, rolling to her other side. All the talk of men and their attributes had her on edge. She needed to put her thoughts elsewhere. The fabric Mavis handed her today was a happy thought to occupy her mind. When she'd been given the paper-wrapped parcel, she'd torn into it like a child on her birthday. The fabric inside, white with tiny blue flowers sprinkled in it, was as light as a whisper, perfect for this stifling climate. Not something she'd use for a ball, but it would make a nice afternoon dress.

Peg would have liked the material. Longing for her missing friend knifed through her. Of all the regrets she'd amassed since meeting her father in his study, this was the one she felt most acutely. None of the women at the Bloomery could ever take Peg's place—and she didn't want them to.

Tears pooled in her eyes and she brushed them away. She needed to focus her mind on more pleasant things or she would never get to sleep. She tried to think about the daily minutia that now made up her life. She imagined the pattern pieces that would be required to make a dress and then envisioned laying them out on the smooth, new muslin. She was mentally cutting the pieces when she finally fell asleep.

Chapter Four

*J*ason pulled his sodden shirt away from his chest and waved the material a bit to make a small breeze. He'd already taken off his coat and waistcoat and rolled his sleeves nearly to his elbows. If he took off any more clothes, he'd offend his butler's dignity. A smile creased his lips at the thought. He was rapidly discovering there was tyranny in a staff's expectations. How did so many of the colonial gentry stand to always be surrounded by hovering servants?

Dipping his quill in the inkwell, he attacked the next column of figures. This was his least favorite chore, but one that needed to be done. He'd hoped to finish it while the sun was still low in the sky, and he'd risen in the murky dawn to get started. The idea was a good one, but the weather hadn't cooperated. It was already stifling.

He wiped his brow and promised himself a reward for finishing this month's books. He'd swim in the lower pond.

They'd already thinned the trees in that quadrant. No one would be around. To float in the cool water would be heaven.

He felt a momentary pang for those working at the furnaces. Even in winter, the furnaces were a foretaste of hell. But in August's steaming heat... He shrugged. He already had the men working only half time. Perhaps he could suggest they enjoy the water down by the dock. Those who couldn't swim could at least dip themselves while holding on to ropes.

His conscious clearer, he returned to the numbers. He knew Conner McAlister would eventually go over the books, but Jason had to be satisfied first. If he didn't have a care for his own business, no one else would.

His concentration was interrupted by the sound of horses coming up his drive. He wasn't expecting anyone. It was hardly the hour for anyone to be visiting anyway. He stood and crossed to the window, but the riders had already passed the side of the house. He turned to walk to the front door and then thought better of it.

If Jason went to the door himself, his butler, Titus, would think Jason lacked confidence in him, and Titus was trying so damned hard to be all that was efficient and proper. It was difficult to believe he'd paid less for the man's entire life than he would for a seven-year indenture. No one had wanted the tall, lanky Negro with a reputation for being shiftless and lazy. When Jason freed Titus but held him to an indenture contract for seven years' labor, the change in the man's personality was amazing. Now if Titus himself could just realize his own worth.

Jason walked back to his desk and was about to regain his seat when there were raised voices and the sound of a scuffle at the front of the house. Whoever had arrived was having more than words with Titus.

Jason left the room, crossed under the stairway, and entered the long central hall. Titus was seated on the floor at the far end with the familiar figure of Sir Peyton Hyde standing over him, poking him with a cane.

"What the hell are you doing here, Hyde?" Jason asked, striding down the hall. His fingers unconsciously curled into fists.

"I'm explaining to this blackamoor that he is never to put his hands on a white man." Sir Peyton looked up and a slight smile creased his face. "Of course, it's understandable that a servant wouldn't know how to train a servant, but you need more reliable help."

"I'm sorry, Mr. Anders." Titus tried to rise to his feet, but Sir Peyton poked his cane into the man's chest with an audible thud. The butler fell back on his ass, his dignity shattered.

"It's alright, Titus. I'll see to Sir Peyton." Jason glared at his visitor. "If you'll follow me to my study, we can be private." Jason turned on his heel and retraced his steps. He could feel Hyde following him. He suppressed the shudder that ran down his back.

When they crossed the threshold of the study, Jason spun around, grasped Sir Peyton by his ruffled neck cloth, and slammed him against the wall, kicking the door closed in the process. "Never lay hands on any of my staff," he said through gritted teeth. "If you make this mistake again, some fisherman will find your body floating in the York River. You have so many people who would like to kill you, I'll never even be a suspect. Or at least I'll be so far down the list that the magistrate will lose interest before he gets to me.

"Do. I. Make. Myself. Clear?" Jason bounced Hyde's head on the wall with each word. The smaller man was grunting and clawing at Jason's hands. With disgust, he released Sir Peyton, who leaned against the wall and sucked in great gulps of air.

Stepping back, Jason steadied himself. He would like nothing better than to choke Sir Peyton until the light left his eyes. The temptation was like a river of flame though his body. But he'd lied when he said that none would think to question him. If Hyde disappeared, Jason would be the prime suspect, and he had no desire to be hanged for murder when his revenge could take an even more painful form. With effort, he modulated his tone of voice. "So, as I asked earlier, why are you here?"

Sir Peyton straightened his clothes and smoothed down his cravat. He, too, acted as if nothing had happened, but his eyes were hot with hate. "Two of my indentured servants have run away. I have it on good authority that you're harboring these men. I'm giving you the chance to turn them over before I go to the magistrate and accuse you of theft."

Jason gave a bark of laughter. "If you really thought they were here, you'd have arrived trailing the magistrate with you. You'd like them to be here, but you know they're not. I hold the articles on every indentured servant here. Every man at the Bloomery works for me."

"One of the missing men has red hair. It's very obvious. He's been seen."

"There's bound to be more than one redheaded man in the colony, and I have one working here. Tim Meyers. If you wish to fetch the magistrate, I'll be glad to show him Tim's articles of indenture. I rather doubt, though, that the magistrate will enjoy being dragged out here for no good purpose." Jason settled one hip on the edge of his desk and crossed his arms in a semblance of repose. "Why have you actually come?"

"As a neighbor, of course. A neighbor concerned that my property is straying onto your land."

"And I've told you this isn't the case, so if you have no other business here, I'll bid you good morning." Jason pushed away from the desk and started toward the door.

"I also thought to warn you, as a neighbor, of course, that pursuing a seat in the House of Burgesses is a waste of your time and your money."

Jason paused mid-step. Here was the real reason for Sir Peyton's appearance. He'd evidently just now discovered, at a rather late date, that Jason would be running for the seat in the Burgesses long held by Sir Peyton. And he must fear that he could lose.

A smile curled at the corners of Jason's lips. Sir Peyton had always lorded it over everyone else in York County, as if being a baronet was important in a country where wealth, more than inherited position, was the key to power. But Hyde's social position was confirmed by his being one of the Burgesses. This was the first thing Jason wanted to take from the man. His power and his prestige.

Then he would work on bankrupting the bastard. Tobacco leached much of the energy from the soil and Sir Peyton's land was getting tired. His yields were down. He'd had to borrow against his next crop and Jason had been quietly buying up those loans. Oh, he had no doubt that Sir Peyton would make the payment on these notes, but next year he'd have to borrow earlier, and then earlier, until even the interest could not be met. And then he would have nothing.

This was ever so much better than killing the man.

"I appreciate your advice," Jason said, his tone indicating he felt anything but appreciation. "But it's unwarranted, since I have every intention of being the Burgess from this district after the next election. I have all of the qualifications. I'm one of the largest landowners hereabout. I have the good will of most of the citizens. I know it sticks in your craw, but you might as well not run this time, since I *will* win."

"Like hell you will! You're nothing more than a jumped-up, transported felon, part of the dregs of London that are sent over here to get rid of the trash. You got lucky that this worthless land you bought had bog iron on it. A thief's luck, that's all you've had.

"You think you can now claim to be a gentleman because you've built yourself a big house? Wait until you entertain your political contributors, and they and their wives see your idea of class. This place looks like a brothel, but I guess those are the fanciest places you've ever visited. You're wasting your time trying for a position that's so far above you."

"I know men who will vote for me." Jason's voice was low and steady.

"Oh, you'll pick up a few votes from former indentured servants who have held on to their puny fifty acres, but the real men of property will run away from you as if you had the plague. I'm going to enjoy beating you into the ground."

Sir Peyton smiled. "Actually, I've always enjoyed beating you. I loved the whimpering sounds you made when you could no longer control yourself. You'd bite your lips and tongue bloody, and still I could make you cry out. I'd kiss you with the whip and you'd sound like a woman being roughly taken. Even your cock would swell, and with every stroke, you looked like you were humping the barrel you were stretched on.

"God, it made me hard just watching you. More than once I thought to take you up the ass, and probably would have done so if there hadn't been an audience. I think I may start telling that story around. That should get you a lot of votes."

Jason's hands were so tightly fisted that his arms shook. He took a step toward Hyde and watched his eyes widen with alarm. There should have been satisfaction in being able to frighten the man, but this victory tasted of ashes. "If you tell that tale, all you will prove is that you're a sadistic bastard. I'm hardly that boy anymore."

Sir Peyton flicked his hand as if dislodging an irritating fly. "Ah, but Jason, inside you still are." Then he turned and fled the room.

Jason didn't follow. He stood in the middle of the room and breathed deeply through his mouth, trying to center himself. If he'd been perspiring earlier, he was now soaked with sweat. The desire to do murder scorched him.

He was *not* that boy. He'd never be so helpless again. He'd been ten years building a defensible position from which to attack that son of a bitch. And attack him he would.

But deep within his flesh and bone, he could still feel the cut of the lash, could remember the utter humiliation of being strapped across a barrel, shirtless, with his breeches pulled down to his ankles. Sir Peyton had wielded the whip, but there had always been others watching. The latter was his fault. When he was a child, it had taken two men to subdue him and strap him down. As a young man, it had taken four.

He sat back down at his desk and picked up the quill. His hand trembled so badly he was unable to get it into the inkwell. "Hell," he said loudly and stood so abruptly his chair fell over backwards.

It was too damned hot to do this work. Instead he'd—he'd what? All he wanted to do was kill Sir Peyton Hyde. But he knew even that would not erase all that had come before.

He'd earlier decided to go swimming in the lower pond. That's what he'd do. But first he'd go by the furnace area and relieve the men of their duties for the day and give them permission to go to the river. If it was too hot for him to work, it was too hot for everybody.

He walked to the door, remembering Sir Peyton's look of fear as he'd banged him up against the wall. Hyde knew he wasn't the helpless boy he'd been. That look proved it. At least Jason hoped it did.

Cassy put down the scissors and surveyed the sections of material lying across the table. Each pattern piece looked right. Put together, the dress that lived in her mind should come into being. She was afraid to start the stitching, however, since her hands were sweaty.

Mavis had been in earlier to say most of the men had been given time off due to the heat and she saw no reason for the women to labor on if the necessities had been taken care of. No sooner had the housekeeper left than word arrived that the truant men were down at the dock, swimming. Speculation among the women about the state of dress such an activity would allow became rampant, causing a good deal of laughter. The exodus to view the sights had started immediately, until only Cassy was left, determined to at least get her new dress cut out.

She carefully folded the pattern pieces, wrapped them in some sheeting, and placed the packet on the shelf. Her fingers itched to begin sewing, but with the heat of the day upon her, she feared ruining the fabric. Night would be the best time to work on the dress, but Mavis meticulously counted the candles, so the light was always uncertain. She wished she could find a lace maker's globe like the one used by the older women in the village near her father's estate. When a clear globe filled with water was placed next to a candle, the increase in illumination was amazing.

Perhaps Mavis would know if there were glass containers that could be used to cobble together something similar. But for now, Cassy would follow the other women's lead and try to find somewhere shady and cool. She had no desire to join in the voyeurism at the river, but on an estate filled with large stands of trees, there had to be a number of enjoyable places to relax.

With no one around to see, Cassy took off her mobcap. Already she felt cooler. She then sought the shade of the tall trees behind the kitchen building. A hint of a cool breeze teased her from the gloom of the woods. She wandered in among the high branches and found a well-used path running into the woods.

Cassy strolled down the path, enjoying the quiet. It was hard to find privacy with so many women crowded into the upper rooms of the kitchen. One could only be alone outdoors. She followed the path for some time and heard the faint tinkle of water running over stones. She was drawn to the sound.

The thick trees suddenly opened into a good-sized clearing surrounding a small pond. A lazy stream flowed into one end, the water making a tiny falls. She started forward with a gasp of delight, already imagining the wondrous feeling of dangling her feet and legs in the water. Her forward motion was arrested, however, by the sight of a man reclining on a rock on the far side of the pond. She immediately ducked back into the shadows.

Jason Anders rested on a large stone slab. Turned slightly on his side, one of his arms was bent at the elbow and his head was cradled in the raised hand. One leg folded at the knee; the other lolled straight along the rock. He was a picture of a man in repose. If sculpted by an artist, the work could have been entitled *Elemental Man at Rest*. The beauty of both the man and the design took Cassy's breath away.

He was not handsome. Cassy had flirted and danced with handsome men in England, and this man was so much more. His shoulders were wide and heavily built. The bicep of his folded arm bulged. Patches of sunlight filtered through the trees, bringing the muscles of his broad chest into relief. A swath of dark hair crossed this expanse and arrowed down a flat, ridged stomach to—

Oh, my God in heaven!

This was what the women joked about. Having never before seen a naked man, Cassy had assumed their talk was exaggeration. This was no exaggeration. His cock lay across the powerful thigh of his straightened leg, a lighter mark against the sprinkling of hair that darkened his leg. Bess had told her a man's cock would grow and stiffen in arousal. If that were the case, she was definitely looking at the ax handle of Bess's fantasy.

She should turn and quietly leave. She knew she should. But she stood frozen in place, unable to look away. The blood that had left her head when she'd first spied him now pooled between her legs, hot and damp. The bodice of her dress constricted her. Breathing was difficult and when she did inhale, her breasts seemed to rub uncomfortably against the fabric.

In an instant, all of the jokes and laughter made sense. Sneaking off into the woods to meet a man no longer seemed such an impossibility—as long as it was a man who looked like this.

He suddenly stood with a fluid motion that moved him from his reclining position to his feet with easy economy. Startled, Cassy edged back into the undergrowth. She heard a splash and the lapping of water. Unable to resist, she again parted the branches and peered out.

Anders lay on his back in the midst of the pond, seeming to float on the water at his ease. His hands moved slightly at his sides, propelling him to the center of the pond. He submerged and then came splashing to the surface. He shot a stream of water from his mouth and laughed, the sound echoing around the small glade. "To hell with him," he said aloud.

Cassy wondered whom Anders was consigning to the devil, but the thought stopped as he stood and walked back toward the shore. Water sluiced from his body, but his back was clear in the stippled light. The ruin there tightened her throat. His back was crossed and recrossed by scars and welts. Some were lighter than his normal skin color, some darker. They showed a pattern of whippings that must have lasted for years. To be flayed so extensively at one time could only have caused death. The jumble of lines even flowed onto his taut buttocks.

She imagined his back would feel hard and ridged to the touch. Cassy had one small scar near her knee, a souvenir of a fall from a tree as a girl, and it sometimes pulled at the surrounding skin. How did the man move so gracefully, carrying that horror on his back?

Like all the women at the Bloomery, Cassy had been curious about their mysterious master. She now knew more than she really desired. But she would keep this knowledge to herself. Anders never removed his shirt, even when doing hard labor next to the men, and she now understood why.

She wondered if she would ever be able to look the man in the eye and keep her face from reflecting this awful knowledge. She realized why Anders' only threat for misbehavior was to sell the offender's indenture to someone else. No one so abused would wish to visit a similar punishment on another.

Sadness slid over her and she dropped back into the trees. She hurried back to her room above the estate kitchen, hoping Anders never realized she'd spied on him. She still wondered how the man could have laughed with such abandon, and she hoped the person he wished damned was the one who had disfigured him.

Chapter Five

September 1755

C assy ran a hand along the seams of her gown, making sure they fell correctly over her improvised panniers. After working with osnaburg and other rough cloth for the past few weeks, the soft muslin felt more luxurious than silk.

"Leave off picking at yerself," Ellie said. "Ya look fine."

Cassy wished she had a mirror, but all she had was Ellie's opinion. The tall, rawboned woman looked her up and down. "I think Mr. Anders'll be impressed with yer fancy work."

"Lord, I hope so." Cassy unconsciously fingered the delicate embroidery that covered the stomacher. "I guess I'd better get on up to the house. I'm supposed to be there at three."

"Ya look like an angel," Ellie said with touching sincerity.

Cassy doubted that was true, but she appreciated her friend's efforts to bolster her confidence.

Although the other indentured women recognized that Cassy was in many ways different from them, they had always been supportive and kind. Ellie and Bess had become her friends, filling the void left by Peg's death during the horrific voyage to Virginia. She valued both women for their pragmatism and optimism. She'd even come to terms with the moral laxity that allowed them to ghost away at night for trysts.

She'd never told the women of her stumbling on Jason Anders at the small pond. If Bess or Ellie had had a similar experience, Cassy was sure they would have attempted to entice Anders with sly looks and actions. Cassy's not doing so would give them a great deal of amusement, so she was never going to mention it. To her friends, sexual congress was an activity to be enjoyed. A sport. A game. And a naked Jason Anders had certainly looked like a prize.

The root of her nervousness lay in the confused feelings she had toward Mr. Anders. Just going up to the big house to have him pass judgment on her sewing skills would have been frightening enough. But the strange feelings she'd experienced when seeing him naked compounded this. She wasn't sure she could look him in the eye without blushing and stammering like an idiot.

She was Lady Cassandra Spathe, she reminded herself. Jason Anders was only an indentured servant who had made good. But since hers was a title she could no longer claim and Anders was the man who controlled her fate, this argument held little consolation.

Her project was finished, however, and Jason had asked to see her work. Cassy took a deep breath, squared her shoulders, and marched to the main house. Mavis had told her to use the front door instead of the servant's entrance. She didn't know whether to be encouraged or frightened by this request. She walked up the front steps as if she belonged there, thankful the weather had broken and the day was comfortable.

At her light tap, the door was opened by a tall, slender Negro dressed like a normal English butler. "Miss Spade to see Mr. Anders," she said, feeling foolish.

"He's expecting you, Ma'am," the butler said. His words were distinct, but the cadence of his delivery was a bit odd.

She was shown into a large center hall running straight from the front to the back of the house. The walls and the heavy woodwork were whitewashed, as if being prepared for a coat of paint. The hall contained little furniture and her footsteps clicked as she walked across the polished wood floors. She followed the butler to the rear, turned right under the cantilevered section of the staircase, and entered a garishly decorated study.

Mr. Anders stood as she entered and, at this polite movement, Cassy felt the familiar mantel of Lady Cassandra Spathe fall over her.

"Mr. Anders," she said, curtsying.

"Miss Spade," he replied with a bow.

And then the two of them silently stared at each other. Anders seemed as confused as to how to proceed as Cassy was.

She was the first to break the stillness. Holding her skirts out to the side she said, "Miss Mavis gave me this material last week and asked me to design a dress that would show my sewing abilities to the fullest. I hope this meets your approval." She did not add that this would have been more easily accomplished had she been given the proper undergarments.

The only stays available on the whole estate belonged to Mavis and could have wrapped around Cassy twice. She'd tried to cobble together a homemade corset using wood strips for the boning, but the effect was not quite right. As tight as money had been in her family, there had always been funds to buy such things from a competent mantua-maker.

Anders continued to stare at her intensely. He seemed to focus on her embroidered stomacher, or perhaps it was her bust line. Cassy surreptitiously glanced down to make sure that one of her improvised stays hadn't popped into view.

Growing increasingly uncomfortable under his wordless scrutiny, she finally said, "Do you want me to make ladies' gowns? I can adjust the style to match the person." She suddenly wondered if Anders' trips to York were to visit a mistress instead of a brothel as rumor had it. Did he hope to impress a lover by supplying elegant gowns? Was this unknown woman the person she was supposed to dress?

Her words seemed to finally animate the man. His dark eyes, sharp and inquisitive, rose to meet hers. "No, I'm not interested in dresses. I was actually hoping you could make *me* more fashionable." To her surprise, a blush stained his tanned face as he held his arms out to the side and turned in a circle. "I wore my finest clothing for your critique. Mavis says that you're familiar with what is being worn by the gentry in London."

Now it was Cassy's turn to stare. His finest clothing was out of date, but the man himself was breathtaking. No gentleman should have such shoulders. They strained the fabric of his coat. Likewise, heavily muscled thighs were evident in the tightness of his breeches. But his waist was trim, his stomach flat. And she knew exactly what he looked like without any clothes at all. She felt her face flush.

"Perhaps some lace at the neck and wrists," she stumbled on the words, "and a more colorful vest with embroidery would bring you more into fashion."

He smiled then, his teeth white against his tanned face. She felt a strange quivering in her midsection that had nothing to do with poorly fitting stays. "It's good to know that I'm not completely a lost cause," he said. "Would you be able to make the type of clothing you described?"

She now knew what the real job was supposed to be. Mr. Anders was in need of a tailor, and she wasn't sure she could sew for a man. It seemed to her to be a different skill than the one she had. She suddenly saw her contract being sold to someone else, someone who needed a modiste and not a tailor. The thought of leaving Anders' Bloomery tightened her throat.

"I, I'm not sure I can make gentlemen's clothes," she mumbled. "I've only sewn gowns."

"You're making men's clothes now. Mavis said you're really good. You've made more trousers in the past few weeks than all of the other women working together have made in the past month." He smiled confidently.

"But those are just rough trousers. There's no actual fitting, no tailoring."

He laughed. "That's not what Hats said. He's delighted to have pants that fit him."

She smiled back, unable to keep from echoing his expression. She'd remembered the small man's complaints when he'd brought her to the Bloomery and had acted on them. "That was hardly tailoring. I cut the pattern pieces down as I would to make a child's clothing."

"For heaven's sake, don't tell anyone that. Hats is telling the other men you personally measured him. It's made him quite a hero."

Personally measured him. Oh, good Lord. Cassy suddenly had a vivid mental image of what it would be like to measure Mr. Anders. Stretching the string down his powerful arms and around those well-remembered biceps. Running her hands across his firm chest to determine its broadness. And to assess the needed length of the fall in his breeches, she'd have to touch... Her pulse pounded through her and her mouth was suddenly very dry.

"The men's trousers were easy to make. I simply took an old pair apart to see how the pieces were cut and assembled. Then I made a few adjustments I thought would make them more comfortable and cut them in various sizes. Hats obviously got one of the smaller pairs." Cassy realized she was speaking very fast and staring at the floor. She took a deep breath and looked up at Mr. Anders. "Before the trousers, I've only ever made women's garments, and I'm well acquainted with how those should fit."

He raised one eyebrow quizzically. "I would have thought clothes were clothes, and between women's and men's, the making of something for a woman would be the more difficult. Men are just straight and women..." He moved his hands, evidently shaping a women's figure in the air. Then he seemed to realize what he was doing and dropped his hands to his sides. "Well, I'd think women would be more difficult to dress."

"Where were these clothes made?" Cassy asked.

"A Mr. Hines in York purports to be a tailor, but you can immediately identify all the men who buy their clothing there. We all look the same. The same material. The same style. And everything has been the same for years. I feel as if I'm wearing a uniform that proclaims I'm from York. When I go to Williamsburg, the men dress differently, and I want to look more like that."

"Then why not use the tailors in Williamsburg?" Cassy was sure money would not be a consideration.

Anders chuckled. "Gossip is more rampant in the capital than anywhere else and there are some things I choose to keep to myself. A man has no secrets from his tailor."

Cassy thought of his horribly scarred back. A proud man would not want to display that to strangers. "If you have some old clothing that fits tolerably well, I could probably take them apart and use the pieces as a guide. I could change things a bit to give the articles more style. Then, with careful measurements, I could make the new clothing have a better fit." Her voice rang with a confidence that gave no hint to her uncertainty.

He smiled. "I could definitely use a better fit. This is my best coat and it restricts movement since it's so tight across the shoulders. And Mr. Hines will not make the sleeves as long as I need." He stuck out his arms, showing how the sleeves receded, leaving a large portion of his wrists exposed. "I want to keep that covered if possible. No need to constantly remind people of my past."

Cassy looked at his naked wrists. Both were banded with scars. Slightly lighter than the surrounding skin, they looked like irregular bracelets. Without thought, Cassy reached out and touched the discolorations. The defects were slightly ridged, but were soft and pliable. She ran her fingers over them, then realized what she was doing and hastily dropped her hands.

"Shackle scars," he said, carefully watching her face.

"Your coat sleeves are too narrow rather than too short," she said quickly, trying to show no reaction. "The place you need more length is in your shirt. Coat sleeves are expected to ride up and down the arm, but your shirt sleeves should stay in place." Cassy found herself looking at his hands. They were large but long fingered, the nails bluntly cut and clean. A light down of dark hair covered the backs and the upper part of the fingers. His hands looked capable of accomplishing all types of tasks.

"Thank you."

She wasn't sure what he was thanking her for. Perhaps for pointing out how his clothes could fit better. Perhaps for agreeing to try to make him some new and more stylish ones. She didn't know what to answer. Silence again settled over the room.

"I'm sorry. We shouldn't be standing in the middle of the room. My manners are in need of improvement as much as my apparel. Please have a seat, Cassy, eh, Miss Spade."

She smiled. "I work for you, sir, so Cassy is totally acceptable." Besides, his treating her like an honored guest would only confuse things. She had to keep reminding herself that Anders was her employer, the owner of her labor if not actually herself. It was best to keep an emotional distance. She walked a few steps to the upholstered chair he indicated and sat down, carefully smoothing her skirts.

"Very good, then, Cassy. Could you embroider a waistcoat something like you've done on your..." He waved his hand in front of his torso.

"Stomacher," she supplied. "I think an embroidered waistcoat would be just the thing, but with a different design. I really don't see you with large, blue flowers on your chest."

He laughed then, an easy, free sound. "I agree. Only a beautiful woman should look like a field in bloom. Of course, it might be a good way to advertise my bloomery." He laughed again, obviously having heard of her initial confusion. Cassy felt her face heat. She wondered what else he knew about her and who the bearer of the tales was.

"But I'm remiss. Would you care for tea?"

Without giving her a chance to answer, he popped out of the chair he'd taken opposite her and crossed the room to a bellpull. Cassy was surprised he didn't just bellow, since that seemed the normal mode of communication here. "Much more genteel than just calling," he said, as if he'd read her thoughts.

The butler immediately appeared at the door. "Tea, please, Titus," he ordered, then he returned to the chair he'd vacated. "I'm working on doing things more properly." His smile was self-deprecating. "I want to take my place in Virginia society, now that I have a fine house, and I was hoping you could give me some direction. Mavis said you'd been a governess, that your father was a parson, so I figured you'd know the rules of society."

He looked at her expectantly. At least he'd identified Mavis as the person giving him information, and she'd obviously told him Cassy's well-rehearsed tale of being forced into service by her father's death and the cruel employer who'd attacked and then dismissed her. Anders' knowledge of this tale thankfully eliminated any need for her to repeat it. "I'm well acquainted with most aspects of polite society," she said. "Although my father wasn't wealthy, we always—"

She was interrupted by the arrival of the Negro butler carrying an elaborate tea tray. Unconsciously, she motioned him to set the tray on an adjacent table and said, "Thank you, that will be all. I'll pour." She instantly knew she'd overstepped. As the daughter of a country parson, she would not have ordered someone else's servant around with such authority. Now was not the time to reveal she was the daughter of an earl, especially one who was wanted for murder.

Anders seemed to notice nothing amiss, however. He simply nodded Titus on his way and said, "I'll take mine with one lump of sugar, no milk."

He carefully balanced the cup she handed him and waited until she had taken a sip of her own. "Is the tea to your liking?"

"It's excellent."

"And those little sandwiches? Are they appropriate?"

"Perfect," she replied, bemused. "Isn't this what you always serve with tea when you entertain?" She didn't understand why he was so tentative.

White teeth flashed in his dark face. "This is actually the first time I've entertained formally. It's sort of a practice for the real thing. Since you've lived in gracious homes before, I thought you might give me some pointers. I have no problem with your being critical. I want to do things right." He took a rather large gulp of his tea. "I mean, are those sandwiches supposed to be so tiny? Cook says she knows how tea sandwiches should look, but they could hardly be sustaining."

It was her turn to laugh. "Mr. Anders, a social tea isn't supposed to be sustaining. It's all about conversation."

"Which is why men go to taverns, so I understand that point. At least a tavern serves real food." As if to emphasize his point, he grasped a small tart and popped it into his mouth. He smiled and licked a spot of cream that had adhered to his lip. The motion brought her attention to his lips. They were thin and in repose looked harsh, but when he smiled, they softened. Cassy wondered what it would feel like to be kissed by those lips. She jerked herself back to reality, nearly sloshing the tea from her cup.

"I suspect the conversation as well as the food in a tavern has more substance than in the drawing room," she said. "In polite society one is to speak of innocuous things: the weather, fashion, plays, books. Any topic that could be considered controversial is to be avoided."

"Well, that's definitely different from a tavern, where controversial topics always ensure the liveliest discussion. I like that about taverns." He put another tart in his mouth. Mr. Anders must have a liking for sweets. "For now, however, I'd like your honest assessments, even if you think they're not polite. For instance, what do you think of this room?"

Cassy brought her cup up to hide her face for a moment, searching for something honest but positive to say. "This room is very colorful. I'd call it cheerful. Your upholstered pieces, such as these chairs, have lovely lines." She floundered as she wracked her brain for kinder, euphemistic terms.

"And the material on these chairs?"

She looked down at the arm of the wingback. It was covered in a flame stitch fabric that combined brilliant, clashing colors. It was garish, really awful. "It's vivid," she said.

He leaned forward and replaced his cup on the tray. His one errant eyebrow arched up again. "That it is, but it doesn't seem quite right. The whole room isn't, I don't know, how I want it to look. I've been told this room looks like a brothel."

Cassy had to lower her head to hide her smile. This mix of colors did seem like what she imagined an expensive bordello should look like. "I've never been to such a place, so I have no comment."

"Well, I have and it does. And I shouldn't have said that, should I? There are a number of areas where I need help to be respectable. Would you help me with decorating my house as well?"

"I'd be happy to make what suggestions I can, but why do you want to change yourself and your surroundings?" The question was honestly asked. For all of her life, Cassy had defined herself by her position in society. Since arriving in Virginia, however, she'd come to realize there were other ways. Here, she was a person in her own right, not just a titled lady who was tightly fitted into a box made from others' expectations. The discovery had been frightening but liberating. She couldn't imagine Mr. Anders wanting to build such a box. She couldn't imagine his being willing to be controlled by what others thought.

"I want to look and behave like someone born into the upper class." He flexed his shoulders and looked somewhat chagrinned. "I've read Jerome Pierce's *The Making of an English Gentleman* at least five times. I've tried to improve in the areas stated as important." He held up his hand and began ticking off items. "I've practiced proper speech patterns. I always wear clean linen. I'm polite to servants." A brief smile flickered across his face. "I often fail at that, but I suspect Pierce didn't have the same quality of servants that I have."

Another finger popped up. "I've built a substantial seat from which to venture forth—by that, Pierce means a large house, but I'm also supposed to develop a good seat on a horse as well. Two different kinds of seats." Again the brief smile. "And I've been establishing a library, to display my interest in intellectual pursuits." He waved his hand toward a nearly empty bookcase. "I have twenty-seven books to date, which isn't very impressive, but I only get those I actually want to read. So, I'm on my way to becoming a gentleman, but I still need help."

"Are you in line for a title?" Cassy asked. The idea seemed plausible and would explain Anders' enthusiasm for what he saw as improvement. More than one noble family had had to cast around for a second cousin once removed to fill its vacant seat.

"Heavens, no!" His laugh filled the room. "I want to get elected to the House of Burgesses."

The answer surprised her. Mr. Anders wanted to remake himself in order to win an election to some small, backwater version of the House of Commons? The idea certainly didn't fit with the image she'd been given of a sharp, hard-driving businessman. Cassy had only been vaguely aware of the political maneuvering that occurred in London, but she'd always thought of politics as a childish game.

Her derision must have shown on her face, since Anders suddenly looked every inch a hard businessman. His dark eyes snapped. His smile was gone. Intensity rolled off him like heat from a banked fire.

He leaned forward and Cassy thought for the first time that perhaps she should be afraid of this man. "The Burgesses make the laws for the Virginia Colony, laws that we all must live under, live with. For the most part, the established planters control this legislative body. But all free men of property may vote. I want those votes."

"And then you could make the laws?"

"Exactly! Fair laws. Ones that don't allow the planters to exploit their laborers, be they indentured or slave. Laws that enable everyone who comes to this colony an opportunity for a better life. We can build something better here than England has ever known."

Conviction burned in his remarkable eyes. With a jolt, Cassy recognized the same pragmatic optimism she'd seen in the indentured women.

"Sir Peyton Hyde has been the Burgess from York County for years. He thinks he owns the position, just as he thinks he owns every servant whose labor he buys. I've beaten him before, however, and I'll beat him at this. But I need the votes of men who are accustomed to being influenced by those they perceive as their social betters. I want them to forget my origins and see only what I've become."

"I'll help you if I can, sir," Cassy said, carried along like a leaf in a torrent by his passion.

The smile again flickered about the edges of his lips. "Good. And would you feel comfortable helping me furnish this house as well?"

"Furnish your house? You mean that most of your rooms are…"

"Empty," he completed, giving her a self-deprecating smile.

That smile made her want to help him become whatever he imagined he could become. If his finances allowed, Cassy could make his home a showplace. She was less sure that she could make Anders appear to be a real gentleman. Clothed by the best tailor in London, his own dark hair covered by the most expensive wig, Anders would still be too large, too expansive, to blend into a ballroom filled with aristocrats.

"I'll do what I can," she promised.

"My thanks. When I bought your indenture, I was sure you could be useful in this endeavor, even if you did look like a starving kitten." Cassy wasn't sure how she felt about this description, even if it were true. Before she could respond, however, he called out, "Titus."

Then he leaped to his feet and dashed to the bellpull, but Titus appeared at the door before he had time to ring. "I need some string so Miss Cassy can measure me for new clothing."

"Very good, sir." The butler left, grinning.

"I have some chalk here," Anders said, going to his desk and rummaging through the middle drawer.

He retrieved a piece, then slipped off his coat, hanging it over the back of the desk chair. Heavens, was the man going to disrobe? Cassy felt breathless at the thought. "You can leave your waistcoat on," she quickly said. "Until it's time to fit the garments, I just need rough sizes." All true, but the thought of what such a fitting would involve was unsettling.

Titus returned with the string, and Mr. Anders walked to the middle of the floor, holding his arms out to the side. This was evidently how the tailor in York measured him. Cassy tried to remember how the mantua-maker had acted the few times she'd had a new dress. Attempting a professional demeanor, she walked behind Anders.

"Drop your arms for a moment," she said. He relaxed his pose. Cassy came closer to his back and stretched up to pull the string taut across the broadest part of his shoulders. The muscles beneath her fingers seemed to bunch and move, but she couldn't feel any scarring. She rocked away from him and marked the place she held on the string. Returning the string to its original position, she said, "Bend slightly at the hips and stretch your arms forward, as if you were reaching for something on a desk."

Anders did as she instructed, but it brought his firm buttocks back into her stomach. The contact made her feel queasy, but not in a sick sort of way. Instead, the fluttering energized her. Anders smelled of something spicy she couldn't identify. She resisted the impulse to drape herself across his back and press against him while breathing in the interesting scent. Instead, she backed away from him while she marked the string. "That should give you a bit more room to move." She assiduously studied the marks on the string as she spoke.

"Arms out now." She measured the length of his arm, then the area around his bicep. Wrapping the string around his forearm, she was amazed at the size. This is probably where the tailor had made his mistake. She walked in front of Anders and pulled the string from his cuff to just under his chin. His pulse beat there. Without volition, her hand lightly stroked the spot.

Anders made a low sound in the back of his throat. Cassy jumped back as if burned. What was she doing? "I think those are all the problem areas," she said, her voice not quite steady. Anders stood like a statue, his eyes closed. "Oh, drop your arms." Cassy was frantically gathering the string onto the ball.

"I'm sure I can get the rest from your old clothes. Be sure to send them as soon as possible and I'll make a rough pattern out of sheeting." And then she fled the room without waiting for permission to do so. This was a very different flight, however, from the last time she'd left a man in haste.

Chapter Six

*J*ason stood unmoving in the middle of the floor. What in the hell had just happened? No, he knew exactly what had occurred. He'd come within a hair's breadth of grabbing one of his own indentured servants and forcing himself on her. When she was standing in front of him, she had to know he was as hard as a pikestaff. His breeches tented out like he had a dog on point hidden there. No wonder the woman had had the good sense to turn tail and run.

He strode to his desk chair and plopped down. He loathed men who took advantage of their power, but, sweet Jesus, he'd wanted to take every bit of advantage he could with Cassy Spade.

He'd been shocked almost speechless when she entered the room. He wasn't sure what he'd expected—but this gorgeous woman with the artlessly arranged, honey-blond hair was not it. She was every inch a lady, graceful, charming.

Her blue eyes sparkled. The soft mounds of her creamy breasts cried out for his questing hands. He'd never before had such a visceral reaction to a woman.

But he'd mastered himself and played his part well. He tried to pretend she was Mary McAlister, another beautiful woman he saw on social occasions. Conner's wife held no allure for him, so he could relax and play the gallant. He'd managed the charade, barely, until she'd touched him.

Her light strokes along his shoulders went through him like a lightning bolt. He felt her touch in his toes. And then she'd leaned into his back. Dear Lord, he could feel her breasts through his shirt and waistcoat. Her cunny was pressed to his ass. He had either to turn and grab her or to act like a man made of stone.

He'd managed to impersonate a statue until she stood in front of him, where all he would have had to do was relax his arms to encircle her and pull her tightly to him. She smelled of laundry soap and lavender, like fresh sheets just taken from the linen press. He wanted to lay her out on those sheets, watch that golden hair spread over the pillow. He could imagine sucking the lush globes of her breasts into his mouth, could envision parting her legs and slipping his cock into her wet warmth.

When she'd touched his neck, bare skin to bare skin, he could not keep a groan from surfacing. And so she'd run away from him. She'd very wisely run. But that didn't explain what he was going to do with her now.

Cassy Spade was every temptation he'd ever faced all rolled together. And he knew from past experience he wasn't always good at resisting temptation.

All those years ago, he'd known he shouldn't try to steal the pocket watch, that he hadn't the experience or the dexterity. But it had winked in the sunlight as the gentleman consulted it, and he'd wanted it so much. He'd cursed that watch for getting him transported—but he no longer did. Instead, he now thought getting caught might have been the luckiest thing that ever happened to him. If he'd remained in England, what would have become of him? Gaol was almost a given. A hangman's noose a distinct possibility.

Now he wanted Cassy Spade with the same intensity he'd felt when he saw the watch. If he took *her*, however, there would be no overt consequences. He'd have to explain his actions to no one but himself.

He tried to picture Kate slung across the dairy table, tried to use that horror to bludgeon down his own lust. But somewhere deep inside, he knew it would not be the same thing. With a little encouragement, Cassy would come to him willingly.

He could never be completely sure of that willingness, however. All the planters and tradesmen who bedded their indentured servants said the women were willing. The possibility that there would be unacknowledged, emotional coercion held him back.

"Bloody hell," he said aloud, as he flung himself out of the chair and crossed to the rum decanter. He certainly wasn't interested in drinking any of the now cold tea.

"Evidently your interview with Cassy didn't go as you anticipated," Mavis said from the door. "You can order her to sew and help you get furniture for the house, but you can't order her to have taste."

"There's nothing wrong with her taste, and she agreed to everything."

"Then why are you acting like a bull stung by a bee?"

"I'm not acting any such way. I just feel..."

"Frustrated?" Mavis smiled.

"Don't you stand there and look all smug. Don't you dare say 'I told you so.' I don't want any of your motherly drivel."

"Jase, I haven't said a thing."

"You may not have actually said anything, but you looked it." Jason realized how ridiculous he sounded and began to laugh. "Oh, hell, Mavis. Get yourself a drink and sit down."

"It's too early to drink spirits. I came to ask you if you wanted supper early or late. You've not eaten supper, if you remember."

"I had tea," he said, "and that's got to count for something. But now I feel like a tot of rum."

Mavis picked up a clean cup, poured some tea, and sat in the adjacent chair.

"That'll be cold," Jason said.

"It will be fine. Sit down and tell me what our Cassy did to anger you. I like the girl. I don't trust the story of her past she tells, but, hell, everyone is allowed to let that ocean they crossed wash away uncomfortable pieces of their lives."

Jason took a seat in the chair opposite. "What don't you trust?" Mavis was very good at reading people. At least, he'd always had a difficult time getting away with a lie.

"Does she seem to you like her papa's a parson? I mean, she never reads the Bible, she never prays at meals. Nothing about her says parson's daughter or even governess."

"You also thought she couldn't be a seamstress, and as far as I can tell, her sewing is excellent. She's really getting a lot of the men's trousers made and I thought that dress she had on was as nice as any I've seen in the capital."

"I admit I was wrong about that," Mavis said. She took a sip of the cold tea and grimaced. "And I was wrong about this left-over tea." She put the cup down and poured some rum into a glass.

"But I wasn't wrong that there is something sensual about the girl that could snare any man. I don't think you're immune and I think that's what has you so out of sorts."

Jason made a noncommittal sound, irritated that Mavis could so easily read him. "I don't think it's something she does on purpose."

"I agree. It's something innate. If I could have taught it to my girls at the Heron, you don't think I would have? I'd be richer than you. Oh, I could teach them some tricks. All good whores know some tricks. But that special allure Cassy has, well, that can't be learned. She makes you hard just looking at her, doesn't she?"

He loosened the ribbon holding his queue back and scrubbed his fingers through his hair. "Mavis, there are some things that are none of your damned business."

The older woman laughed. "Just as some of what I do is none of yours. But back to my question. What are you going to do about her? If she stays here, you know you'll bed her, and then all your posturing about not molesting indentured women will come back to bite you in the ass. So your best choice is to sell her contract."

When Jason moved forward in his seat to rebut what Mavis had said, she held up her hands for silence. "There's bound to be some nice lady who needs fancy sewing. Now Cassy's all cleaned up, placing her would be no problem. Hell, you'd probably make a profit."

"And the husband, or son, or neighbor of this 'nice lady' is going to give Cassy a wide berth? I think not. You know her employer attacked her in England. The same thing could happen here."

"At least that's what we've been told," Mavis said. "I think we've been given a fantasy. Cassy was born to privilege, if not wealth. That's obvious in the way she acts. You said it yourself that when you fetched her from the ship, she flared at you like she was the lady of the manor. Well, those who are high have farther to fall, and I think fall is what Cassy did. Society is willing to forgive a few things, but those people never forgive a scandalous lady. Our Cassy has had a lover, or lovers, and it is one of them she's fleeing."

"Even then, none of this could be seen as her fault." Jason couldn't disagree with Mavis's evaluation, but he didn't go along with her conclusion. There was no way he was selling Cassy's indenture. There was no way he was going to put her in danger. Hell, he should be honest with himself—there was no way he would let her go, period.

"I'm not looking to find fault," Mavis said, sounding aggrieved. "You know me better than that. All I'm saying is that if you keep Cassy Spade here, then you're going to end up in bed with her, and that'll not lead to happiness. You'll eat yourself up with guilt."

"I can control myself," Jason said, "and you know me better than to think otherwise. I'm going to use Cassy to help me become more of a gentleman and for nothing further."

"And so you might." Mavis upended her glass and set it on the tea tray. "But you do make me sorry I sold out of The Blue Heron, because you're going to be visiting there a lot—and that will make the owner a good deal of money."

She stood and walked to the door. Before exiting, she stopped and asked, "Are you going to want supper later?"

"No, I'm going out."

"Give my best to the girls at the Heron." Mavis gave him a saucy smile and strolled from the room.

Jason had the childish urge to throw something at her retreating form. The trouble with Mavis was that she told him things he knew were true but didn't want to acknowledge. The idea of Cassy running away from a lover— or worse, lovers—curdled his stomach. He hated the thought of her being with any man.

He downed his own rum in one swallow. He had no right to feel possessive of Cassy. He didn't own her in that way. *But you want to*, whispered an insidious voice in his head. He felt again her slight weight on his shoulders and back, the brief touch of her hand on his bare throat. And he wanted to own every damned part of her, to use every damned part of her until his unruly prick would lie sleeping in his breeches and he wouldn't notice her any more.

Shit, he was already stiffening just thinking about her, and an erection made poor company on the ride into York. But it was a ride he would take. He was sure his problem was that he'd been too long without a woman.

Chapter Seven

$\mathcal{C}$assy hummed as she folded the last of the trousers currently needed at the foundry. Barring a major accident, this should hold the men at the forge and the furnaces for a while. They were the ones who most often ruined their clothes, although Mavis had said the charcoal-makers were now complaining that they had nothing to wear but rags. Everyone wanted something new.

But for today, the needles were put away. She was going to town with Mr. Anders to choose material for his new clothes. She felt almost lightheaded about visiting a provincial village. How the people she'd known in London would laugh.

She was surprised when Ellie and Bess came into the room. "Aren't you supposed to be doing laundry today? Mavis will be testy if she finds you're not in the washhouse." The minute the words were out of her mouth, Cassy felt guilty. She was getting an outing and should be more thoughtful to the people who were stuck here doing their work.

Neither of the women seemed to notice any slight, however. Instead, they were both grinning like idiots. "Ruth wanted ya ta use this." Ellie whipped a wide-brimmed straw hat from behind her back will all the skill of a conjuror. "Ain't it pretty? That Tim ya turned up yer nose to got it for her, sommair."

"He probly stole it," Bess said, "so iffen some woman starts ta scream atya, run."

Ellie swatted at Bess, who easily moved out of the way. "I think he found it. An it'll be perfect for a ride inta town. E'en it's spossed to be fall, the sun is still warm."

"I couldn't take Ruth's hat," Cassy said. "She's already helped me so much." Who would have thought that Ruth, who worked in the dairy, would know how to make stays? Cassy could now wear her new dress without being poked from beneath.

"She wants ya to use it. Truly. That a way, it's like we're all goin' on a trip." Ellie's face had taken on a stubborn look.

Cassy took the hat. If wearing it in some way gave the other women a vicarious pleasure, Cassy would enjoy the shade under the large brim.

"Bess an me brung ya some fresh mint. Jus' picked it. It's not so nice as a hat, but it's what we got." Ellie held out a small packet of cloth.

"Why thank you both. I'll enjoy chewing it. I've been given an abundance of riches." Cassy was touched. She had no idea the other women would think going into York was so special.

"*An abundance of riches*," Bess parodied and they all laughed. "An Cook said to tell ya she's got plenty of tansy for tea. A course, ya won't be needin' it right now, but jus in case ya miss yer courses."

"Miss my courses?" Cassy had no idea what this had to do with gifts for a trip.

"A course. Ya can't be tellin' a man like Mr. Anders he's got to pull out afore he's done," Bess said. Ellie nodded her agreement.

The gist of the conversation suddenly became blindingly clear. All of the women thought she and Mr. Anders were going off for an assignation. And they were all pleased about it.

"Mr. Anders and I are just going to York to buy fabric," Cassy said emphatically, feeling her face blush scarlet.

"Doone be embarrassed, Cass," Ellie said, patting her arm. "There's not a woman here that wouldna get round heels iffen Mr. Anders gave her a look. We're all right proud a ya. Snaggin' him away from those trollops at the Heron."

Cassy felt she should argue that nothing had happened between her and Mr. Anders. And she doubted anything ever would. She'd actually been afraid he was angry with her for some reason. Ever since she'd had tea with him, Mr. Anders had disappeared. She'd been invited up to the big house to look at the vacant rooms so she'd have some idea of what was needed, but Mavis had shown her through. A very grumpy Mavis, at that.

She suddenly realized she was fulfilling a fantasy that all the women shared. Mr. Anders was unavailable and inapproachable and the epitome of the powerful male, so all of the women had probably imagined what it would be like to be intimate with him. "Thank you for your good wishes," she said, uncertain if she should laugh or cry.

"He's commin," said Bess, peaking out the window. "An he's drivin' a little carriage instead a the wagon."

"Oh, my," said Ellie, also going over to look out.

"Help me get the hat on straight." Cassy's comment brought them back like dogs to a bone. Cassy removed the long hat pin from the crown and waited until Ellie was satisfied it was level before replacing it through her coiled hair.

"Yer a picture," Ellie said in tandem with Bess's "Now git." Cassy followed Bess's advice. She whisked down the narrow stairs and out the door as Mr. Anders got out of the carriage.

Even in London, the two-wheeled gig would have been considered smart equipage. The paint looked new and the gray horse in the traces shone like burnished pewter. "Good morning, Cassy." Mr. Anders gave her that quick little smile that squeezed something near her heart. "Nice hat."

"Thank you," she said, as he helped her into the carriage. "The hat's borrowed." She heard a slight noise from behind her and turned to see the shadows of Bess and Ellie looking out the window. Even Cook was hovering near the door. She had to control the impulse to call out "Thanks for the offer of the tansy," and might have done so, if she'd not suspected Mr. Anders would know its use.

Anders clucked to the horse and they moved off. Cassy felt a well of happiness bubble up inside her. It was a beautiful day, warm without being oppressive. She was going shopping and there was a handsome man at the reins. She cut her eyes to the side. Yes, Mr. Anders was indeed looking handsome.

He had on the same clothes as he'd worn when they had tea—a tobacco brown coat, lighter tan waistcoat, buff breeches, and blindingly white shirt, stock, and hose. Cassy knew the entire female population of London would have given him a second look if he'd driven by. It was no wonder the women on the Bloomery fantasized about him.

She wondered what he'd think if he knew it was the general belief that they were lovers. Would he be appalled or find the circumstances humorous? Of course, she wasn't sure how she felt about it. But it did make a nice daydream.

"Do you ever powder your hair?" The question just came out of the air, but once asked, she was curious about the answer.

"No, powder's messy, and I hope I live long enough to eventually have a lot of my own white hair. I see no reason to start the process early."

"Do I need to ask about wigs, then?"

He chuckled. "Probably not. I know some see wigs as a sign of a true gentleman, but if that's the test, then I'll never pass. They're hot, they itch, and the only way to make them look right is to shave your head."

"Maybe you'll go bald instead of white. Then you could wear a wig to keep your naked head warm." She suddenly had a clear image of Mr. Anders without hair. She snorted a laugh, but she didn't find the look unattractive. "I've heard that a man's hairline will match that of his maternal grandfather."

"If that's the case, then I'll have a full head of gray hair when I'm an old man."

"You knew your mother's father?" Cassy was surprised. She thought he was an orphan. Had he said this, or had she picked it up from the gossip that abounded on the Bloomery?

"I saw him from a distance," Anders said. "He was a carter. A big man. I really didn't know him except by reputation—which suggested he was a mean son of a bitch."

"If you want lessons in gentility, I should point out that gentlemen don't curse."

"All the ones I know do."

"I guess all the ones I know do, too." They both laughed, and something that had been missing in the day was suddenly added. Cassy felt some tension go out of Anders' body and she felt herself relax as well.

"You grew up in London?" she asked.

"Yeah. The story of my life isn't exceptional. As I said, my mother was a carter's daughter. She learned how to read and write to help with her father's business after her mother died. Then she got pregnant with me and had no husband, so her father threw her out onto the streets before I was born."

"Do you know who your father was?" Once the question was out of her mouth, Cassy wished to take it back. Anders had admitted to being illegitimate. There was no need to rub his nose in it.

"I used to imagine he was a duke and would someday return and shower my mother with gifts. In my youthful fantasy, he'd set me up on a fine horse and call me 'son.' But all Mam ever told me was that he was a soldier." He shrugged. "So I don't think he was actually a duke."

"If you grew up in London, how did you end up here?" Cassy was as curious about Mr. Anders as anyone else on the estate. The various rumors about him didn't add up. They seemed to be about a number of different people. She felt privileged he was willing to give her this private information.

"Transported for theft, but you guessed that by looking at my wrists." Anders stared out over the horse's head as if his past flickered there. "I was indentured for seven years, but I managed to stretch it to ten by running away a couple of times. When I was young my behavior was often counterproductive. The man who owned my contract thought he owned me, body and soul, and I resented that attitude.

"My contract holder did one good thing, though. As punishment he put me to work with his estate blacksmith. Hiram was the smith's name, and he turned out to be the closest thing to a father I ever had. He taught me all there is to know about smithing and iron."

"Did he die?" Cassy thought of Peg, her surrogate mother, and felt her throat close.

"No. He got sold away to someplace in Georgia, and I've never been able to find him. You see, Hiram *was* owned. There're a lot worse things than being indentured, Cassy girl. At least you can see an end to it, no matter how far away it looks. To be a slave is something altogether different. You never belong to yourself. If I'd been one, I'd have run every time I got the chance. They would have had to kill me to make me stay."

Cassy thought of the ruin that was Anders' back and knew he was telling the truth. Even being indentured had about killed him. She looked over at the man so competently driving the horse. He definitely belonged to himself. She suddenly realized that for the first time in her life, so did she. Anders had made it clear that he'd purchased only her labor. She knew other planters didn't think this was the case and treated their indentured servants like slaves, but she'd been lucky enough to end up at the Bloomery, where she was free to make personal decisions as long as she did her work.

Growing up she'd always been under others' control. First her Aunt Amelia's strict rule had circumscribed her life. Then she'd been handed off to her father, who viewed her as something he owned and wanted to get the best value for.

He'd been comfortable selling her to Lord Tilton to do with her as he willed.

The other women at the Bloomery, most of whom had eked out a living on the London streets, had been freer than she'd been. Cassy had been privileged but caged. To her chagrin, at the time, she hadn't recognized *how* privileged, since she'd been so absorbed with the restrictions.

She now knew her life had been easy, but part of her was almost glad she could not return to it. Here, indentured though she was, she still had a heady feeling of freedom. Perhaps Anders' conviction that something better could be built in this raw land was right.

She realized they'd been traveling in companionable silence for a while and were already approaching the outskirts of York. "This trip has certainly been much faster than the one I took going the other way," she said.

"Yeah, the trip from the ships to wherever you're going seems like a lifetime. The Bloomery isn't that far from town. Our wagons go back and forth daily. York is a busy harbor, which makes it easy to ship our iron."

He slowed for a dray filled with hogsheads of tobacco. He nodded toward the cumbersome wagon. "I should be beholden to the planters for establishing York as an important port. I couldn't do the business I do without ready transportation. But I do get tired of hearing how my iron takes up too much cargo space and that it's too heavy. The planters seem to forget that every one of those damned barrels weighs about a thousand pounds when packed with tobacco."

He clucked to the horse and they picked up speed, passing the lumbering dray. Cassy put a hand on her hat to make sure it wasn't unseated, but relished the rush of air by her face. Anders slowed to a more sedate pace and eventually pulled to the side in front of a yellow painted building with large windows in front.

"Here we are. Jeffries' Dry Goods. They have the best selection of fabrics." He tossed a coin to one of the handful of boys who seemed to materialize when they stopped. "Take good care of my horse and there'll be another when we come out." He handed Cassy out of the carriage and ushered her into the cooler interior of the store.

Upon entering, a sharp combination of scents nearly overwhelmed her. The pungent odor of various dyes competed with an assortment of spices. A clerk came bustling up with an effusive greeting. Mr. Anders explained their errand, introducing her as "Miss Spade, my seamstress," and bolts of costly material were magically displayed. Cassy ran her fingers over the rich fabrics with care, conscious of how her hands had roughened, but the soft plush of the velvets still felt like fog and the shimmering satins like she held her hand in a trickle of water.

Mr. Anders seemed to prefer more subdued shades. When the clerk unrolled a bolt of puce brocade, they looked at each other and laughed. "I trust your taste," he finally said, shifting his weight from foot to foot. "I'm off to look over the new shipment of books." He started to move away, then turned back. "Oh, and get something for yourself to make another dress. When we go to Williamsburg to look at furniture, you should have more than one."

He moved away, leaving her staring blindly at a serviceable, dark broadcloth. *When we go to Williamsburg.* So easily said, but for Cassy, breathtaking. He was not avoiding her as she'd thought. He'd planned a days' long trip with her. If the women she lived with needed further proof of an affair, this would do it. But what was Anders' intent? She worried the question around in her mind. He was always carefully polite, but occasionally a heated look came into his eyes before the veil of polite civility fell over them. And her own intent? That was also murky.

She looked over to where he was talking with two other men amid much backslapping and gesturing. Both of them were better dressed than Anders was. She would do something about that. When she got through with Mr. Anders' wardrobe, he would be resplendent, but definitely not a macaroni. "Both of these," she said, pointing to some more brightly hued fabric, and then she continued her search.

She was trying to decide between two materials for herself when she felt a light touch on her elbow. "About done?" Anders asked.

"I'm trying to choose between this solid and this stripe." She pointed to the samples on the table in front of her. Both were heavier fabrics than the dress she now wore. Even in Virginia, the weather was sure to turn cold at some point.

"Get them both," he said. "We need to leave. Clouds are building to the east and that generally means rain. Chas Elliot pointed out that we're here in what he calls 'my little open toy,' and we could have a damp ride back to the Bloomery if we don't hurry." He transferred his look to the hovering clerk. He waved his hand over the display. "Both." And it was decided.

They left the shop in a flurry of clerks carrying wrapped parcels. Cassy hadn't realized she'd committed Anders to such a huge expense. All of the purchased fabric cost many times the price of four years of her labor. The man didn't look in the least concerned, however, so she told herself not to worry. As she exited the door, she looked to her right into the bowed front of the shop window. She froze, transfixed. There lay her mother's locket.

"Cassy?" Anders touched her arm.

"That's my mother's locket." She gestured toward the window display.

He leaned over to peer in. "Are you sure?"

"Absolutely. It has a central 'H' surrounded by a smaller 'E' and 'P.' My mother's initials before she married. The locket was in my luggage that went missing on the voyage."

Straightening, he said, "I'd say stolen is a more accurate description than missing. Just a moment."

Mr. Anders squeezed past her and returned to the shop. Cassy watched as a hand appeared and lifted the locket from the window display. Then Anders was behind her, his mouth near her ear, saying, "Bend your head forward," causing the fine hairs on her neck to stand on end. She felt him fasten the locket behind her and the familiar weight settle just above her breasts. The locket was warm, either from the memory of the sun in the window or from his hands. She shivered.

"The wind's picking up," he said, misinterpreting her reaction. "We'd best hurry."

The ride through the town was sedate because of all the traffic, but once the road cleared in front of them, Anders brought the horse to a lope. Cassy noticed he didn't use a whip to accomplish this. The horse in the traces leaped to his commands by voice and reins alone. They were flying before the wind. One of the ruts in the road threw her up in the air and she grasped her hat with one hand and the seat with the other. Laughter bubbled out of her. Next to her, Anders grinned wildly.

Her joy came to an end when the first fat drop of rain hit her in the face. "Oh, dear, some of the fabric I chose for you will be damaged if it gets wet," she called over the sound of the wind. Even stored under the seat, there was no way the packages could survive a deluge.

"I'm to be dressed in clothes that must always stay dry?" Anders looked appalled.

"Yes."

She thought he muttered, "Dear God," but he said nothing else. They had no choice but to continue on, rain falling faster around them. She was surprised when Anders slowed the horse and turned off into a field covered with the stubble of corn. The small carriage bumped and lurched across the furrows, but she could see a small barn ahead of them that must be their goal.

He stopped before the structure—up close more of a large shed than an actual barn—and leaped to the ground. "Get inside," he called over to her. "I'll get the parcels of this damned picky fabric."

She pulled the door open and entered the dark, musty interior. The faint odor of rotting vegetation, pungent but not offensive, permeated the air. Rounded burlaps bags were stored at the rear. A lopsided wheelbarrow stood to one side. Otherwise, the building looked empty.

Anders was right behind her. He pushed passed and unceremoniously dumped the wrapped packages on the ground. One he retained and carefully placed in the wheelbarrow. "Books," he said with a self-deprecating smile, then went back out the door. Anders might scoff at fabric that was damaged by rain, but he felt no compunction in saving his precious books from a soaking.

He returned, leading the horse out of the sluicing rain. The horse and its traces could fit through the door, but the carriage had to stay without. Cassy moved to the back of the building, taking off her now sodden hat and shaking it. If it had been ruined, she didn't know what she'd say to Ruth. Her hand reached up to stroke the locket. It was hard to lose a prized possession, regardless of what it was.

Mr. Anders joined her in the rear of the shed, slipping out of his coat and shaking it before draping it over a nail in the wall. "Cassy, it's going to be damned hard for me to wear something that can't get wet."

It sounded like criticism and unexpectedly angered her. "I was worried about a fine, light satin I'd chosen for a waistcoat. It's for eveningwear. Not when you're working." She realized he'd moved to stand next to her. Turning slightly, she looked up into his dark eyes. "I wanted you to stand proud."

"I always stand proud," he murmured, his voice husky. He ran a thumb over her bottom lip. Her breath caught when he brought his mouth to hers. His touch was soft, tentative. Heat raced through her, warming her damp skin. She put her hands on his wet waistcoat for balance. How had she ever thought his lips were thin and stern?

He nibbled at the edges of her mouth. His tongue stroked her lower lip. In surprised response, she relaxed her lips and his tongue slipped in to tickle along the sides and roof of her mouth. Cassy had been kissed before, a quick pressing of lips together in a secluded corner of a room or garden, but she'd never experienced anything like this. Anders' kiss was wondrous, intoxicating. Why had she not known a kiss could be like this?

He straightened, moving his warmth away. "Sorceress," he muttered.

The loss of his lips was like pain. Sliding her hands up to his neck, she pulled him back down toward her and reclaimed his mouth. She did to him what he'd done to her, caressing his lips and the velvety texture of his mouth with her tongue. He groaned softly, tightening his arms around her, pulling her flush to his body.

Breathing became difficult. The solid wall of his chest pressed against breasts that tingled and throbbed. She remembered what he had looked like sitting near the pond, the symphony of his sculpted muscles. She longed to run her fingers over every polished inch. She rose onto her toes and then back to stand flatfooted again, rubbing her aching breasts against him. It felt wondrous.

Not breaking the kiss, Anders lifted her and settled her back against the burlap sacks behind them. The dry contents of the bags crackled as he lowered his bulk to hers. He moved slightly to one side, but his weight still trapped her. Cassy felt a moment of panic, started to push him away, and then realized she wanted to feel him against her.

His lips left hers, moving to kiss the side of her jaw, her ear, and slowly down the column of her neck. Simultaneously, his hands moved over her body, sending tendrils of heat to lodge between her thighs. Her hands copied his movements, roaming, stroking along the broad plain of his shoulders, feeling the muscles bunch and quiver. He trembled at her touch and her hunger grew. She realized, at this moment, she was as powerful as the man above her.

He brought his head lower, running his warm, silken lips along the tops of her breasts, moving the locket from side to side. His hand encircled one of her breasts, his thumb slowly stroking the sensitive tip through her dress. She pressed up into his hand, enjoying the friction, feeling her nipple tighten into a nub. Her soft gasps made a counterpoint to the thrumming rain. Her skin burned.

When he worked one breast free of her bodice, her heart stilled in anticipation. She quivered in his embrace, impatient to feel his mouth on her bare skin. As if responding to her unvoiced request, Anders gently kissed her breast, running his tongue across the throbbing tip before taking her fully into his warm mouth.

She arched up into him, strange mewing sounds coming from her mouth. She wanted. Dear God, she wanted. She wasn't sure what, but she was sure Anders could give it to her.

The horse stomped and snorted near the door, rattling the harnesses, the sound rising above the pounding rain. Anders came to his feet in one smooth movement. His expression seemed stunned, but when he looked back at her, she thought she saw a glimmer of disgust cross his face. She could imagine what she looked like through his eyes, wantonly sprawled on a pile of sacks, one breast exposed. Her hands instinctively came up to cover herself.

"Sweet Jesus," he said, turning to walk near the horse and stare out at the sheeting rain. Cassy didn't know what she'd done wrong, but it must have been something that disgusted him . Tears welled in her eyes and rolled down her cheeks like the rain. She sat up, trying to straighten her dress, making the bags rustle.

Anders leaned against the doorframe, his back to her. "Tell me about your mother's locket," he said, his voice tight.

Her mother's locket? After thrusting her away, he wanted to know about her mother's locket? Through a fog of distress she said, "It was the only good piece of jewelry I owned. All of the supposed gems were paste. I thought if I had to, I could sell it. But I didn't want to. It was all I had of my mother. As a young girl, when my Aunt Amelia scolded me for some misdeed, always punctuating her disparagement by saying I was just like my father, I'd run my fingers over the initials and repeat my mother's name, Elizabeth Patience Hargrove, over and over, like an incantation. And I'd feel better, knowing I was part her."

As she talked, Cassy's fingers played with the locket. As of old, she felt connected to a lady who had always been described as good, kind, and beautiful, if not necessarily wise. She'd been loved by her mother, she was sure of it.

She felt her emotions settle. Cassy also tried hard to be good and kind. Those were attributes she could control. She supposed she was beautiful—others thought so—but that was simply a trick of bone and skin. Beauty had made her valuable to her father, beauty had attracted the vile Lord Tilton, and it was probably beauty that prompted Mr. Anders to kiss her and do what came after.

She looked down to make sure all of her clothing was again decently arranged. She wished Anders could see through her beauty to the Cassy who lay beneath. He might not find the inner Cassy as easy to dismiss. She looked up and found Anders now staring at her.

"I'm sorry. I behaved inappropriately. I certainly don't want you to think I redeemed your locket with the idea that I was purchasing your favors." He stumbled on the last two words. "You're under no obligation to ..." His voice trailed off. Then he laughed. "I'll never make a gentleman. I have no idea how a gentleman would approach this topic, so I'll just have to be blunt. The money I paid for you on the ship was to buy your labor. Any gifts I give you are gifts, freely given with no expectation of any repayment. In no way are you obligated to give me access to your body."

He ran a hand through his hair, pulling part of it free from his queue. "I want to bed you. That's bluntly said, but I don't know of any way to sweeten the topic. You're my servant, however, and this makes any carnal relationship impossible. So I ask you to forget what happened here and to say nothing about my lapse in behavior. I've always kept my relationship with women on the Bloomery businesslike and wish to continue to do so. Do you understand?"

Cassy understood only too well. She was now a servant and Anders was embarrassed by his attraction to her. He imagined she was like the other women at the Bloomery and was someone he could bed at will. Only his innate honor kept him from doing so. The irony of the situation would have made her laugh if it hadn't saddened her. If she'd seen Anders in London, she'd have admired his looks, but would have thought him beneath her.

"I understand," she said.

"Good. Then we'll wait out the rain and return to the Bloomery as if nothing has happened."

Anders turned back to stare out the door. Obviously, he thought all had been said about the subject that needed to be said. Cassy knew she would never tell any of the women what transpired. Not for the reasons Anders wanted, however. She'd keep her silence and smile when her friends questioned her about the day. The other women would be horribly disappointed if she admitted to this farce. It was better to let them have their fantasy.

Chapter Eight

*J*ason was up before dawn—not that he'd necessarily slept. He'd been haunted by Cassy. The damned woman would not leave his mind. He kept seeing her lolling on the corn sacks, one pert breast exposed, the nipple wet and furled like a rose bud in the early morning. Her mouth, so generous and soft, swollen with his kisses. God, he'd never seen anything so tempting in his life.

If the jingle of the horse's harness hadn't brought him back to his senses, he would have tumbled her right there in that storage shed, pumped into her to the accompaniment of breaking barley stalks and thought it a lovely sound. He was losing his mind. For years, he'd tried to overcome acting on his baser impulses. Now he was failing.

Cassy Spade was a puzzle he had to figure out to keep his sanity. With this in mind, he was leaving for Williamsburg today—alone. He needed to talk to someone with clarity of vision, someone whose opinion he could trust, and Conner McAlister was his choice.

He crept out of his own house like a thief and made it to the barn with no one the wiser. The last thing he wanted to do was try to explain himself to Mavis. He'd left her a note saying he'd be gone a few days and that would have to suffice.

He saddled Jack, a dark bay gelding with a roman nose, not the most impressive of his horses, but one with an easy gait. Jack could get him the thirteen miles to Williamsburg in comfort. At the first hint of light in the eastern sky, Jason was in the saddle and on his way.

Without pressing his mount, he arrived in the capital before noon. He left the horse in the livery at Christina Campbell's Tavern and walked a few blocks behind the establishment to McAlister's office and home. When he was shown into Conner's private office by one of the clerks, Conner unfolded his tall, slender frame from his chair, a welcoming grin splitting his freckled face.

"Jase, how delightful to see you. We didn't have an appointment today, did we?"

"No, this is a spur-of-the-moment visit. I have some information I want you to check," Jason said.

"Have a seat." McAlister waved toward a chair facing his desk and regained his own seat. "I hope you've not come about anything serious."

"No, no, nothing drastic. I just find myself in need of both some legal advice and the wise counsel of a friend."

"I'd hope my legal advice would be wise as well," Conner said, laughter brimming in his eyes. Jason had been blessed to have Conner as a friend, and his advice to date had been unvaryingly wise. When Jason had first started buying up what others thought of as useless land, Conner had made sure that all of the title changes were legal and could never be challenged. The latter had proved essential when those whose land he'd bought discovered the inexpensive property, deemed unsuitable for tobacco, was filled with bog iron. Most had been impressed with Jason's business acumen and wished him well. A few, led by Sir Peyton Hyde, had been angry and claimed Jason had cheated them. Some of this rancor persisted.

"Any opinion you give me is always wise," Jason said. "The first thing I need is a confidential enquiry. And I mean confidential, even from Mary. I don't want to put you in an awkward position with your wife, since I know you talk over most things with her, but it's necessary at this juncture. I need you to get me some information on a woman who left England about four months ago." Jason paused when Conner shifted forward in his chair. "You can put your eyebrows back down, if you please. She's one of my indentured servants."

McAlister pulled a piece of paper in front of him and dipped his quill, ready to take notes. He was unable to subdue a grin. "I'm fascinated by your interest in one of your indentures. I'm sure she hasn't stolen the silver, since the last I knew you didn't have enough for it to be worth anyone's while. So let's start at the beginning. Name?"

"Cassy Spade. I think that's genuine. Or her real name is at least something close. She has responded to it easily from the beginning."

"Occupation?"

"Seamstress. And she's a good one, but says she was a governess in England."

"Ah, I can see where this is going," Conner said. "If you can come up with references, you could make a tidy amount by letting her out to all those planters and merchants who are crying for some basic education for their children." The grin suddenly dropped from his face. "Don't tell me she was transported. That would definitely decrease her value."

"No, she was not. And I have no desire to make money on her contract. Will you shut up and listen? To give me wise counsel, you have to know enough to be wise."

Unoffended, Conner waved his quill at Jason and said, "Continue then, by all means."

"To begin again. Her name is Cassy Spade. The tale we've heard is that she was a parson's daughter, a gentlewoman fallen on hard times. She found work as a governess but was attacked by her employer and sacked without references. In her naivety, she accepted an indenture to get to the colonies and start anew. Her manners, her pattern of speech, even the way she moves, all say she's educated and from the upper class. Her speech particularly might be a little too polished for a provincial parson's daughter, but it is possible." Jason paused and looked up.

"What? Am I now allowed to speak?"

"I can hear your silent questions shouting in my skull, so go ahead."

"Well, the most obvious question is, does she have the looks that would motivate some unknown employer to attack her?"

"Yes." Jason knew damned well that Cassy's looks could cause an otherwise sane man to act like a brute, but there was no way he'd admit that, even to his closest friend.

Conner's caterpillar eyebrows again lifted toward his receding hairline. "Ah, this is getting interesting. Continue."

"Get your mind away from the topic that's showing in your eyes. I'm simply interested in finding out the truth. Yesterday, when I'd taken her into York to look at some fabric, she saw a gold locket in Jeffries' window that she identified as having belonged to her mother. Evidently, she had personal items that went missing on the ship over and the locket was among them. So I bought it for her."

"You bought it for her?" Conner's voice increased in volume. "Are you now buying all of your servants trinkets, or only the ones who are pretty enough to provoke an employer to misbehave?"

"It was hardly a trinket," Jason said, choosing to ignore the second half of Conner's question. "The locket is gold, heavily engraved, on a gold chain."

"Definitely not a trinket," Conner muttered. Jason chose to ignore this comment also.

"The important thing is that, when looking at the initials, she gave me her mother's maiden name, Elizabeth Patience Hargrove, and I thought that would make tracing Cassy easier. She also mentioned that all her other jewelry was paste. Now I ask you, what type of governess or parson's daughter would have a lot of jewelry, even if it wasn't real?"

"Why do you want to know?"

"I guess it's the mystery of the thing."

Conner looked skeptical. "I'll take that lame excuse for now. If you want my honest assessment without ever meeting the woman, I'd say it's more likely that your mysterious Cassy was a wealthy man's mistress instead of a governess. Or perhaps a not-so-wealthy man, if the gems were paste."

"That was Mavis's impression."

"Well, my God, man, who would know better? I'd believe Mavis."

"But her speech, her general demeanor..."

"Can be learned. Haven't you worked hard to erase the London slums from your accent? And succeeded, I might add."

"Only because I've tried to emulate you, and this sometimes makes people think I'm a Scot."

"My father sounds like a Scot," Conner said. "I sound like I've been to Oxford, which I have."

"You can't act touchy about your accent. Not after the things you've said to me."

"True. We all have our sore points. I get damned tired of other men lapsing into an imitation brogue when I come around. But give me a description of the woman. I'm sure anyone I write in London would need that to make any sort of identification."

Jason was silent for a moment. What could he say about Cassy that wouldn't immediately give away his interest in her? Captivating. Gorgeous. A sorceress. None of those would do. "I'd guess she was about twenty years old, maybe a little less. Blond hair, wheat colored would probably be more accurate. Blue eyes. About middle height, but very well rounded in the, eh, top section. Pale skin with no discernible marks. And she has a laugh that..." That what? Made him hard as a pikestaff. He could hardly say that.

Conner looked up from his note taking. There was no humor in his face. "That makes you want to tumble her?" he asked.

"Yes." Even with care, he'd evidently been obvious.

Conner leaned back and wiped the nub of his quill with a rag. "So, all of your curiosity about this woman is really an effort to come up with some reason that excuses your wanting to bed her?"

When Jason opened his mouth to rebut this uncomfortable truth, Conner held up his hands. "If she's a high-class whore, your conscious can be clear. Is that the idea? You could convince yourself you've simply hired her to continue her former trade. But if she truly is a ruined governess, what will you do? Continue with the ruin? You're damned either way."

Jason wanted to refute Conner's assertion, but no logical argument came to mind. Before he could marshal his thoughts, Conner cut him off. "You want to be elected a Burgess and part of your platform is reformation of the indenture laws to make it illegal for an owner to demand anything more from his servants than normal labor. You've spoken over and over about the immorality of an owner bedding his female indentured servants, since these women aren't in a position where they could say no if they wanted to. If you carry through to where I think you want this to go, you'll be a joke and not a candidate. You know you can't keep something like this secret."

Jason got out of his chair. He needed to pace. He needed to move away from uncomfortable truths. "I guess that rather succinctly covers it."

"Bloody hell, Jase, what has this woman done to you? I've never seen you so susceptible to big tits and a throaty laugh before."

He shrugged, feeling foolish. "I don't know why, but she's like a fever in my blood. I try to ignore her. I try to stay away. But I can't. And when I'm near her, all I can think about is having her. All I can see is the image of her sprawled naked across my bed. I feel like a damned stag in rut. It's driving me mad."

"So your constantly hard cock has not yet found the promised land?"

"Correct."

"Then stop pacing and let me think for a moment."

Jason returned to his chair with difficulty. He'd always been better at making decisions on his feet than on his ass, and he couldn't understand how Conner could be so different.

Conner tapped the end of the quill on his front teeth, a habit that often left him with spotted lips and stained linen, both to Mary's irritation. "All right. I have some ideas. Since leaving the woman in your employ is courting political disaster, you'll either have to excuse her articles of indenture and send her on her way or you can sell her indenture elsewhere."

"I thought about voiding her articles of indenture, but then where would she go? How would she support herself?"

"You said she was a competent seamstress, so how she would make money is obvious. As for where she'd live—I'd suggest some place far from you. If you just set her up in a nice little house in York or even here in Williamsburg, you can yell that you've released her at the top of your voice and it will make no difference. The perception of the situation will outweigh the facts. And I suspect if you set her up in a house of her own, you'd do so in the expectation of her being your mistress. The only way this would work is if you married the girl. Is that what you want?"

For some reason, Jason had never considered marriage. No, that was a lie. It wasn't for *some* reason. He had a very definite reason. When he saw himself as a Burgess, he also saw the daughter of a planter or a prosperous merchant gracing his arm as his wife. To marry such a woman would be a sign of his respectability, a sign he'd been accepted by those who had the power to control lives.

And what if it turned out Cassy had indeed been someone's mistress and her flight to the colonies one to avoid scandal? If he married her and this information got out, he'd look like a fool. He was sure his enemies would look for any scandal in an unknown wife's background. Commerce and gossip between Virginia and England were slow in coming, but they always arrived.

He wanted Cassy Spade in his bed with every fiber of his being, but he wasn't sure he wanted her to be the mother of his children. He didn't know how he felt about the idea of her being a permanent part of the empire he was slowly building.

God, such thoughts branded him an elitist and a hypocrite. He was as bad as the bastards he wanted to impress. The question was which was more important, bedding Cassy or rubbing the noses of Sir Peyton and his cronies in his success? The latter had been the goal that had sustained him for years. Was he ready to give that up for a woman?

Jason squirmed in his chair, uncomfortable with the ugly picture of himself his mind was painting. He wasn't without character. He liked Cassy as well as lusting for her. In the end, he wanted to do what was right.

"Selling her contract would probably be the wisest thing, but I'd hate to put Cassy in the same situation I'm trying to free her from," Jason said slowly, knowing his comment made his rejection of marriage clear to his friend. "I don't think you'll understand until you see her, but Cassy Spade has an allure that's irresistible."

Conner continued to tap his teeth. "Sell her contract to Mary. She'd enjoy having a seamstress at hand, and if this woman is all you say, maybe she could act as a lady's maid. Mary would love that. And I can guarantee she'd be safe from a lustful employer. My wife would have my balls on the chopping block if I even had lascivious thoughts about the girl."

Jason knew what Conner said was true. Mary wouldn't put up with any misbehavior on her husband's part. Most men envied Conner his strikingly beautiful wife. But all they saw was her slender, dark beauty. Jason was a good enough friend to know Mary had a ramrod for a backbone and could be a wildcat when angered.

Conner was offering a viable solution. It was probably *the* solution. This would mean he would occasionally see Cassy, but she'd no long be part of his everyday life. This was what he wanted, wasn't it? Temptation would be removed and he could get on with the careful plans he'd made for his future.

But he hated the idea.

He could no longer stay in the chair. He got up and paced from window to door and back again. "I'll bring her to Williamsburg next week to meet Mary. If your wife thinks Cassy would work, we'll draw up the papers."

"I know a good lawyer," Conner said in a sad attempt at humor. "Are you staying at Christina Campbell's tonight? I know the food at the tavern is good, but Mary would be disappointed if you didn't come for supper."

"No, I think I'll head back to the Bloomery. Please say hello to Mary and tell her I'll expect to be fed when I'm in town next week."

"Good God, Jase, it will be dark before you can get home. Why not stay the night here?"

Jason knew Conner was right, but it suddenly seemed imperative he go home. He needed to hole up in a familiar place to lick his self-imposed wound. But his decision was made. He'd sell Cassy's contract to Mary McAllister and they would all be much happier.

"The post road to York is in good shape," he said, "and once I'm on Bloomery land, I know every inch of it. So I can make the trip easily."

He made a hasty goodbye and was soon on the road. He should have felt better now that a decision had been made, but his pulse beat with the same dread he'd felt as a young convict boy when he'd been loaded on the ship that had taken him far from all he knew and loved.

Chapter Nine

*T*he click of the latch falling on the door at the bottom of the stairs sounded like a shot and brought Cassy from her restless slumber. She listened for the rustle and snores of the women around her and heard only silence. Without getting up to check, she knew she was the only person in the rooms above the kitchen. She should have recognized the edgy, humming energy whispering among the women at dinner. Now all of them had left to find comfort in the arms of their current lovers.

Perhaps they'd been affected by the broad moon that slanted though her window. Perhaps the cooling of the weather had heralded a general urge to mate. Whatever the impetus, Cassy was alone. Alone after a trying day that had left her limp with exhaustion.

Mavis's casual announcement that Mr. Anders had gone to Williamsburg had been a knife in her heart. He'd told her they would go together and then he'd decided otherwise. As she suspected, her behavior in the shed had disgusted him. He evidently thought her no different from the other women at the Bloomery whose attentions he avoided. And now he was going to avoid hers as well.

She should be pleased. Intellectually she was. At least, that's what she told herself. But emotionally, it was difficult to feel this way after she'd spent the day pretending she and Anders had a relationship. Anything less would have disappointed the others, who'd been as delighted with her locket as if it now belonged to them all. She hadn't told the women the locket had been her mother's and had silently smiled at the insinuations that it had been a gift for services rendered.

She reached up and rubbed the familiar golden surface. She was completely adrift in a sea of confusion. Something about Anders sent the blood singing in her veins, and she'd thought he'd felt a similar attraction. But that was evidently not the case.

What if they'd completed what they'd started? Would it have been bad? Her former self would have pronounced such behavior immoral, but that wasn't the consensus of the other indentured women. They looked on such trysts as normal, as a way to assuage loneliness. And she wanted Anders. She was willing to follow wherever he led.

But he'd rejected her. There was no other way to construe what had happened. Her sadness evolved into anger. Damn the man. Who did he think he was to reject her? Half the eligible men in London had been interested in her. She'd been the toast of the season. Yes, fate had intervened, and her circumstances had changed, but she was the same person she'd always been. Anders, however, was really nothing more than a lowborn thief. He should be beneath her.

That she continued to want him, to relive the glory of his lips on hers, only angered her more.

She freed her legs from the tangled sheets and sat on the side of her low trundle bed. With her feet on the floor, her knees were nearly even with her eyes. She wrapped her arms around her legs and hugged them. Everyone else had found someone who cared for them, if only for a few hours, and she was alone, her affections thrown away by a man who wasn't worthy of them in the first place.

She stood and walked to the window, drawn by a freshening breeze. The big house glowed a ghostly white in the moon-washed darkness. Standing stark on the landscape, the house cried out for the shrubs and flowers that would anchor it to the land. Over time, the newness would disappear and the property would take on the patina of gentility. That was what Anders wanted. He wanted it much more than he did some indentured woman. He should have been able to look deeper and see Cassy's intrinsic value—but he couldn't.

She leaned her head against the wavy glass in the window. Off to one side she saw a horse and rider arrive at the stables. She easily recognized the broad-shouldered figure as Anders. If he'd gone to Williamsburg, he'd certainly returned quickly. Maybe Mavis had been wrong about his destination. Hope shuddered through her, followed by irritation for feeling the emotion. Where was her pride?

She wouldn't skulk here in her room. She'd confront Anders and let him know what she thought about his high-handed behavior. Without further thought, Cassy belatedly joined the exodus from the kitchen rooms. She grabbed a shawl for modesty's sake, then marched down the stairs and out the door. She was oblivious to the softness of the night. She didn't feel the coolness of the grass on her bare feet or hear the call of a whip-poor-will from the adjacent woods. She went unerringly to the stables but came to a halt at the door.

Inside, Anders carried on a low-pitched conversation with a rangy gelding he was brushing. The interior of the stables, although lighted by a pieced tin lantern, was actually darker than the moonlit exterior. There was something so homey, so comfortable, about the scene that it gave her pause.

"Anders," she said, bringing the heads of both the man and the horse around to look at her.

"Cassy?"

"Yes." She boldly walked inside.

"What in the hell are you doing here?"

He didn't sound pleased to see her. "Did you go to Williamsburg without me?"

"I wasn't interested in furniture or fabric on this trip. I had private business to attend to."

His response was reasonable. Of course he'd have business in the capital that had nothing to do with her. He was hoping to be active in the government and Williamsburg was the seat of that government. She felt some of her anger melt away. "So we'll be going to look at items to decorate your house next week?"

He patted the gelding on the neck and took a few steps away, placing the currycomb on the ledge of a stall. "We'll be going to Williamsburg next week, but you'll be going to stay. I made arrangements today to transfer your articles of indenture."

Panic and fury washed over her in equal measure. He was selling her indenture? He no longer even wanted her to stay at the Bloomery? Her hands clenched at her sides. She wished she had something heavy to throw at the bastard. She noted he'd put more distance between them before calmly announcing that he'd completely rearranged her life.

She charged toward him, one hand poking him in the chest. "You can't do that!" Her voice had risen to a yell.

He grasped the hand she continued to pound into his chest. "Cassy, get a hold of yourself. I can sell your indenture and I have. It's for the best."

"For the best? How can you think such a thing? I've made friends here. I have my work here. Work I'm good at. And you want to send me away—to do what?" She had a horrible thought that Anders was so anxious to get rid of her, he didn't care what she'd be doing.

"I'm sorry you're unhappy with my decision," he said, his tone low and carefully controlled. "You seem to be under the illusion that you have some say about your life for the next four years, and that's not the case. You sold that option away on a dock in Bristol when you voluntarily signed the articles of indenture. But I've taken care to place you with good people. I'd never sell your papers to anyone who treats their indentured servants like slaves. You have no idea what your life could be like."

"I can imagine what it could be like since I've seen ample evidence written on your back." The words popped out of her mouth before her brain was engaged. What a stupid thing to say. Anders' reaction was immediate. It was as if a shutter had fallen over his face.

"When have you seen my back? You've been spying on me!"

"No. It was an accident. I saw you down by the small pond." Naked remained unsaid, but he had to remember he wore nothing when he was swimming.

He jerked on her captured hand, pulling her forward. His other arm wrapped around her waist and settled her snugly against him. "If I hadn't seen you on the ship myself, I'd think Sir Peyton had sent you here to torment me." His voice was low, almost a whisper. "You want to know why you have to leave? Well, here's a perfect example. You show up in the stables in the middle of the night wearing only a shift and a shawl. Every delectable part of you is pretty much on display. And I'm supposed to be able to resist you. No way in hell."

He lowered his mouth and took hers. This was no seductive kiss. This was possession, pure and simple. She instinctively fought against his control, but he only pressed her more tightly against his solid body. One large hand held her head still as his tongue knifed into her mouth. With a slight undulation of his hips, he rubbed an obvious erection across her stomach.

Her anger dropped away and fused into a primitive, shimmering heat. Her hands slipped up to hold his head as he held hers. Her fingers threaded through his silky hair. Her tongue dueled with his. Tendrils of fire sliced through her and her pulse accelerated.

She felt him lift the bottom of her sleeping shift and slide a hand up her thigh to cup her buttocks. The calluses on his fingers gently abraded her soft skin and forced all the heat she felt to pool between her legs. She realized he no longer held her tightly. She was the one who pressed against him, rubbing her body across his by her own volition.

He broke the fevered kiss and leaned back. The loss of his lips opened a deep void within her and she attempted to pull his head back down to hers. He stopped her from doing so, looking deeply into her eyes. His had darkened until the pupils seemed to cover the entire irises. "I need to be inside you," he whispered. "For just this one time, take me inside you."

All she had learned, all she knew, told her to reject him as he had her. But when she opened her mouth, she said, "Yes," a promise floating on a sigh. And she knew this was what she wanted. *For just this one time*, he'd said, and if this was all she could ever have of this compelling man, it would be now.

He seemed surprised by her answer and kissed her more gently. The apparent tenderness fanned the heat within her until she felt consumed.

"Come," he said, taking her hand and leading her along the row of stalls and up a narrow set of stairs. He pushed open the door to a small room illuminated only by the bright moon beyond the window. She saw a narrow bed, a dresser, and a group of pegs along the wall from which hung an assortment of hats.

"What is this place?" she asked.

"Obviously Hats' room," he said with a chuckle. "As chief groom, he lives up here."

She hesitated, wondering where the little man was now. She quickly searched the shadowed edges of the room. Anders must have felt her uncertainty. "He isn't here. Hats spends every night with Mavis in her room in the basement of the big house." He gave a rueful laugh. "Many nights I feel like I'm the only man on the Bloomery who's sleeping alone. I have to go into town to the Blue Heron to find a counterfeit of passion." He pulled her into his embrace. "Tell me this is real for you. Tell me there is no pretense and that you want me as badly as I want you."

His hair, loosened from its queue and falling around his face, cast moon shadows on the sharp contours of his cheekbones and highlighted the arrogant bridge of his nose. Cassy could imagine no more wondrous sight. "I want you," she said, her voice low and hoarse. "I want you more than anything I've ever wanted in my life."

He kissed her again with soul-destroying tenderness. Then he moved his lips to roam her face. He traced her cheeks with butterfly kisses, softly tugged on her ear lobe, and kissed his way down her neck. She trembled in his embrace. She felt cherished, as if she were something of great value that he'd never hoped to win.

He loosened the tie at the neck of her shift and pushed it down. The sleeves momentarily trapped her arms, and she helped him shed the garment from her body until it pooled around her feet. She should have been embarrassed to stand naked before a man, but as his eyes roamed her body, she felt the rightness of it all.

He cupped her breasts in both hands, seeming to weigh them. Then he rubbed the sensitive tips with the pads of his thumbs, watching her face instead of his hands. She arched into him with a moan. He lowered his head and licked one and then the other, the dampness of his mouth pebbling her nipples, the coolness of her dampened flesh contrasting with the heat that hammered through her.

"God, you are beautiful. The most beautiful thing I've ever seen."

How could she tell him he was equally beautiful? She suspected he would find offense in the phrase, even though it was true. The planes of his face were finely sculpted. She could feel the structure of his powerfully built chest beneath his clothing. "You've too many clothes on," she said.

"Indeed I do." His laugh was carefree and boyish. "Come, lie down, and I'll get rid of this unneeded material."

As though bewitched, Cassy did as he said, lying down on the bed. The counterpane was rough beneath her. She reached for him, but he chuckled and eluded her grasp, sitting down on the edge of the bed near her feet. He quickly heeled off his tall riding boots, unbuckled the legs of his breeches, and rolled down his hose. He then stood and stripped off his coat and waistcoat and pushed his breeches to the floor. Stepping out of the pants, he turned and lowered himself to the bed next to her.

"Shirt," she said, pulling at the offending article. His long, billowing shirt hid most of his body.

"No." He removed her hands, kissed them, and placed them on top of his shirt on his chest. "You said you've seen the ugliness that is my back. There is no need to let that intrude on your beauty and the beauty I hope we can create together. Forget what you've seen. For now, for this one night, imagine me whole."

He leaned down and drew one breast into the warm interior of his mouth. He suckled harder, gently nipping her nipple with his teeth. A moan she didn't recognize wavered in the air, and her hands gripped the top of his shoulders in rhythm with the action of his mouth. The fabric bunched in her hands, but she could feel the play of the powerful muscles hidden by the cloth.

His hand stroked down her stomach until he came to the juncture of her legs. When one finger slowly slipped into her cleft, she involuntarily jumped and pulled her legs tightly together.

"Open for me, Cass," he said, as he drew his finger back and forth. "You're wet for me. You weep for what you want. Relax your legs and let me give it to you."

She did as he asked, but more in reaction to the sensations caused by his caresses than to his words. His fingers circled the nub at the top of her cleft. Her breath caught in her throat and her pelvis arched. Spirals of delight circled from the area he touched. Anders gave a soft, chuffing laugh. "The little man in a boat likes to have his boat rocked."

Cassy tried to reconcile what was happening to her with the talk she'd heard in the kitchen, but no one had mentioned little men or boats. Whatever Anders was doing, though, the sensations were marvelous. One of his fingers entered her, but there was no feeling of invasion. Instead, it further added to the tension building in her midsection. He moved his finger in and out, in time with the stroking of her nub.

He shifted his position, the bed creaking in protest. She opened her eyes to see him kneeling between her splayed legs. His face was taut, as if he too could feel the tension coiling within her. He watched the hand that fondled her. His shirt had rucked up and she could see his cock jutting from a thatch of dark hair.

Unable to reach him, Cassy clenched the bed covers on either side of her body. Her breath came in pants, each exhalation a whimper. She felt herself further stretched as a second finger joined the first pumping her opening. "Come for me, Cass," he panted. "Flood my hand with your juice. You're so damned tight and I don't want to hurt you."

And then he did hurt her. He reached up and pinched one of her nipples between strong fingers. Pain and pleasure combined, and the tension within her shattered. She cried out, the sound like a hunting hawk that had found its prey.

Anders' hand disappeared and she felt the broad head of his cock pushing against her opening. He stretched his body above hers, supporting his weight on his elbows, and in one quick flex of his hips, fully entered her. The pleasure became all pain and she jerked away from him, but he held her steady beneath him. "Bloody hell, why didn't you tell me?" he asked in a strained voice.

Then he kissed her hard, his tongue moving in and out of her mouth in rhythm with his cock. Pain diminished and the joyful feeling returned. Her hips moved up to meet his thrusts. The linen of his shirt tickled her breasts and she wanted, needed, to feel his skin next to hers. Her hands floated down to his hips and found the bottom of his shirt. She pushed it aside and stroked his buttocks, feeling the smooth skin and the muscles moving as he pounded into her.

The exquisite tightness she'd experienced earlier returned, this time with greater intensity. She wrapped her legs around his hips, straining against him. She knew now what lay on the other side and actively sought it. She climbed higher and higher until she once again flew apart, her legs instinctively molding him to her as her interior muscles contracted around his cock.

Anders jerked back against the restraint, surprising her. Then he again lay prone over her, rubbing his hard cock across her stomach a few times until his body stiffened and she felt the warm gush of his seed. His breathing was harsh as he nestled his head next to hers. She tenderly kissed his sweat-slick cheek. The smell of warm male and clean linen reminded her of the first time she'd seen him and he'd carried her across the hot deck. It was just a few short months and yet a lifetime ago.

When his breathing became more regular, he rolled to one side and pushed her damp hair from her face, his fingers staying there after the job was done to rub the side of her jaw. "Don't ever hold me inside you," he said. "You feel too damned good and I almost didn't get out in time."

"Oh, Anders. That was something that Bess said you didn't have to do."

A wistful smile twisted the corners of his mouth. "First of all, I think it would be best if you called me Jason, don't you?"

Cassy nodded.

"Say my name."

"Jason."

His smile broadened. "And as for the other, I'm no different from any of the other men. Only a fool plants a child when it can be avoided. It's probably become habit for me. During those long years of my indenture, all I had to offer was pleasure and careful behavior. The exodus to the woods is not a new thing, you know. And there have always been many more men than women, so I had to build a reputation for satisfaction and safety if I wanted someone to fill my nights."

Cassy looked at him in surprise. Didn't he know his looks attracted every woman on the Bloomery? It wouldn't have been any different when he was younger. His allure had nothing to do with his now being a landowner. "Women wanted you because you're beautiful."

He gave a rueful chuckle. "Only if I stay partially dressed." He rolled from the bed, crossed to the dresser, and poured water from a pitcher into a bowl. Cassy wondered at his familiarity with the room. Did he meet other women here?

Jealousy nibbled at her brain. Ridiculous! She had no claim on Jason. But that didn't calm the emotion.

He returned to run a cold, wet cloth across her stomach. She jerked to a sitting position with a quick shriek. "I'm just cleaning you up a bit before you go back to your room. I thought you'd prefer that the others not know of your activity tonight, since it's obvious you've never done anything like it before."

She took the cloth and vigorously rubbed her own stomach. She was sticky and sore between her legs, but she definitely wasn't washing that area until she was alone. Jason picked up her shift and handed it to her. She shrugged it over her head without standing. Strangely, she was now embarrassed by her nudity. Perhaps feeling the same discomfort, Jason slipped on his breeches.

He settled on the bed next to her. "Why didn't you tell me you'd never been with a man before? I heard you'd been attacked by your employer, at least that was the story you gave to the other women, and so I assumed this would not be your first time. Was that tale a lie?"

"No. I was attacked, but it didn't go that far." Her voice trailed off.

Jason looked away, his eyes focused on nothing in the middle of the room. He ran his fingers through his hair. "Shit! If I'd known, I could have done things differently."

Cassy couldn't imagine how things could have been different. She certainly didn't think they could have been much better. The feelings he'd engendered in her were glorious. She could now understand why the other women left their rooms at night. But she didn't think she would have felt the same had the man in bed with her not been Jason

Anders. No other man called to her as he did. "I thought it was nice," she said, placing her hand on his arm.

He barked a laugh. "Nice? Ah, Cass, you certainly know how to damn a man with faint praise."

"But it was wonderful," she protested. And magical and incredible and life-altering, but she couldn't bring herself to say those things. "Since you were selling my contract to someone else, I wanted to have this experience with you, and I'm glad I did." She felt tears gather in the corners of her eyes and blinked them away.

"I may have to rethink the selling part," Jason said. He stood abruptly and held out his hand to help her rise. "I may have to rethink a number of things. But for now, you need to get back."

Cassy took his hand and came to her feet. She turned and began smoothing the cover on the bed. Even in the faint light, a dark spot was visible. She leaned over further to check the stain, her butt bumping into Jason behind her. He put his hands on her hips and pulled her back against him. He kissed her on the back of her neck. "Dear God, woman. Stop doing that if you hope to get to your room before daybreak."

He stepped back, grasped her shoulders, and turned her in the direction of the door. "Go. I'll see to the room."

"Hats is bound to know we were here," she said, worrying her lip.

Jason was also eyeing the bed cover. "Well, he'll know someone was here, but not who it was. I'll go through the motions. I'll have to talk to a few of the men at the forge, warning them away from Hats room and suggesting they stay to the bowers that scatter the woods. That should take care of it."

He took her hand and led her down the stairs as he'd led her up. At the door, he kissed her gently on the forehead and nudged her outside. She walked with haste toward the kitchen building. She was almost there when she looked back. She could just make out his white shirt in the waning moonlight. He looked as insubstantial as a ghost. She shivered and walked on.

Chapter Ten

Jason swung the long-handled ax high above his head and brought it down with a satisfying whack onto the log balanced on the chopping block. The log neatly split into two pieces that fell to either side of the block. He leaned down, retrieved both halves, and took them to a growing wood stack. Picking up another log, he repeated the process, enjoying the sensation of his muscles tightening and releasing. There was a great deal of pleasure in a mindless, repetitive task. The woodpile was tangible proof of accomplishment while his mind was free to examine various problems.

The motion was much the same as forging iron, a task Jason had eventually found liberating. All of his plans, which were slowly coming to fruition, had been made as he changed a shapeless piece of metal into something useable. He couldn't work at the forge now, however. It caused too many curious stares. He was an important landowner and supposedly beyond such menial labor. But here, in the woods behind the house, he had the privacy to think and plan as he swung the ax.

He'd made the basic decision quickly. As he lay replete, breathing in the faint lavender scent that clung to Cassy's skin, he'd known he'd have to marry her. A man didn't breech a woman's maidenhead with impunity. There was a price to pay for such behavior and that price was marriage. He told himself it was out of his control. This was how a man of honor behaved.

But he knew this was a rationalization, an excuse to follow his heart. If he were honest, he'd admit he *wanted* to marry Cassy Spade. Honor had nothing to do with it. He could see her gracing his yet-to-be-purchased table. He could imagine her talking with him by the fire on a winter's night. And he could definitely envision her lying across his bed. The banked passion of the woman found an answering passion within him. He wanted to spend a lifetime exploring the different ways he could make the soft whimpers emerge from her throat.

She'd been a virgin. Jason had never thought this was a possibility, or he would have done things differently. He'd been told she'd been attacked and secretly suspected she'd been some powerful man's mistress. That she had never lain with a man had not been a consideration.

He chuckled at his thoughts and swung the ax again. Certainly, he would have done things differently, if he'd had the slightest idea what those differences should be. He'd bedded women since he was sixteen, more than he could individually remember, their appearances now a confusion of different body shapes and faces, but he'd never before been some woman's first man. He'd been given the gift that could only be given once. When he'd made that discovery, there was no way in hell he was going to let Cassy get away from him. Irrational possessiveness flashed through him. He was Cassy Spade's first lover, and he would be her last.

Yes, that decision was made. The problem that remained was how to implement this marriage. Again, he was confounded by the repercussion of marrying one of his own indentured servants. It would lower him in the estimation of what passed for the colonial aristocracy, and he would not—could not—give up his dream of rising to a position of power. The impetus to destroy Sir Peyton Hyde, both emotionally and financially, was too strong. There had to be a way he could accomplish both his desires. It just required more thought.

With a slight grunt he hefted the ax and watched it fall, splitting the log with ease.

"I thought you'd be hiding here," Mavis said.

He straightened from picking up the halves and carried them to the pile. "I'm in plain sight on a bright day. I would hardly call this hiding."

"But this is where you always come when you have something to mull over. You do realize you employ men to do this job, don't you?"

He grinned at Mavis, surprised that his behavior was so transparent to her. "I'm well aware of who I hire," he said.

Mavis stood with her hands on her hips. "I doubt you are. You seem to have forgotten that Cassy Spade is one of your indentured servants. After all your pretentious pronouncements about not messing with your servants, you bedded Cassy, didn't you? Tell me I'm wrong."

He shrugged, caught between confessing and brazening it out. "What makes you think that?"

Mavis held up her hand and began ticking reasons off on her fingers. "Well, to begin with, all morning, Cassy's had a shaky smile and eyes that want to fill with tears. And then, someone used Hats' room last night for a trysting place. They tried to clean up, but I can recognize both come tracks and blood on his bed covers. I can't think of anyone but you who would have the nerve to use Hats' bed for that purpose. The main reason, however, is that for weeks you've been following her with hungry eyes, like she was a fine meal and you were starving. This morning you look like you've supped well. So, what do you have to say to that?"

He let the ax hang at his side and frowned at his housekeeper. "I say what I do is none of your damned business. And in the case of Cassy, that will soon be taken care of."

"God, Jase. I never figured you for such a cold-hearted bastard. I already know how you plan to take care of her. You're selling her contract to someone in Williamsburg. Cassy told me this morning when I asked her what was wrong. So, from my way of seeing it, you had your way with the girl and are getting rid of the evidence. I can't believe I so misjudged you. You make me want to puke."

Since that was exactly what Jason had originally planned, it was hard to deny these accusations. He'd thought if he could just bed Cassy, he could get her out of his mind. He thought she was an itch that once scratched, would never itch again. Was there ever a man who was such a fool? "Well, before you lose your breakfast, you might as well know that I'm out here deciding how I'm going to marry her."

Mavis got the same look he'd seen on a steer when he knocked it in the forehead with the big forge hammer. It was a job he hated, which was why Sir Peyton assigned him to it, but he'd never forgotten the look of shocked disbelief that crossed a cow's eyes in that split second before it fell over dead. He was almost afraid Mavis's knees would buckle, but she only stared with her mouth open. "Now that's an interesting twist. I guess that's why Conner McAllister is pacing a hole in the rug in your study and why he sent me out to find you."

"Conner is here?" And more importantly, Conner was pacing? Conner was a tooth-tapper, not a pacer. Alarm shot through him.

"Didn't I just say so? God, Jase, are you so far gone about that woman that your brains have fallen into your prick? McAllister is here. I assumed you'd sent for him."

"No, I have no idea why he's here." Jason's gut tightened in apprehension. Conner couldn't be here to pick up Cassy and take her back with him. That wasn't going to happen.

He hefted the big ax and buried it in the middle of the chopping block. Wiping his hands on his breeches as he walked, he hurried into the house. If Conner was going to arrive unannounced, he'd just have to accept a sweaty Jason in shirtsleeves.

When he entered his study, Conner wasn't pacing, but he was rocking back and forth on his feet as he looked out the window. This was indeed alarming behavior for Conner. Jason was the one who tended to stay in perpetual motion.

"Conner. I'm surprised to see you again so soon. I hope there's not a problem. Is Mary all right?"

McAllister turned from the window, a broad grin splitting his face. No one in difficulty could smile so widely. Jason felt himself relax. "Actually, Mary is very fine. She informed me just after you left that she's expecting our first child. If you'd stayed for supper, we could have had a celebration."

Jason crossed the room and clapped his hands against his friend's shoulders. "That's wonderful news! Congratulations to you both. And I think this is worthy of a celebratory drink, even if it is still morning." Jason knew Conner had been concerned that after nearly three years of marriage, Mary had yet to conceive. They both desperately wanted a child. Jason shared in his friend's joy. He suddenly had a mental image of Cassy holding a child to her breast, and his happy smile matched his friends.

"Would you care for Madeira or rum?" Jason asked, eyeing the decanters resting on the decorated tray.

"Madeira, please."

Jason poured a glass for his friend, but his hand paused over the second glass. If this was to be a celebratory drink, it might as well be something palatable. He replaced the wine decanter and poured himself a tot of rum. "Do you really like this stuff?" he asked, handing Conner his glass.

"What's not to like? Unless you're telling me you have some sort of substandard vintage." Conner took a sip. "This is excellent."

"Mavis keeps telling me it's what gentlemen drink, but I find it so damned sweet." He raised his glass toward McAllister. "I figure with you I needn't pretend to be the gentleman, so I toast your happiness with some good Jamaican rum."

The two men took a drink. "This isn't the news I hurried here to give you, however," Conner said. "I've found out some interesting things about your mysterious indentured servant."

Jason's grip on his glass tightened. For all that his friend was smiling, he felt what he was about to hear would not be good news. "Sit down and tell me what you've discovered," he said, motioning toward a chair. "I know you haven't heard from your contacts in England unless you're involved in sorcery."

"No, nothing supernatural." Conner settled himself into a wingback by the cold hearth. "Last night I met some friends at Shield's Tavern. I was anxious to tell them my happy news. Among the group that eventually settled in the taproom was David Lyle, newly arrived from London. In the course of the evening, someone asked him for the latest gossip from the capital. You'd think we'd not care about what happens so far away, but we both know that isn't the case." Conner paused to take a drink of his Madeira.

"And," Jason prompted. He knew he wasn't going to like whatever Conner had to say, but like a child fascinated by a boiling pot, he couldn't resist sticking in a finger to see if it was hot.

"Well, in the course of a rambling account of the rampant stupidity of our king and those who govern, Lyle mentioned that when he left London, society was agog over the disappearance of Lady Cassandra Spathe, the Earl of Chelle's daughter. That immediately got my attention. Cassandra Spathe, Cassy Spade, the names just seemed a little too close for coincidence. So I asked him to describe the missing lady, and when he did, his description sounded very much like the one you'd given me of your servant. Though I must say Lyle's version was a bit more laudatory of her physical attributes than yours."

"Be that as it may, how did this woman, eh, lady, go missing?" Lady Cassandra Spathe. Dear God, what if Cassy were indeed this lady? It would explain many things—her speech patterns, her innate confidence, her carefully guarded virtue, which he'd relieved her of just last night. The rum he'd drunk turned to acid in his gut. He could feel it eating its way through his stomach with an almost debilitating pain.

"The best theory seems to be that the lady was kidnapped. Lady Cassandra came to town at the beginning of the season and cut a wide swathe through society. She had beauty and wit and impeccable bloodlines. A number of eligible men had made their interest known to her father, but he was being very choosey, and evidently sent most of them packing. The frontrunner for her hand seems to have been Lord Tilton. Now here's where the story gets interesting." Conner leaned forward in his chair.

Interesting? How about nauseating? Jason was sure the rum had bored a hole through his stomach.

"According to Lyle, this Tilton is known as a gamester, but he has plenty of money to lose, although he seldom does. The man is ruthless and has the devil's own luck. Some would say perhaps a bit too much luck for honesty. At any rate, at the same time Lady Cassandra goes missing, Lord Tilton is attacked and nearly killed by ruffians. The official version is the attack was a robbery gone bad. The man was left blind in one eye. But the whispers are that his beating was retribution for his participation in a crooked card game. Of course, no one will admit to that, so it's speculation. But one theory about the lady's disappearance is that Tilton's enemy spirited away his lady love."

"So this alliance between Lord Tilton and Lady Cassandra was a love match?" Jason rubbed a hand across the front of his shirt in an effort to ease the pain that had settled there. His gut now felt cold rather than hot, but it hurt all the same.

Conner laughed. "Love match? Hardly. As I said, Tilton has a lot of coin and Lord Spathe had a desperate need for some. As I understand it, the match was to be more of a financial transaction. The description Lyle gave of Tilton wasn't complimentary. He made the man sound like a hog that's been fattened for the table. With this in mind, I think it possible the lady fled on her own, but that hardly explains how she could have ended up an indentured servant."

A tiny hoped flared. This could just be a confusion caused by a similarity of names. His Cassy need not be Lady Cassandra, a noblewoman so high above him it was laughable. "Obviously the only way to be certain is to present this information to the lady herself and see what she says."

Jason was proud of himself when he used the bell pull instead of bellowing for Titus. When his butler arrived, he asked him to summon Cassy immediately. There was a strange, knowing look on Titus's dark face. Dear Lord, did everyone on his estate know what he did in the night and with whom? He began pacing. He should have made this room larger. He could only get in eight good strides before turning and retracing his steps. And where the hell was Cassy that it was taking her so long to get here?

Then, Jason heard a slight noise at the door and turned. Cassy stood in the doorway in her normal work clothes, and she still took his breath away, she was so beautiful. Her face was flushed and a few tendrils of golden hair had escaped her cap and bounced around her face. She looked at him with radiant delight until she noted Conner's presence, then her face became more guarded. "Are you Lady Cassandra Spathe?" he blurted out.

All the color left her face and he knew. Dear God, he knew.

Next to him he heard Conner mutter, "I can see your problem."

Chapter Eleven

"*A*re you Lady Cassandra Spathe?"

Cassy had expected any number of things when she rushed to the big house at Jason's request, but she had never imagined she would be asked *that* question.

She'd been stitching together the cream-colored waistcoat when one of the younger boys from the house found her. She had a clear vision of the embroidery she wanted to do on the front and was pressing to get it to the place where she could begin the fancy work. She wouldn't have started on the waistcoat if she thought she'd be leaving the Bloomery, but after last night, she hoped that wouldn't be the case.

Last night had been the most magical of her life. She knew it was possible to have sex without there being any meaning. The behavior of most of the women who lived over the kitchen confirmed this. But her time with Jason had been more significant than she'd ever imagined. She cared for him in a way that had nothing to do with sex, and she thought he had similar feelings.

As she hurried to the house, she'd thought he was going to tell her that she'd be staying at the Bloomery indefinitely. Somewhere in her secret heart, she saw him going down on one knee and asking her to marry him. It was a foolish fantasy, she knew that, but the dream persisted because it was the desire of her heart.

When she entered the study, a stranger rose to his feet. He was tall, slender, fair, and very serious-looking. Was this the person Jason was going to sell her contract to? Sweet heavens, was Jason actually going to get rid of her after...?

The thought was interrupted by Jason's question: "Are you Lady Cassandra Spathe?"

Her pulse stuttered to a stop. This was much worse than being sent away. Cassy immediately knew who the other man was. He was the magistrate, come to take her to jail. How had the authorities found her so quickly? She wavered and had to catch hold of the doorframe to keep from going to her knees. Should she lie? If she'd already been found, it seemed of little purpose.

Cassy straightened her shoulders, lifted her head, looked directly at the magistrate, and said in her haughtiest tone, "Yes, I am Lady Cassandra Spathe."

Jason made an odd choking sound and she turned to look at him instead of the man who would soon place her in irons. Jason seemed shocked by her answer, even though he'd asked the question. She noticed he stood in shirtsleeves. This should have put him at a disadvantage when compared with the elegantly attired intruder, but it didn't. Jason Anders in anything was the most completely virile man she'd ever seen.

"Would you have a seat, Lady Cassandra?" Jason asked in a strained voice. He motioned to the wingback next to the one the unknown man stood before. "I believe we have a number of questions that need answering."

Cassy gracefully lowered herself into the chair and straightened her wrinkled work dress as if it were a ball gown. If she were going to jail, she would go with dignity.

She glared at the stranger, her expression identical to the one her Aunt Amelia had perfected to put lesser mortals in their place. "And you are?"

The look must have worked. The man gave her a graceful bow. "Conner McAlister, Esquire, at your service."

"Ignore the esquire part," Jason said as he pulled his desk chair up so he sat between Cassy and McAllister. "He's just a jumped up merchant's son with an Oxford education. He's also my attorney, by the way."

"You're not the magistrate?" she asked, relief flooding through her in a dizzying rush.

"At the moment, no. But I hope to be. It will just take a while to get Simon Jessup's broad ass out of that chair." He got an odd look on his face. "I'm sorry for the cursing, my lady. Colonial manners can sometimes be rough."

"Sweet Jesus," Jason said. "You're supposed to be helping me get to the bottom of this mystery, not courting. Kindly remember what you said Mary would do to your ballocks if you stepped out of line and don't worry about a few curse words."

"As you most obviously aren't worried," McAllister rejoined, sitting down.

The two men stared at each other for a moment, then Jason leaned forward in his chair until he was almost touching her. She could feel his heat and wished he'd take her hand or in some way acknowledge his concern. Both men looked at her as if she were a prisoner in the dock.

"Cassy, can you explain how you came to be here? The truth now. None of this nonsense you've told everyone here so far. What have you done that you think should involve a magistrate?"

"I don't want to talk in front of Mr. McAllister," Cassy said, stalling for time. If they didn't know she'd killed a man now, they would when she finished her tale. She felt in the end Jason would protect her. She was less sure of McAllister.

"You can say anything you like and, as your attorney, I can't testify to any of it. In this respect, telling me something that might be criminal is actually safer than telling Jason."

Jason glared at McAllister, but only said, "Consider yourself hired as Lady Cassandra's attorney. Now can we just get to the truth."

Cassy looked down. "I don't know where to start."

"Start anywhere, but for God's sake, start." Jason abruptly got up and began roaming around the room.

"My father is the Earl of Chelle." Cassy's voice wobbled. She would shorten her tale to the essentials. Jason said his friend was trustworthy, but right now, she wasn't totally sure of Jason, who continued to pace the room with a scowl on his face.

"After my mother's death, I was raised by her side of the family. Last year, my father visited my Aunt Amelia's estate in Wiltshire and said he'd decided to take me to London for the season. I was very excited. I thought I'd find a place in society, meet the man of my dreams, and then marry him to live happily ever after. As it turned out, this was all just a fantasy. My father's plans also included my marrying, but he was looking for a wealthy husband for me who could inject some needed capital into the Spathe coffers."

She realized she was picking at a loose thread on her skirt and stilled her hand with difficulty. She did not want to discuss this part. She tried to imagine this had happened to someone else and that she was just reciting a tale she'd heard. "My father's choice was Baron Tilton. When I refused him, the baron attacked me with my father's complicity. I assume the idea was that after he had ruined me, no other man would have me, and I'd be forced to marry Tilton. I tried to fight him, but he was a big man and forced me back across a desk. There was a quill knife on the desk and I grabbed it and stabbed it into his eye. I killed him."

She stopped and the room settled in silence. Even Jason was frozen where he stood. McAllister shifted forward in his seat and said, "This explains your concern about the magistrate coming to call, but it leaves out the whole tale of how you came to be in Virginia."

"I knew I had to flee. My maid Peg had heard that you could get free passage on a ship to the American colonies by agreeing to an indenture contract. I had a friend in the military who'd been posted to Boston and I thought we would go there. I was sure he would pay the ship's captain our fee and I'd be safe from prosecution. But when we got to Bristol, the only ship immediately available was going to Virginia, not Massachusetts. I had no idea these places were so far apart, so we took passage. And then the voyage was horrible. We were locked in a hold and I was deathly ill and Peg died." Cassy sobbed out the last word. Her friend's death lay on her like a stone. It was her fault. All of this was her fault alone. A large, tanned hand appeared in her line of vision, holding a plain handkerchief. She looked up into Jason's stern, controlled face.

"Who was the man you were hoping to meet in Boston?" he asked, his voice tight.

"Gilbert Michaels. Lieutenant Michaels with the Fifty-Fifth Regiment of Foot. I'd met him in London." Cassy didn't add she could no longer bring Lieutenant Michael's face to mind. He'd been charming. He'd danced well. He'd kissed her in a garden before he left to join his regiment. Now it seemed foolhardy to cross an ocean on such a slim acquaintance.

"Why didn't you apprise anyone of your circumstances once you were here?" McAllister asked.

"I was afraid." It sounded so simple, but her reasons were actually more complex. Initially, she'd held her silence out of fear, but in a short time, her motivation changed. Cassy had certainly never really worked before in her life, never risen with the dawn and been given a day's worth of chores. But she'd discovered she liked it. She liked the structure, the feeling of accomplishment. And she liked the people around her. She'd made real friends where before she'd primarily had acquaintances. She didn't want to explain this to these two men. They saw a life of privilege as something to aspire to. They would think her mad.

"There are a few things you should know before you decide what to do now," McAllister said. "First of all, Lord Tilton is not dead. You did manage to blind him in one eye, but he is very much alive. He put about that he was injured by footpads. The gossip suggests your disappearance may be tied to his attack. There are those who believe both events were the result of someone's anger over Tilton's allegedly cheating while gaming. At any rate, you'll not be charged with murder since none was committed."

The air whooshed out of Cassy's lungs and she slumped in the chair. She'd not killed Tilton. She was free of the fear of incarceration. But she also knew she didn't want to be anywhere near the baron. He knew exactly what had happened and she suspected he would take reprisal on her for what she'd done. "I'm relieved I'm not wanted by the authorities," was all she said.

McAllister suddenly stood, crossed to the desk, and picked up a quill pen lying there. He returned to his seat and began methodically tapping his front teeth with the dry pen. She must have looked at him quizzically, since color washed up his neck and across his fair face. "I'm sorry. I do this to think." He gave her a brief smile. "It works rather well as long as the nub is dry. And it certainly takes up less room that Jason's incessant pacing."

She could make no comment on this, so sat silent amid the tapping and pacing. Why was she worried these men would think her insane? Neither was exhibiting much stability.

"I've been trying to think of a scenario to explain your being here," McAllister finally said. "I think we can use the perception that you were the victim of foul play. We could say you were drugged and put on the ship to Virginia and when you got here…" He tapped his teeth a few more times. "You had amnesia. Yes, amnesia is good. Maybe you could have had it before you were placed on the ship. That might work better. Hit on the head and whisked to the ship and waking up not knowing who you were. I like it. It works. Then you regained your memory, but no one would believe you. We could even pull in your unusual name." He turned to look at where Jason silently prowled. "You know that in Greek mythology, no one believed Cassandra?"

"I haven't had the benefits of an Oxford education," Jason said sharply, "but I do know who Cassandra was. I thought no one believed her predictions of the future, however."

"Close enough," McAllister said.

"You really don't think anyone would believe this preposterous tale, do you?" Cassy asked.

McAllister looked genuinely perplexed. "Of course I do. I've found that the more fanciful a story is, the more people will think it's true. They love to be involved in something amazing, if only peripherally."

"Since you both are blithely rearranging my life, don't you have any questions or comments?" She looked pointedly at Jason, who had said very little. Why was it that men thought they could make decisions for her?

Jason stopped and frowned at her. "Yes, I do have a question. How is it that a fine, blue-blooded lady could pass herself off as seamstress? I'm no authority on making clothes, but what you've done shows competence."

Cassy felt inordinately pleased with the compliment. "I had to appear in a wide variety of clothes while I was in London, and my father's purse wasn't plump enough to have these gowns made by a mantua-maker. My maid Peg knew of a shop where lady's maids sold their mistresses' castoff clothing. We bought the gowns and other things we thought had potential and then made extensive changes so they appeared newly made."

"Enterprising," Jason said, and Cassy again felt the glow of his praise. She suspected this was the trait he held in the highest regard.

"Lady Cassandra's sewing ability is not important at this juncture," McAllister interjected. "We need to establish the amnesia story to protect her reputation up to now. Of course, she'll have to come and stay with Mary and me in Williamsburg, and we'll have to send the happy news of her recovery to her father in England and arrange for passage—"

"No." Cassy cut him off. With that one word, she felt the old Cassandra resurfacing. She'd resented and fought against her father's control, and she would not hand over that control to some other man. In this case, one she didn't even know.

McAllister looked nonplussed. "No? No to what?"

"To all of your schemes. So, no, I will not be returning to England. I came here to escape my father and will not again place myself under his control. If no one knows what happened to Lady Cassandra, why can't we leave it that way?"

"And you do what? Stay here as an indentured servant? Don't be ridiculous. You are who you are. We get enough visitors from England that you're sure to be recognized at some point. We have to figure some way to return you to your place in society." McAllister was adamant.

"*We* don't have to figure out anything," Cassy said with equal intensity. "*I* have to decide. And I find it very difficult to come to any sort of decision when you're sitting there creating fairy tales about my life. Now that I know Lord Tilton is alive, I realize I can have a life. One of my own choosing."

McAllister threw his hands in the air in a gesture of frustration. "Jason, are you going to continue to act like a hovering vulture or are you going to add something to this discussion? You always have opinions shooting out of every orifice and now you've suddenly become mute. What do you think?"

"I think I never realized that you were such an Oxford educated snob. And that whatever is decided, someone is going to owe me four pounds for loss of labor." With that, Jason turned on his heel and stalked out of the door.

Cassy and McAllister stared at the empty doorframe, expecting him to return. When it became apparent he wasn't, McAllister said, "Well, I guess that's that."

That's that. It sounded like the epitaph engraved on the headstone of her silly dreams. It was obvious Jason didn't care what she decided. He'd already determined he was going to sell her contract. He wanted nothing so much as to get rid of her. What had happened between them had no meaning to him.

For years she'd been warned to guard her virtue. Aunt Amelia had reminded her constantly that without a decent dowry, all of the men circling her wanted only one thing. And once they'd gotten it, they wouldn't care anymore. Her aunt had been proven correct and the knowledge was bitter on her tongue.

Jason had bedded her, period. He'd been upfront about his desires, had even tried to be noble and stay away. She was the one who had pressed him, had made herself available. She'd wanted the experience and she'd wanted the experience with him. It had meant something to her, but obviously it had meant nothing to Jason. He'd gotten what he wanted and was done with her.

And now the rest of her life lay before her. It was an empty map on which she could draw the lines. This should have been a heady realization, but all she felt was adrift, alone. She shook herself and contemplated the concerned man opposite her.

"If you'd be so kind as to advance me four pounds, that will clear my obligation to Mr. Anders."

"Of course. That won't be a problem."

"Good. Then I think I can work with a version of your amnesia idea." Cassy leaned forward and emotionlessly began filling in the map of the rest of her life.

Chapter Twelve

*J*ason brought the ax down with more power than was needed and the pieces of the split log bounced away to the edge of the clearing. He didn't know exactly in whom he wanted to bury the ax, but it was decidedly a person and not a log.

Anger was a living flame inside him. This burning fury had been the familiar companion of his youth, but one that he thought he'd caged, if not extinguished. He'd forged his hate toward Sir Peyton Hyde into an instrument of cold revenge. But he didn't know where to turn this particular anger.

Perhaps toward himself.

Had there ever been such a deluded fool? Here he was figuring out a way he could explain marrying an indentured servant, and all the time she'd been *Lady* Cassandra Spathe, socially so far above him that marriage could not even be considered. He'd been overwhelmed with remorse at taking the virginity of a servant. But Cassy was of a class that guarded this prize even more jealously. So how had she ended up in his bed—and what was he going to do about it?

Drifting into the stables clad in a nightshift, she must have known he couldn't resist her. Hell, he couldn't resist her, period. If she'd been some other woman of her class, he might have thought she'd just been looking for a quick roll in the hay with one of the lower orders. He'd heard that fine ladies sometimes coupled with servants to enjoy their brutish energy. Dear God, with his ruined back, he would easily qualify as brutish.

He balanced a log and swung the ax. The very fact of her virginity removed her from this type of scenario. He couldn't imagine her laughing about him with other highborn ladies, balancing tea cups as they compared the various performances of low class studs. No, this was an unlikely reason for Cassy ending up in bed with him.

The more logical explanation—that she cared for him—was equally unpalatable, however. Last night had meant much more to him than a quick tup in the dark. He was actually looking forward to having Cassy Spade always in his life. The impossibility of this now happening was fuel for the fire in his gut. An earl's daughter did not marry a transported convict. Regardless of his accumulation of wealth and his ridiculous ideas of improvement, this fact was immutable. Oh, she might have thought she wanted him when she believed she'd killed someone and had no other options, but now...

Set. Swing. Set. Swing. He'd been imagining a fairy tale more improbable than anything Conner could come up with. He'd seen them walking hand in hand into a distant happy life. God, he was an ass.

"Mavis said this is where you come to sulk." Conner's voice intruded on his dark thoughts.

"Think, not sulk." Jason gripped the ax handle firmly. He had a terrible desire to take a swing at his friend. It made no sense, but he felt Conner was in some way complicit in what had happened.

"Well, do you mind putting the ax down while we talk? You look like you'd enjoy using it on someone."

Jason leaned the ax against the chopping block and ran a hand across his face. "So talk. I assume you and Lady Cassandra have reached some decisions."

Conner looked around for some place to sit down. Seeing none, he leaned back against one of the woodpile supports. "She's come to some conclusions and I think they'll work, but we need your help to establish her story."

"Just ask anything. I'm entirely at the lady's disposal. I may leave off tugging my forelock, but I'll be as helpful as I can."

"Oh, stop the bullshit, Jason. You've never tugged your forelock in your life, not even when it would have been the smart thing to do. Sir Peyton certainly would have been more amenable if you'd done a bit of tugging."

"I don't think it was a forelock he wanted me to tug."

Conner shifted his weight and rolled his eyes. "What Cassy needs…"

"Cassy, is it?"

"For heaven's sake, she said to call her Cassy. It's what she goes by with friends. Stop being a pompous ass and listen. What she needs is the temporary use of the old house you lived in before you built the new one."

"Isn't that a bit small for someone of Lady Cassandra's consequence? She's the daughter of an earl, after all." Jason knew he was being an idiot, but he couldn't seem to help himself. Maybe he *was* sulking. What a horrible thought. "I'm sorry. This whole revelation, and watching you gush all over my former servant because of her connection to nobility, has put me out of sorts. Why does Lady Cassandra want my old house?"

"Well, we've come up with a plan that should work. Cassy's going to go with the hit-on-the-head, amnesia story. In this version, when she regained her memory and told you, you immediately acted. You wrote her father in London, you wrote her lieutenant in Boston, and you established her in her own dwelling with the proper chaperone. For the chaperone she suggested..." He dug a small piece of paper out of his pocket. "Ellie."

"Ellie?" Jason snorted. "Having Ellie act as a chaperone would be like the proverbial fox guarding the hen house. Ellie's bedded most of the men working here. I hear she's indefatigable."

When Conner elevated his bushy eyebrows, Jason said, "Just because I don't participate doesn't mean I don't know what happens on my own estate in the dark of night. And why in the hell would Lady Cassandra continue to live here, anyway? Did it ever occur to either of you that I might not want her here? It makes much better sense for her to go back to Williamsburg. There's no question of Mary's suitability to act as chaperone."

"Cassy doesn't want to be 'put on display,' as she calls it, and feels being in the capital would cause this to happen. Here at the Bloomery, she can, in essence, hide from society. We'll put out that she's recovering from her mental injuries and is embarrassed at having been in a servile position."

Jason turned a choking sound into a smothered cough. So Cassy was embarrassed at having been in a servile position. She was evidently quickly reverting to everything he loathed about the aristocracy. "I don't suppose I'm actually supposed to write those letters."

"No. They're just part of the story we're putting about. She doesn't want her father informed of her whereabouts at all, and she'll take care of contacting the lieutenant. All you need to provide is lodging."

"She can't stay here for very long," Jason said. "I fixed up the old house for Joseph Hanrahan and his family. They're coming from Ireland and should be here in the next few weeks. I built my new furnace to his specifications and want him here when it goes into production. It's costing me a fortune to get him to come to Virginia, and he probably wouldn't have if he weren't Irish. It seems our mother country isn't enthusiastic about exporting blast furnace technology and no Englishman would come. Anyway, part of the package Hanrahan agreed to included the use of a house."

"I don't think she'll be there all that long. Once she hears from that lieutenant…"

"Michaels," Jason supplied. "Lieutenant Gilbert Michaels of the Fifty-Fifth Regiment of Foot." It suddenly occurred to him that it was Michael's head he wanted to imagine on the chopping block. Too bad he didn't know what the man looked like. But he could definitely envision the pretty red jacket and the shiny gold trim. He was sure Michaels was slender and supple, a man built for fencing and dancing. He'd be a thoroughbred and not a bull with oversized muscles from swinging a blacksmith's hammer.

"Yeah. Well, once she hears he's expecting her in Boston and sends her funds to get there, she'll be gone. When she gets to the Massachusetts colony, she can act as her normal self. The whole story we've made up is primarily for local consumption. And, of course, if any word of the affair gets to Boston. I explained to her that the colonies aren't isolated and, along with commerce, gossip is an item greatly in demand."

Jason nodded. "I'll have Cook send over the regular meals to Lady Cassandra and Ellie. It may not be what blue-bloods normally eat, but since I'm served the same fare as everyone else on the Bloomery, it's not that bad. Just be sure she understands I do not want to see her. If she needs anything, she can send Ellie."

Conner looked contrite. "I'm sorry. I know you were attracted to her. Any man would be, but it was to avoid her temptation that you were going to send her to Mary. In the end, this will be for the best. If you ever wanted to establish social equity with the other planters, having an earl's daughter visit isn't a bad thing. And that's how we'll play it. She's now your guest."

His friend rummaged in his pocket again. "And since she is now a guest, Cassy asked me to give you this." He held out a hand in which four gold coins glinted. The price he'd paid for Cassy's indenture.

"That's not necessary. Besides, what you're offering is too much. I paid pounds, not guineas."

"Take it, man. Let's make this completely legal. I'll pull her articles out of those I have on file and have them marked satisfied at the court house."

Jason walked over and let Conner drop the four coins in his hand. His first impulse was to hurl them into the woodpile, but his fingers closed around the money, and he decided he would keep them on display in his bedroom as a reminder of what happened when he lost sight of his goals. They could be his version of Judas's forty pieces of silver, but between him and Cassy, he couldn't decide which of them was the betrayer and which the betrayed.

"Oh, and tell her she can use whatever material we bought in York to make up some dresses for herself. If she's going to Boston as Lady Cassandra, she'll need to look the part. Most of the fabric she chose was really too fancy for the likes of me anyway." *I want you to stand proud*, she had said. Well, by God, he was proud in the clothes he already had. And if his sleeves rode up to show the shackle scars, what difference did it make? Every potential voter in this district either knew or suspected he had them.

He pocketed the money and picked up the ax. Turning his back to Conner, he placed a log on the block and swung. He'd chopped that red-coated bastard in Boston into a million bloody pieces before he heard Conner leave. He continued at a killing pace until he was positive he was alone, then he dropped the ax head to the ground, leaned on the long handle, and pulled huge draughts of cool air into his lungs.

He straightened and pushed his loosened hair out of his face. The area around the chopping block was littered with split logs. He'd get one of the men over here tomorrow to stack them and tidy up. He didn't have to do it. He was a substantial landholder, the owner of Anders' Bloomery, and he hired people to do the work he didn't want to do. Soon he'd have the new furnace up and running, hopefully the first of many. He'd no longer have to ship his blooms to England and buy the more highly refined English iron from which to forge useable implements.

He'd made a lot of money and he was sure to make a lot more. He surely had more pounds and pence than any effete lieutenant in His Majesty's army ever would. He squared his shoulders and strolled back to the house. He was master of all he surveyed and would keep his eye on the prize.

"Titus," he shouted when he entered. "Bring up hot water and lay out some clothes. I'm going to York for the evening."

He went up the stairs two at a time, anxious to shed his sweaty clothes and get into town. He'd go to the tavern first for supper and conversation. He needed to keep his ideas circulating so like-minded voters would know he was their man. And then he'd visit the Blue Heron. One woman was pretty much like any other, and he imagined the girls at the Heron had missed him. He chuckled as he stripped off the last of his garments. At least they'd missed his money.

When he heard Titus's sharp intake of breath, Jason realized that this was the first time the man had seen his naked back. He always kept his shirt on unless he was sure he was alone. "Not a pretty picture, is it?" he asked his butler.

"No, sir, it's not."

"What's yours look like?" He turned to face the former slave.

"I s'pose it's 'bout the same."

"That's what I thought."

Titus gave him a cheeky grin. "But I also s'pose we make up for it wid what we got hangin' in front."

Jason threw back his head and laughed. "I'm hoping to make up for a lot this evening, and I don't think I'll be hanging when I do. Get my clothes laid out so I can be on my way."

Titus chuckled as well.

The echo of this laughter buoyed Jason's spirits and carried him out of the house. The evening air was cool. Autumn was finally arriving. The dogwoods showed a blush of red on their leaves. Before long, he'd have the first pour from the new furnace, and this would continue throughout the cold weather. By spring, he'd ship the first of his forged implements throughout the other colonies, items made in America for Americans. And then in summer, he would be elected to the House of Burgesses.

Sir Peyton had to feel him nipping at his heels. Over time, Jason had bought up nearly all of Sir Peyton's notes, confident that eventually the planter would flounder and lose all he held dear. By the time he'd exacted his revenge, Jason would still be in his mid-thirties and at the pinnacle of colonial society. This would be the time to find a wife and build the dynasty he envisioned. He'd choose a local girl, strong in body and mind, compassionate, a helpmate to walk next to him throughout the rest of his life and provide him with children. If she weren't the grand passion of his life...

He shook his head and tried to get that sentiment out of his head. He'd had a close call and should be thankful of his reprieve. He and Cassy would never have worked out. It was time to celebrate, not grieve. Jason reminded himself of the fact with every step his horse took into town.

The tavern was full when he arrived, a lively discussion of new taxes already underway. There were always new taxes. The more wealth that was accumulated in the colony, the more the British Parliament thought a large portion of this wealth belonged to them. Nothing could galvanize men like the government taking what the men considered to be theirs.

After a good beef pie and innumerable glasses of the cloying Madeira, Jason felt the tension draining from his body. Here was where he was meant to be, among the company of men, not wallowing in self-pity because of a woman. He'd nearly convinced himself he didn't need to visit the Blue Heron when the late September wind blew in Sir Peyton Hyde and two of his cronies.

Jason and Sir Peyton greeted each other with equanimity, although antagonism rolled off both of them in waves. He realized that his peers felt the change in the atmosphere. Most of the surrounding men, friends and foes alike, wore an avid look most frequently seen at a cockfight.

But Jason would be damned if he'd give the men the fight they wanted. The tightness of the scars across his back reminded him of the cost of losing his temper. He was no longer Sir Peyton's to command, but lack of control would make it easy for the man to claim that Jason was still an unreasoning brute who had no place as a leader in the community.

"I see you're here trying to convince some of *my* voters to come over to your side," Sir Peyton said with a false smile.

"With the political positions you hold, it's not taking much convincing. People are ready for a change that better reflects how they think," Jason calmly replied, pleased with his iron control.

Peyton puffed up like a threatened toad. "I'm sure that I know what men of property consider important, since I and my entire family have been in that category for generations, while you're, eh, what? Oh, yes, you're a convicted thief who got lucky."

Jason couldn't argue with Sir Peyton's basic assessment, since he *had* been convicted of theft. That he had been eleven at the time, and starving, made no difference. He'd been transported to the Virginia colony and indentured until he was eighteen.

Since his articles had been purchased by Sir Peyton, it was not surprising that years had been added to his term of service for willful disobedience. He'd not been a free man until he was twenty-two. But by that time, he'd completely worked out his articles, and there wasn't a damned thing Sir Peyton could do about it.

"Well, I do admit to being lucky," Jason said with a laugh, relishing the ironic truth of his words. He had been lucky because he'd carefully prepared himself to be.

"Your biggest piece of luck was buying the contract for that hot little piece I saw you escorting around York before any of the rest of us got a look at her." The comment came from the far side of the room. Jason couldn't identify the speaker.

"Oh, no, gentlemen," Sir Peyton said with false sincerity. "You must be wrong about this. Jason would never use one of his indentured servants as his ladybird. He's castigated all of us who have done so and wants to pass laws that would make it illegal. Our Jason here is too morally upright to do such a thing. Or did you discover that you were more upright than moral?"

Sir Peyton's question garnered a hearty laugh all around. Jason noticed that even his supporters smiled. He throttled back the desire to bury his fist in Sir Peyton's face and smiled as well.

"As it happens, I was recently in town with Lady Cassandra Spathe. That's evidently who you saw. She and her chaperone are currently my guests until arrangements can be made for her to join her fiancé in Boston." Jason was amazed he could keep a straight face as he uttered such twaddle. But the men around him smiled and nodded as if he were making complete sense.

Sir Peyton was one of the few who exhibited obvious disbelief. He could see questions and rebuttals forming on the man's lips. Before Sir Peyton could voice them, however, Jason decided it was time to beat a retreat. He could only tell so many of the lies Conner and Cassy had concocted without vomiting.

"For those who saw her in town, you'll know that Lady Cassandra is stunning. She's also one of the leaders of London society. While she's here, she's agreed to help me finish the decorating of my house. Sir Peyton here is right. I'm a lucky man to have found someone with such superior taste to aid me. But since decorating is the only service the lady in question will be doing for me, I'm going to have to take my upright portion down the street to the Blue Heron."

More laughter followed and Jason left the tavern amid ribald comments, thankful no one had thought to question a story that made not the slightest bit of sense. But talking and thinking about Cassy had removed any desire to visit The Heron. One woman really wasn't like any other. Instead of ambling on down the street, he turned his horse toward home.

He wouldn't think about his guest. He'd concentrate on other things. He was mentally reviewing all he knew about blast furnaces when he approached his house. The small house he'd originally built stood off to one side. Without volition, he stared at it, but no candle flickered through the window. All was dark. He could easily ignore the fact that anyone was there.

But three hours later, he was still pacing his darkened bedroom, his pretense that the old house was empty proving to be an impossible feat.

Chapter Thirteen

October 1755

Cassy adjusted the beaker of water to focus the candlelight on the material she was stitching. Mavis had found the clear glass container and Hats had cobbled together something similar to a lacemaker's globe. The oddly designed contraption worked surprisingly well. Now that the sun was setting earlier, the device had been a godsend.

"Yer goin' to end up blind," Ellie said, entering the large main room from her smaller bedroom. Then she belatedly added, "Milady." Ellie had been *milady*-ing Cassy ever since they'd taken up residence in the little house two weeks earlier. Nothing Cassy said could make her stop. She had managed to halt the incessant curtsying, which was at least a little progress.

"If I go blind, I'm sure I can count on you to take good care of me," Cassy replied.

"Tha's the truth." Ellie now fancied herself a lady's maid and believed it was her job to make sure Cassy did nothing. The raw-boned woman seemed to have forgotten that she and Cassy had worked side by side for months. Instead, Ellie acted as if putting *Lady* in front of Cassy's name made her instantly incompetent. This attitude was slowly driving Cassy insane. At least Ellie didn't think that personal sewing was beneath a lady. Her friend was adamant that Cassy have "lots of pretties" before she left for Boston to join her fiancé.

All of the women at the bloomery had conveniently forgotten their assumption that she was having an affair with Jason Anders. Their romantic fantasies had now attached themselves to Gilbert Michaels. Sight unseen, they'd decided he was handsome and dashing and madly in love with Cassy. She evidently had Jason to thank for Lieutenant Michaels' elevation to the role of fiancé. Bess was the first to bring this happy news when she came to help clean and gossip.

"Ya shoulda tol' us," Bess exclaimed. "Then we'da known nothin' was going on wid Mr. Anders."

Cassy often wondered what they thought of the tale making the rounds that she'd had amnesia. The women were in a position to know that tale was patently untrue, but they acted as if amnesia were contagious and they all now suffered from it. Unanimously, they pretended that Cassy had always been an honored guest.

"I thought I'd take a stroll," Ellie said in elevated tones that gave a good impersonation of a duchess. Then she ruined the effect by giggling as she removed her shawl from the pegs by the door.

"Yes, I think it would be a lovely night to take the air," Cassy responded, winking as she did so, which sent Ellie into another fit of giggles. They both knew Ellie would not be back until nearly sunrise. Ellie's strolls were legendary. Cassy was simultaneously appalled and envious. "Enjoy yourself," Cassy called as Ellie exited the house.

Cassy stared at the rust-colored velvet she was working on. The material seemed to undulate in the magnified candlelight and gave a hint of how it would look in a brilliantly lit ballroom.

With careful cutting, Cassy had managed to get all the pieces needed for a gown out of the amount of fabric she'd bought to make a suit for Jason. The area for the exposed petticoat was perhaps a little wider than was standard, but Cassy doubted anyone would ever notice. The gown would be beautiful—the color rich without being gaudy. She could use it as an example of her craftsmanship when she reached Boston. Of course, she would only need such a dress as an example if she intended to make her way as a seamstress. But if she arrived in Massachusetts as Lady Cassandra Spathe, that would not be an option.

Cassy was unable to divine her own future. She had no doubt that Gilbert Michaels would send her money for the fare. Her departure was assured. It was the arrival that remained nebulous. Exactly who should disembark at that northern port—Lady Cassandra Spathe or Cassy Spade?

She felt she was two women inhabiting one body. She had, of course, been Lady Cassandra her whole life—but this was a life she had no desire to return to. She would never again place control of the way she lived into her father's hands. England, therefore, held no allure and made Massachusetts her obvious destination. But as Lady

Cassandra, would she be safe from her father's machinations there? She could trade on her position in society, but would have no money—or acceptable way of earning it—unless she accepted a position as a companion or governess. Or married.

She wondered what Lieutenant Michaels would think of his assigned role of loving fiancé. Theirs had been a flirtation without serious intent. Cassy doubted she'd be interested in marrying him, even if he were so inclined. Lieutenant Michaels had simply been a straw she'd clutched at in a moment of panic when she needed to flee.

Marrying anyone, of course, led to the problem of her no longer being a virgin. Men of her class would expect as much, and only a few would accept the tale of assault she'd decided to use if necessary.

If she arrived in Boston as Cassy Spade, seamstress, her life would be very different. By necessity, she would probably have to be a widow, but as a tradesman, she would not be particularly noticed. Cassy Spade would have more freedom and could earn her own way. But could Lieutenant Michaels be convinced to go along with this charade? And would Cassy herself be satisfied to be considered one of the lower class, even in a colony that was much more egalitarian than England?

All of these problems whirled in her mind, robbing her of sleep, and so she sewed while others trysted.

The little house creaked around her as the timbers adjusted to the cooler night temperatures. The hearth fire kept this room comfortably warm, but Cassy was still glad for the robe she wore over her shift. It was odd that, after the heat of the summer, she now felt so cold.

She tried to imagine Jason living in this house. Mavis had told her he'd done so for years until the big house was built. One side of the small dwelling was a general living room and kitchen. Mavis referred to it as the hall, which was altogether too grand a name for the area it covered. The other half of the house was divided into what were now two bedrooms, although the smaller one at the front had been used as a study during Jason's tenure. A small bookcase had been built into one wall to hold Jason's precious collection of books. Perhaps that was why this particular room still seemed to echo his presence.

Cassy was very glad that room was Ellie's bedroom and not her own.

After enough time had passed to ensure that Ellie would not be returning early from a disappointing assignation, Cassy carefully folded the velvet and took out the light ecru silk she'd chosen as Jason's waistcoat. She did this work only when she knew she was alone, uncertain about how the others would view her continuing to sew for Jason. In honesty, she wasn't sure why she did so herself, except that she wanted to leave him something beautiful to remember her by.

She'd heavily embroidered the front and the bottom of the waistcoat with a flowering vine. The flowers were fanciful. Nothing grown in any garden could compare; the colors were vibrant and the shapes angular and severe. She was in the process of placing similar flowers on the pocket flaps. Then she'd finish by scattering small sprays around the body of the garment.

She thought the effect would be stunning, especially spread across Jason's broad chest. Would he think it too bright? Or he might reject it simply because she'd made it.

Jason continued to avoid her. She felt she was back to her early days at the Bloomery, when the mysterious owner was seen only from a distance.

She'd tried to stay angry with him. She was the one who had been used and discarded, after all. But the embroidery she'd so carefully planned called to her and she felt compelled to work on it. As she did, her feelings toward Jason softened. He once again seemed isolated in the midst of so many people. She wanted to finish the waistcoat as a gift in thanks for the many kind and thoughtful things he'd done.

She reached up and stroked her mother's locket. His giving it to her was so typical of his behavior. It reminded her of a happy time before whatever had soured their relationship had occurred. Could Jason harbor a reverse form of elitism? She'd heard that self-made men often felt superior to aristocrats, who they believed were useless drones, taking from society as a whole and giving nothing back. Since his behavior had changed when he learned who she really was, the theory was plausible.

But his distance had also followed on the heels of the night they'd spent together. What if he'd simply lusted for her, and once that lust was exercised, wanted nothing more to do with her? For her, the time spent in the room above the stables had been a profound experience. What if he'd found it mundane and boring? She didn't know which of these potential reasons hurt less. She hoped there was another explanation and wanted the waistcoat to be a remembrance of a happier time.

She planned to give it to him right before she left, and she expected to leave fairly soon. A courier had taken her letter to Lieutenant Michaels directly to a ship leaving for Boston.

The money for her passage should arrive shortly, depending on the vagaries of tide and wind.

And then she'd be gone, once again on a ship taking her into the unknown.

Her hand wavered and she pricked her finger. With a curse, she jerked it back before she could stain the light-colored silk. Sticking her finger in her mouth, she sucked on it, the action tightening her midsection. It was not only her concern for the future that kept sleep away. Memories of her time in that small bed with Jason heated her blood and kept her awake.

She lusted for him. There was no way to pretty up what she felt. She had waking dreams of his warm, wet mouth on her breasts. She could vividly recall the glorious feeling of his thrusting into her. And she wanted those feelings again. More specifically, she wanted Jason Anders, and there wasn't a damned thing she could do about it.

The one impossible future she actually wanted was to stay in Virginia with Jason. Now that everyone knew her identity, however, she couldn't be his mistress. She'd be cut by society and probably not accepted by even the servants. She'd be a joke. The fallen noblewoman who was ruled by her lust instead of her brain. She would make of herself what her father and Lord Tilton had wanted her to be.

The truth was—she wanted marriage. But again, everyone would see this as a mésalliance. She didn't care as long as she was in Jason's bed and held even the smallest piece of his heart. Her being Jason's wife would hurt his political goals, however. She wouldn't ask him to give up his long-held dream. She was not surprised that Jason had never mentioned marriage.

She suspected she had given him her heart while his remained solely his. This knowledge hurt more than she thought possible. She ran her fingers tenderly over the silk threads in the flower she was working on, realizing she couldn't see it that well. The magnified light was making her eyes water. If she weren't careful, she would indeed go blind and prove Ellie correct.

With a sigh, she folded the waistcoat and hid it under some other fabric. She blew out the candle behind the globe and the room descended into shadows. Only a glow from the banked hearth lighted the room. It was restful, and she leaned back in her chair and looked out at the big house across the lawn.

From this angle, she could see the windows of both the study and Jason's bedroom. Illuminated by the candles in those rooms, his movements at night were visible. She knew she'd become a voyeur, watching a life she dreamed of pass before her as she sewed, but she couldn't help herself. Tonight, both rooms lay in darkness. Jason must sensibly be in bed.

She was starting to get out of the chair when a flicker in the study window caught her eye and she sat back down. Perhaps Jason was having as restless a night as she was and had returned to the study for a book. She stared at the speck of brightness, hoping to see his figure pass by the window.

The weak light suddenly expanded, filling the window with brilliance. It took Cassy a minute to realize what was happening; then she leaped from her chair and dashed to the door. Once outside she shouted, "Fire! Fire in the main house!" Her voice seemed a weak thing to throw against the flames growing in the window.

She ran, yelling "Fire!" with every other step, fighting for breath to both hurry and shout. Someone had to hear her. There were people ghosting about the estate at all times of the night. Why was no one responding to her cry?

She imagined Jason coming down for a book, perhaps half asleep, stumbling and dropping the candle. He might have actually set his clothing alight before the fire spread to the room. She screamed like a banshee and hurdled up the long, front steps, panic lending speed to her feet.

The entry hall was dark, but an ominous glow came from behind the stairway where the entrance to the study lay. She thought she heard shouts from outside the house and was heartened when an alarm bell began clanking out its cry for help. She sped to the study door and stopped, attempting to take stock of what was happening.

With relief, she ascertained there was no Jason-sized figure writhing on the floor. The room, bright with flames, seemed to be empty. The drapes on two of the windows flared to the ceiling, making columns of fire and billowing smoke. She had no plan. All she could think of was Jason's small collection of carefully selected and much-loved books. She knew that in some way they were a symbol of his rise in the world. She needed to save them if she could.

Cassy pulled her robe from around her and used it to begin frantically beating at the flames. So intent was she on her task, she didn't realize anyone else had entered the room until strong hands grasped her shoulders and threw her away from the fire.

"Get back, you idiot," Jason yelled. He snatched the flimsy robe from her hands and began beating at the flames himself.

It seemed a scene from hell. Jason, dressed only in a nightshirt with his loose hair whipping around his face, was a huge, dark shape silhouetted against the fire. His shoulders bunched and released as he swung the billowing robe. The bright colors of the fabrics in the room moved and shifted in the light of the flames. Smoke began to fill the space.

Suddenly, the room was alive with shouting men armed with brooms, quilts, and water. Cassy was pushed back toward the door by the swirling chaos. She felt a gentle touch on her arm that was at odds to the previous shoving. Mavis, her gray hair forming a wild corona, stood next to her.

"You need to get out of here," Mavis said, her sharp eyes taking in Cassy's night shift and plaited hair. "There is only so much gossip Jase can deflect with either laughter or silence. I'll not have you ruin all he's tried to build or destroy all he's tried to be."

The hand on her arm grasped her tightly and dragged her into the hall. The further they got from the study, the less smoke filled the air. Mavis took her to her room in the basement, which showed no indication of the chaos above them.

"Sit down," Mavis said. "Do you need something to drink?"

The idea of some cool water was very appealing, but Cassy shook her head and sat on a dainty gilded chair with a crimson velvet cushion. She was conscious of the soot on her shift and hoped she didn't soil the bright red material.

Mavis shook her head. "I'm very disappointed in Jason, but there's no need to make the rumors worse by the two of you, dressed in night clothes, being seen together by everyone on the Bloomery."

"Disappointed?" Cassy was confused. "Jason didn't start the fire."

"Of course he didn't." Mavis' tone was dismissive. "This night's evil was undoubtedly the work of those in the hire of

Sir Peyton Hyde. This isn't the first time that he's tried to punish Jason for rising above his birth and threatening Hyde's assumed superiority.

"No, I'm disappointed that Jason persists in taking you to his bed when you can do him nothing but harm. Oh, you're obviously beautiful. I can see why he's tempted. And I can see this damned attraction isn't one way."

"It's nothing like that," Cassy said, breaking into the housekeeper's torrent of words. She realized Mavis assumed they'd both come down from Jason's bedroom. "Mr. Anders wants nothing to do with me. I saw the flames from the old house and came to investigate."

Mavis gave a grunt that might have been a laugh. "It's possible you were in your proper place, I'll give you that, even though I'm not sure you know what your proper place actually is. I can tell you it isn't anywhere within tupping distance of Jase. But as to the first part, about Jase wanting nothing to do with you. Girl, you're either a deluded fool or a liar. I watch you both look at each other with hungry eyes when you think no one else will notice. The attraction between the two of you is palpable."

Mavis settled her bulk into a much sturdier chair covered with the same velvet. Cassy suddenly had a vision of Mavis and Hats resting in this room, talking over their day like an old married couple while sitting in these chairs. Cassy was occupying the one undoubtedly used by Hats.

"Cassy, before I came to Virginia and established The Blue Heron, I was the, eh, companion to wealthy men. Now, don't think I was a common whore like the girls I hired at the Heron. I was kept in style and made a tidy packet off my endeavors. But there was never a man who didn't get value for his money. It was a living and something I did well.

"I entered into a business arrangement with each of my gentleman friends. And that's all it was ever supposed to be—business. But occasionally a man became special. I craved his touch. I lived for the sound of him opening the door. I was wet for him even before we even got to the bedroom, and he couldn't pound into me hard enough or long enough for me to ever tire of it."

Mavis leaned forward, the chair groaning in protest. "So I want you to understand that I'm familiar with the fever in the blood. And I sure as hell can recognize it when I see it. But the only thing worse than Jase's taking one of his indentured women as a mistress would be his bedding an aristocratic lady. You can't hitch a draft horse together with a thoroughbred and expect the wagon to go anywhere. So if you care anything about Jason Anders, you need to remember you're the lady you were born to be and let him go."

"I don't have to let him go. He's already severed any connection. There's nothing between us." Cassy tried to believe her statement, but the woman Mavis had described sounded uncomfortably familiar.

"Are you all right?" Jason strode through the door, immediately kneeling in front of Cassy, making her last words sound like a lie when he tenderly brushed her hair back from her face and looked deeply into her eyes.

His face was smudged with smoke, but his eyes were bright and filled with concern. He was the most wonderful thing she'd ever seen. Cassy's hand involuntarily reached out to stroke the night beard that shadowed his jaw.

"Oh, good heavens," Mavis said, her voice seeming to come from a great distance.

"Leave," Anders said, not breaking eye contact with Cassy. "And close the door behind you."

"You ass," Mavis exploded. "This is my bloody room. If you're so hot to jump each other and screw up your lives while you're at it, you'll have to go to your own room." She crossed her arms across her ample bosom and glared.

Cassy was only vaguely aware of Jason helping her to her feet, leading her into the lower hall, and shutting the door behind them. All of her attention was focused on the feeling of one of Jason's hands moving down her neck and over her shoulders. His hand was warm in the chill of the basement; the calluses on his palms scraped her skin and made all the fine hairs on her body stand on end.

It was what she'd dreamed, especially when he leaned forward and brushed her lips with his own. He rested his forehead against hers. "The fire's out," he said. "Only a few of the draperies were destroyed. But I was so frightened when I saw you surrounded by flames."

Cassy slipped her hands from his cheeks to his neck and pulled him back toward her face. His lips again touched hers, this time with more assurance. He nibbled at her lower lip. When she relaxed her mouth, his tongue slipped in, stroking her palate and the insides of her cheeks.

Heat blossomed within her, burning its way down to settle at the apex of her legs. She moaned, running her hands over his heavily muscled shoulders.

He began kissing her face randomly—her eyes, her nose, her cheeks—heat spreading wherever his lips touched her. He worked his way down one side of her neck with little nibbles that stole her breath. She felt as though she sat too close to a blazing hearth. "Please," she whispered, now knowing exactly what she begged for.

His hands came up to cup her breasts, tenderly stroking them, sending spirals of desire shooting through her. His mouth replaced his hand as he suckled one of her hard peaks through her chemise. She bucked against the wet warmth, her back arching toward his questing lips.

Jason raised his head. His eyes, dark as a moonless night, reflected her desire. "I want you," he said in a hoarse voice. "Lord help me, I want you more than all the earth."

And then he tucked her hand against his arm as if they were promenading a ballroom and led her up the stairs.

Chapter Fourteen

*W*hen they reached the main floor, Jason wrinkled his nose at the strong odor of smoke. It would take days and a lot of cleaning for the smell to dissipate, but eventually it would be gone. Nothing of real value had been lost. He stopped and swept Cassy up into his arms. She made a quick sound of surprise and then settled against him, her arms around his neck.

He now held what he valued. When he'd seen Cassy standing there with the flames all around her, he'd thought he would die from the fear. He had her now and he would not, could not, let her go. He didn't give a damn that she was too far above him for there ever to be anything permanent. He refused to think of that effete military bastard waiting in Boston to give her back the life that should be hers. He'd keep her and hold her for as long as he was able, and not count the loss of anything that came after.

He carried her up the stairs. She felt so right in his arms. Her head lay on his shoulder with her face tucked into his neck. Her breath was warm and sure on his throat. He resisted the urge to clench her tightly to him, the memory of the flames and his fear for her still bright within him.

When they got to his room, he reluctantly set Cassy on her feet and pushed the door closed behind them. She leaned back against him as if she, too, wanted to retain the contact, but her inquisitive eyes moved around his bedchamber. "What do you think?" he asked, looking over the top of her head to see what she saw.

He could feel her chuckle more than hear it. "This doesn't look much like the rest of the house."

"Probably because the rest of the house is mostly empty. Well, except for my now destroyed study."

"The colors are restful. This room looks more like you."

He laughed. "Mavis's fine hand hasn't chosen anything here. Years ago, when I was visiting Conner McAllister's house, I leafed through a book that belonged to Mary. In it was an engraving entitled *A Gentleman's Bedchamber*. I liked the way it looked and when I built this house, I recreated that room."

The furniture was heavy and masculine, with a massive bed taking pride of place along one wall. The bedposts were intricately carved and the hangings, a soft grayish green, matched the drapes. Jason always felt comfortable here.

"And what is that?" Cassy asked, nodding her head toward the inner corner of the fireplace wall.

"My bathing tub." He looked at the big wooden trough with a feeling of pride. The huge tub was both an indulgence and a necessity. "I designed the tub to be like a watering trough with a lead lining. I made it large enough so I could stretch out in comfort." He didn't mention that soaking in the warm water and then rubbing his back with a lanolin-covered cloth kept the skin on his back supple.

When the fire had been extinguished, Jason realized he smelled as smoky as the study and had asked Titus to fill the tub. Hot water now sent wispy tendrils of steam into the air. He'd not thought to share his bath with Cassy, but it seemed a wonderful idea.

"I don't think the smoke came up here," he said, sniffing loudly into the back of her neck, calling forth a girlish giggle. "But we both have a decidedly singed odor about us. Would you care to bathe?"

"In there?" Cassy's voice was unnaturally high.

"That's what I use it for. Would you like to try it?"

Cassy looked uncertain. He was already imagining her floating naked in the water and his cock hardened appropriately. "Don't you like to soak in warm water?"

"Never in anything half that large."

"I promise I won't let you drown," he said with a laugh.

She chuckled and turned a sparkling smile in his direction. His breath caught in his throat. "I think I'll give it a try," she said. "I suspect I do smell like a wet fireplace." Without further comment, she stepped away from him, untied the laces at the neck of her chemise, and let the garment slither to the floor. Then she walked to the tub, the rope of her plaited hair swinging across her back, the end just brushing the top of her firm ass. Jason completely forgot to breathe.

She paused at the tall side and he hurried after her. Dear God, if she threw her leg over the edge of the tub, he'd come right then and there, and that would certainly delay some of the night's activities. "Here, let me help," he said, lifting her and slowly lowering her into the water.

She stretched out and leaned back against the sloping rear of the tub. Her eyes involuntarily closed, her long lashes fanning over her cheeks. "Oh, my heavens," she sighed, "this is incredible."

"We colonials have to find our pleasures where we can." Jason found his pleasure in just looking at her. Cassy, naked in his bath, was nothing less than exquisite. Her body made a long, pale line within the water, the thatch of honey-blond hair at the apex of her thighs marking a slightly darker area. Her full breasts seemed to float on the surface of the water, the areolas perfectly round, dusky pink circles. His mouth was dry and his hands itched to touch her.

Almost without thought, he unfastened the breeches he'd hastily donned before going down to Mavis's room and dropped them to the floor. The sound caused Cassy to open her eyes and stare at him. "I thought I'd bathe you and didn't want my clothes to get wet," he said. From her quickly suppressed grin, it was obvious she recognized the lie for what it was.

His hands paused as he began to lift his nightshirt over his head. For years he'd hidden his back, ashamed of the ugliness there. But he now realized the shame belonged to the man who had marked him and not to himself. He wondered again if Cassy thought him brutish. It made no difference. If his scars were part of his attraction and that was what it took to keep her with him, he'd let her look her fill.

His arms moved up, pulling the shirt over his head, and he watched it drift to the floor. When he looked back at Cassy, she wasn't trying to see his back. She was staring very pointedly at his rampant cock. She licked her lips and he had a vivid picture of those lips circling the object of her interest. He stifled a moan.

"If you'd move to one side, I think I could get into the water as well." The words came out as a growl. At least he could still make words—he suspected he was rapidly losing the ability.

She shifted to her left and he slipped into the tub next to her, pulling her on top of him as he took up most of the available room. The water sloshed perilously close to the rim, but Jason was unconcerned, since the painted floor cloth beneath the tub would protect the floor.

The warm water flowed over him and he stretched out with an audible sigh. He cradled Cassy above him, the water slightly supporting her so her breasts softly slid over his chest. "I thought you said you were going to bathe me," she said.

"I am." He pulled her up until he could easily reach her mouth and kissed her. The melding of lips and tongues was slow and languorous. He wanted tonight to be a gentle seduction. He hoped to bind Cassy to him with banked passion and exquisite pleasure.

As they kissed, his hands freely roamed her slippery body, skimming the contours of her buttocks and side, shaping the breasts so tantalizingly near. Her wet skin felt like silk. When he circled her nipples she groaned into his mouth.

Breaking the kiss and drawing back from her slightly, he said, "Support yourself with your arms over the edge of the tub. I want to bathe your breasts." She looked at him quizzically, but did as he asked. He slid his head and shoulders further down into the water, bending his knees up like twin peaks rising from a lake. He submerged his face, took a mouthful of water, and came to the surface, squirting an arc of water at Cassy's breasts as if he were a stone fish on a fountain.

Laughter gurgled out of her. God, he loved her laugh. She shifted, as if she wanted the use of her arms. "No, don't move," he said. "I'm nowhere near finished." He submerged and repeated the process, this time lifting his head further out of the water and taking one of her rosy nipples deeply into his mouth. He relaxed back into the water and released her breast with a wet pop. He repeated the process on the one that had been neglected.

"There are ravenous fish from the depths that love feasting on your breasts. But now they want your lips." He pushed himself up straighter as she lowered her head. His lips closed over hers and his tongue slipped in and out of her mouth like the fish he imagined. His hands came up to play, tweaking the taut, furled buds of her breasts.

Bereft of the use of her hands, Cassy rubbed her pelvis against his straining cock. The current from her movement eddied around his balls. "Keep your arms up," he said, and kissed his way down her dripping body. His hands floated between her legs, fanning the water across her pubic thatch. He stroked along her cleft and she raised herself up even more, moaning softly. Her straightened arms trembled.

He ran a finger over her nub and heard her quick intake of breath. He slowly circled the stiff little point and felt her hips undulate. He dropped his hand further down and slipped in a finger. Inside, she was as wet as the water around them and twice as hot. She whimpered in protest when he withdrew his hand and ran it up the side of her body.

"Can you ride me, Cass?" His voice was breathless and hoarse.

"What?" Her eyes looked heavy and the word was almost slurred.

"Sit up a bit more and put my cock in you. And then I'll show you how to ride. If I don't get inside you soon, I may die."

She followed his direction, looking down the length of her body to see what she was doing. Her hand closed tentatively around his shaft and she positioned herself over him. Then she slowly lowered herself onto his pulsing cock. His words were true. He did think he might die.

When she was fully seated, he grasped her around the waist and rocked her up and down. She got the rhythm and moved of her own accord. His hands dropped away to hold tightly onto the side of the tub. The feeling was incredible. This wasn't fast and hot animal lust, this was something different—and immensely satisfying. Her hands folded over his on the rim, gripping them tightly. Her eyes were partially closed. She seemed to be concentrating on the sensations they were creating.

She increased her speed and Jason could not keep from rising to meet her downward thrusts. Water lapped over their joined hands and dripped to the floor. He felt the pressure of his release building in time with her ragged pants. Her firm breasts bounced with her movements. Her head was thrown back. She looked to Jason like a goddess rising from the sea.

He knew she was near her release but still unprepared when her inner muscles gripped him and she called out. He reached to move her up and off him, his hands sliding on her wet skin until they lost their purpose and he could only cry her name as he pumped into her and her rippling inner muscles milked him dry.

She collapsed forward, stretching out across his chest. He was sure she could feel the thunder of his heart. He gently kissed her forehead.

"I didn't know it could be done like that." She stroked the crisp hairs on his chest.

"What? In the water?"

"Yes. Well, partially. I mean with my being on top and going slowly and all."

"But you liked it, didn't you?" He turned her face up so he could see her expression. Was there ever a man with enough confidence not to ask, or at least, want to know?

She gave him a slow, secretive smile. "I dare not tell you it was nice or your feelings will be hurt," she teased, "so it was better than nice."

He made a humph sound. "If that's the best you can do, then that will have to be enough." He made to press her head back to his chest, but she resisted, looking at him.

"What's the little man in the boat?" she asked earnestly.

He scooted up a little straighter. "Where did that question come from?"

"Well, the first time we, eh…" He saw her flounder on the word tup, and he wasn't sure it was quite accurate anyway, so he just nodded encouragement. "The first time," she began again, "you touched me there and said that the little man in the boat liked to have his boat rocked. And then tonight, you touched me there again and I liked it very much. It makes everything inside me get all crinkly, and so I wondered what it was."

Jason paused, unsure of what he should say. "It's just a part of you that can give you wonderful feelings. You've figured that out already. It probably has a fancier name, but I don't know what it is. Hiram, the smith, told me about it when I was first starting to meet women in the woods at night. He told me if I was good to the little man in the boat, the women would be good to me." He smiled at the memory. Hiram had taught him much more than just how to forge, and this advice, as most of his other suggestions, had proved to be true.

"But why does it have such an odd name?"

"I guess because that's kinda what it looks like."

She glanced down her body to look at her submerged pubic area as if she could see the nub for herself.

"Haven't any of the women mentioned it?" he asked hopefully. From what he understood, no topic was forbidden when servant women talked about the men they met in the night.

She laughed. "Not so I could understand it. Much of what they whisper about doesn't make much sense."

"All right, let me see if I can explain." He felt a flush of embarrassment move up his throat to his face. It was ridiculous to be embarrassed about these things. But doing and talking about doing were two different things. He reminded himself that Cassy had not been fortunate enough to have a Hiram in her life.

"The little man is a bit like a man's cock. Oh, not in the way it looks or how it acts, but in how it feels. You like it when I touch that spot; well, you'd also like it if I licked it or sucked on it."

"And you'd like that if I did it to your cock?"

He groaned aloud. The body part in question was still nestled snuggly in Cassy's sweet quim and it was rapidly stiffening again.

"I take that as a yes," she said with a laugh. Her eyes sparkled with mischief and discovery. "So, could I try?"

Could she try? Better ask if he would object if the heavens opened and showered him with gold. He was now fully erect and it was all he could do not to start pumping away. "Well, the first thing we need to do is get out of this tub and dry off. The water is cooling."

He helped balance her as she disengaged and got out of the tub. The water had indeed cooled, but even that couldn't dissuade his ever-eager cock. He got out, keeping his back to her to hide his excitement. Cassy would think him a satyr.

His back. Bloody hell, what was he thinking? He grabbed up a piece of sheeting to wrap around his waist when he felt her cool hand stroke his scars.

"Does it hurt?" she asked from behind him.

"No." He stood stoically as her soft fingers traced the whorls and ridges. His back didn't hurt, not now. But there had been times when the slightest breeze across the surface could make him want to howl. Hiram had tended to the damage, smearing ointment all over the scoured flesh, always saying, "You'll live," and then continuing on with whatever he'd been doing.

Ugly. He knew it was ugly. By using his shaving mirror to look into a wall mirror, he'd examined the unattractive landscape of his back. He thought it repulsive. But Cassy's hands were gentle, and her silence felt more like curiosity than disgust. When she placed a tentative kiss between his shoulder blades, emotion nearly brought him to his knees.

He turned and gathered her into his arms. She had sheeting wrapped around her like a slender ball gown. But what he most noticed was that her eyes were filled with tears.

"It doesn't hurt," he repeated. "It just is. A part of me I generally cannot see and, therefore, can ignore. You should do the same." He rubbed a teardrop from her thick lashes and said, "Forget this. Let's go to bed and concentrate on other body parts." He didn't want her feeling sad about him. He wanted her laughter.

He grabbed the end of the sheeting she'd tucked around her and pulled. She'd wrapped the material around herself a couple of times and the process of unwrapping caused her to spin away from him. Her surprised laughter trailed over her shoulder. It was the sound he'd so wanted to hear. He rapidly followed her and tumbled her onto the bed.

His kiss was more savage than tender and she matched his passion. He wanted to drive away any sorrow she felt for him and replace it with searing heat. Their legs, arms, torsos were in constant motion. It was as if each were trying to consume the other. Jason realized the playfulness was gone and they both heedlessly dashed toward the hard, fast encounter they craved.

He knelt over her and entered her in one firm stroke. She arched, matching him move for move, both of them making deep, guttural sounds at the back of their throats. She brought her legs up high on his hips to allow deeper penetration. Her fingers bit into his shoulders. His buttocks bunched with every powerful thrust.

When she shattered, calling, "Jase" in a mournful wail, he barely had time to pull out and immediately spilled his seed on the sheet between her legs. The arms supporting his upper body trembled and even his hair was sodden with sweat. He rolled to one side so he wouldn't smother her and collapsed. He pulled her close, thinking she, too, felt boneless.

"Nice," she said in a sleepy voice. He wondered if she said it to tease him. Before he could ask, she was asleep.

He lay unmoving and alert beside her. This night could have consequences. When they'd been in the water and she'd been in control, he'd left his seed inside her. Years of caution had failed him with the one person he cared about. The repercussions were still troubling him as the first, faint light of dawn filtered into the room.

Chapter Fifteen

*E*llie looked out the carriage window at the gray, wet day beyond and fidgeted in her seat. "Do ya think we'll be there soon?"

Cassy disguised her chuckle as a sharp cough. Excitement rolled off her friend in palpable waves. She'd asked the same question six times. Having never been to Williamsburg herself, Cassy had no idea where they were in relation to their destination. Hats, who was driving the carriage, would know, but he was in the driver's box, and the only way to speak to him was through a trap door. She didn't think letting rain into the interior of the carriage was worth asking a question that would in no way hasten their arrival.

"Is there anything particular you want to see while we're in the capital?" Cassy asked in an effort to change the subject. She, too, was excited, and the trip had seemed to take forever. Jason said their travel time should be about four hours, and Cassy was sure that amount of time had passed long ago. Maybe the road conditions were slowing their progress.

She also wished Jason were with them, but he'd left the day before saying he wanted to report the suspicious nature of the fire to both the magistrate in York and to the military in the capital. He would meet Cassy in the capital where she could help him choose suitable furniture for the house. The need had become even more pressing. The smoky pieces from the study had been left outside to air, and the lack of other places to sit quickly became irritating.

And so he had ridden away only a few hours after she'd left his bed the morning after the fire. She hoped these sudden disappearances weren't indicative of a pattern. In this case, however, Cassy thought his leaving was out of necessity rather than rejection. He'd certainly not seemed distant when he'd departed. If anything, he was almost boyishly excited about showing her Williamsburg and shopping with her.

Had it been a sunny day, the ride would have been enjoyable. The leaves were beginning to change; some of the trees at the Bloomery were becoming quite brilliant. But with the rain, all was sodden, brown, and dull. When Mavis was talking to Hats before they left, she'd called it an English day, and Cassy supposed it was.

"Oh look, Cassy, eh, milady, another house. We must be getting to town." Ellie pressed her face against the window. Cassy also surveyed the area with interest. The homes had become more closely spaced, although each was still surrounded by sufficient acreage to support a kitchen garden and perhaps a milk cow. The traffic had increased as well, mostly open wagons with huddled, dripping drivers.

The wheels soon rattled on cobblestones, and a few hardy people hurried down the walkway into various stores. The town looked prosperous but not particularly cheerful, the latter characteristic undoubtedly the product of the dark day.

"Is this all the town?" Ellie turned from her study out the window with a look of disappointment.

"I imagine we've only traveled through a portion of it," Cassy said.

"I thought it'd be like London, but this's jess a village."

Cassy laughed. "I think most of the larger towns are located in the northern colonies. But I understand the citizens here are very proud of their capital, so you would be wise not to disparage Williamsburg while we're here."

Ellie nodded but didn't look any happier. She'd evidently dreamed of a teeming metropolis similar to the one she'd grown up in. Cassy suspected the town would undergo a magical population growth before Ellie recounted her adventures to the other women at the Bloomery.

The carriage slowed and then stopped in front of a tidy if not palatial home. A steeply pitched roof with dormers covered the second floor. Cassy would be staying with Conner and Mary McAllister. Jason had earlier explained that McAllister's law office occupied one side of the building.

Cassy knew Jason held McAllister in esteem, but it was obvious Jason was the wealthier of the two. The big house at the Bloomery, for all its emptiness, could have contained this property many times over. Disappointment, probably akin to what Ellie felt, washed over her. Good Lord, now that the term "Lady" was again placed before her name, had she become a snob?

One of the Bloomery men, who'd been pressed into the role of footman, lowered the steps and opened the carriage door. Cassy hurried through the rain and into the house, which immediately made her adjust her assessment of the McAllister's wealth. They certainly hadn't stinted on the candles, and all was bright and welcoming against the gloom of the day.

Mary McAllister was a tall, striking woman with dark, nearly black hair and arresting features. She came forward and took Cassy's hands, her face smiling and friendly. Then she seemed to pause, dropped Cassy's hands, and sank into a graceful curtsy. "Welcome, my lady," Mary said.

"I liked the impulse of your first welcome," Cassy said honestly. She'd never noticed the artificiality of people around her until she'd been without it. She'd discovered she preferred genuine reactions over those that were deemed proper to her station.

The smile returned to Mary's face. "That's good, since I'm not used to entertaining nobility and have to keep reminding myself how to act. You will have to make allowances if everything isn't done exactly right."

"This is your home and you've been gracious enough to invite me to stay, so anything you do will be right."

"Such as leave you standing in the entry hall and impeding the servants' duties," Mary said with a rueful laugh. She took Cassy's arm and led her into an attractive salon. Behind her, Cassy heard movement and low conversation in the hallway. She and Mrs. McAllister had indeed been an impediment to the flow of servants taking care of luggage and other chores associated with the arrival of guests. She realized Ellie had been whisked away from her and set to her duties.

"What a lovely room, Mrs. McAllister. It gives me confidence that Mr. Anders will be able to find quality furnishings for his home. You must tell me where your pieces came from so I can be sure he takes me to those places."

Mary's face flushed with pleasure. "Thank you, Lady Cassandra. Some of the pieces have been in my family for years, others were ordered from England, and a few were bought used. Tippet's has the largest catalogue selection for ordering furniture and Shockley's has an excellent choice of previously owned furniture. I gave Jason a list of the best stores to visit months ago, but he's never done anything about decorating his empty rooms. You've done him an immense kindness by agreeing to help him chose furnishings and decorations."

Mary moved them toward a cheerfully burning heath. When they were both seated and tea ordered, conversation continued. Cassy pointedly asked about the furniture pieces that were obviously heirlooms and watched Mrs. McAllister relax as she recounted tales from her girlhood that each table and chair seemed to elicit. By the time tea arrived, they were Mary and Cassy, and there was easy laughter between them.

Cassy genuinely liked Mary McAllister. She was as beautiful inside as she was out and utterly lacking in pretension. When Cassy commented on the loveliness of her dark hair, Mary told her that family legend said her great-grandmother had been a native.

"My grandfather swore his mother was Welsh, but the story persists. I always thought it was more exotic to think of my ancestress as being a dusky Indian princess who stepped out of the forest and captured my great-grandfather's heart,"

Mary said with happy sincerity. Cassy couldn't think of anyone she knew in England who would admit to any "dusky" progenitor, much less desire it to be true.

On the topic of Jason, Mary was a font of knowledge. Cassy tried to steer the conversation in that direction without being obvious.

"Jason was one of Conner's first clients," Mary said. "He was working as a blacksmith in York at the time, having recently been released from his indenture. The first time they met, Jason had walked all the way from York looking for an up-and-coming attorney. I think the friendship was immediate." She laughed. "Conner really wanted to be thought of as 'up-and-coming.'"

"But why would Mr. Anders come all this way? Aren't there attorneys in York?"

"Oh, most assuredly, but Jason wanted someone who was not beholden to the older families in that area. He required complete confidentiality and, of course, found that in Conner." Mary's pride in her husband was obvious.

"So I assume their business remains secret?"

"Oh, not what they did at the time. It's now common knowledge. Jason arrived with a map in hand and used Conner to buy up tracks of land he'd specified. Jason would arrive with clinking bags of coins and leave them for the purchases."

"Where did Jason, eh, Mr. Anders, get the money?"

"From the items he forged, of course. Jason made all sorts of useful items that no one else did, as well as some truly beautiful ones. I have one of his chandeliers in my dining room. Would you like to see it?"

Cassy definitely wanted to see it, and when she did, she was awestruck. Most formal chandeliers were made of brass or crystal. Those made from iron or tin were considered substandard and utilitarian. But there was nothing utilitarian about the object that hovered above the McAllisters' dining table.

The chandelier was a riot of vines and leaves. It seemed like something that had grown rather than been forged. In addition to the ring of candles that circled it, other candleholders were scattered at intervals in the interior of the graceful and airy fixture. It was unique and arresting, a true work of art.

"When the candles are lit," Mary said, "the area of the table is very bright, but there are also interesting shadows on the walls. It's like dining in a secluded bower."

Cassy had trouble reconciling the maker of the very sensible, big tub in Jason's room with the designer of this fairy creation. Every time she thought she had the measure of the man, the real Jason elusively slipped away.

"You'll get to see what I mean this evening. I hope you don't mind that I've planned a small supper party. Nothing elaborate, but I thought you might like meeting some of our friends. I suspect living at Anders' Bloomery is rather isolated and thought you'd enjoy company." A blush stained the dark complexioned woman's face. "I also must admit, I wanted to show you off a bit. It's not often that a lady of your rank visits Williamsburg. I hope you don't mind."

"No, of course not. I'd like to meet more of society here."

"Oh, this won't really be what you think of as society. I haven't invited the governor or anything. Ours will just be a collection of professional men and their wives, as well as a few planters who live close to town. I'm afraid you'll find us quite provincial."

"Good heavens, Mary. While my memory was gone, I worked as an indentured servant, so part of me will be pleased I'm not serving the dishes."

Both women laughed, but somehow Cassy could tell Mary knew the truth about the whole amnesia scheme. Evidently, even confidential information was impossible to keep from one's spouse.

"With our little party in mind, you will probably want to rest a while before you change. I've put you in our guest suite at the back of the house. Like most things in this house, it was added higgledy-piggledy, but it opens onto the garden, which makes it nice. Unfortunately, my gardens aren't very attractive at this time of year. The two Chinese maples are a glorious red, however. I hope we have some sun tomorrow so you can enjoy them."

A maid showed Cassy through a narrow hall to the area designated as the guest suite, which turned out to be very nice indeed. The room itself was large. One wall contained a pair of French doors leading to the garden. Opposite was a fireplace with a handsome mantel and a comfortable seating area. A large bed with elegant hangings of crewel embroidery took up the third wall, and the fourth contained a door to a dressing room that held a bed for her maid. All in all, the accommodations were as fine as those provided at most of the homes she'd visited in England.

Ellie had evidently finished with her duties, since the woman was sprawled in one of the chairs near the fire, snoring away. Cassy's entry must have awakened her, however, since she broke off in mid-snore and leaped to her feet.

"Let me tell the chambermaid ya'll now be wantin' hot water for washing," Ellie said, wearing her guise of a lady's maid and bursting with efficiency. "I've shaked out the wrinkles in yer blue gown for this evenin' and doon think it'll need ta be ironed, but ya kin check it if ya like."

"I'm sure I'll be satisfied if you are," Cassy said. The blue dress was the nicest of those she'd finished sewing. It was a good choice for a small supper party, not too dressy or low-cut, but festive. Ellie must have gotten the schedule of the evening's activities from the other servants and used it to guide her choice.

"Have you met many of the other servants?" she asked. Cassy knew Ellie had had visions of rows of handsome footmen standing about like a banquet on display and hoped she wasn't too disappointed the McAllisters' wasn't that type of establishment.

"Mosely slaves." Ellie wrinkled her nose. "I kin see why Mr. Anders doon hold with havin' slaves. They seem a pretty loose lot. But, then, as Mr. Anders says, why should they care? Got nothin' ta look for but mora the same. He an Mr. Mac have words about it a lot. Mr. Mac says Mr. Anders has ta keep quiet on it oren he caint get elected as e'en a cesspit cleaner."

Cassy smiled at Ellie's outspoken opinions and then realized she was only saying what she, or someone else working at the Bloomery, had heard Conner say. "There are few secrets at the Bloomery, aren't there?"

"Oh Lord, Cassy. Ya know tha's the truth." Ellie flashed a cheeky grin and then her face grew grave. "I mean, milady, and no Bloomery tales get told elsewhere without some fixin'. Fer instance, we all know ya were overcome wid the smoke the other night and ya had to stay in Mavis's room. An every man-jack on the place will swear to it. But I doon know what yer goin' ta do wid that handsome colonel up north." At Cassy's frown, Ellie muttered "water" and fled the room.

Cassy wandered over and sat in the chair Ellie had recently vacated. She wondered if Lieutenant Michaels would ever know he'd been promoted as the tale of Cassy's engagement circled among the gossiping Bloomery staff. But she didn't know what she was going to do with Gilbert either, and she now secretly hoped she'd never have the opportunity to find out.

A new variable had been inserted into her plans. Jason had brought her to Williamsburg and he wasn't ashamed to have her meet his friends. Maybe he thought her ridiculous tale would be believed and she could somehow fit into his life. A glimmer of hope flared that her most fantastic dream of the future might come to fruition. What squeezed her heart was the fear that this possibility might be as doomed as Ellie's expectation of footmen arranged every three feet.

Chapter Sixteen

J ason watched Cassy from across the room. She was in conversation with Marcus Lee's wife and had, miraculously, made the woman smile. Jane Lee always looked as if she'd just eaten a worm along with her apple. Jason couldn't remember her ever saying a kind thing about anyone or anything. He suspected poor Marcus had become involved in politics so he'd have an excuse to escape the presence of his wife as much as possible. And Cassy had somehow made her smile.

He hoped Mary wouldn't saddle him with Mrs. Lee as a dinner partner. Again. He was sure he'd threatened Mary with some form of horrible dismemberment after the last time, but he remembered doing the same thing the time before, and it had done no good. "You're so good with her," Mary had said. "Mrs. Lee is much more relaxed talking with you since she feels she is naturally superior and doesn't have to prove to you that she is."

Now that was a backhanded compliment if he'd ever heard one. He doubted Mrs. Lee was even capable of a pleasant expression—perhaps because her hair was scraped back too tightly to allow her face to move. And now Cassy had her smiling. My God, had Mrs. Lee just covered her mouth to hide a laugh? An impossibility.

"She's amazing. I'll give you that," Conner quietly commented near his ear. He was looking in the same direction as Jason. "Jane Lee is convinced that Lady Cassandra has singled her out because they are both aristocrats destined to be surrounded by peasants."

"I don't think Cassy has singled anyone out. She seems to be working the room like a good politician."

Conner smiled. "As I said, amazing."

"It was kind of you and Mary to put together this dinner on such short notice. It's a good place for Cassy to try her wings after her *harrowing trials*." Jason grinned, since most of these harrowing trials were the product of Conner's imagination.

"It was really for you as much as for her. I thought you might like to see how she fit in with people in the Virginia colony. Just in case you mean for her to stay here instead of hurrying off to Massachusetts."

Conner gave him a slow, considered look. Jason schooled his face and showed no reaction. How did the man know Cassy's leaving was not what he wanted? His friend had the irritating ability to see things Jason would have preferred to keep hidden.

When Jason didn't say anything, Conner just raised his eyebrows. "I also have something to say to you privately. If you'd come to the office, this will only take a minute. We both know if we're not here when dinner is served, Mary will kill me."

Pretending an ease he didn't feel, Jason followed his friend. Had Conner somehow heard that Cassy had spent the night with him after the fire? Everyone at the Bloomery undoubtedly knew of it, but with outsiders, his employees were generally closed mouth. If the rumor had reached Conner, however, Jason suspected he was going to have to both listen to a dressing down and eat crow before going in to dinner.

The minute the door to the office closed, Conner surprised him by letting out a low whoop of joy and slapping him on the back. "You've got him!" Conner exclaimed. "You've got that bastard Hyde by the balls and there's nothing he can do about it."

"What are you talking about?"

"You've still got Sir Peyton's notes of payment, don't you?"

"Of course. I thought he'd have sold his tobacco crop by now and the whole county would have heard his scream when he went to his regular creditors and discovered I'd bought up his notes. But he hasn't yet come blustering to me with his redemption money."

"He won't be coming," Conner chortled. "He can't pay."

"What?"

"He's kept it quiet, but his crop has failed. He has nothing to sell. He's got mold in all his barns and there's not a single hogshead of good leaves to be salvaged."

"Oh, my God!" Jason was glad he was standing near a chair because he collapsed into it. The information was staggering. If Sir Peyton didn't have a crop to sell, the only way he could repay his seed loans was to put some of his property on the block.

Jason had thought it would take years for this part of his plan to arrive. He knew Hyde's land was becoming exhausted; tobacco leached the nutrients out of the soil and Sir Peyton was too greedy to let his land rest, so his yields were lower every year. Jason had planned to slowly bleed the man. But to lose an entire crop was to hemorrhage.

Mold was the scourge of the tobacco planter. It could strike at any time. Tender seedlings could get mold. Mature plants could get mold. But this could be somewhat controlled by destroying the affected plants. Mold in the curing barns, however, was catastrophic.

"He picked his leaves too green," Jason said, a statement rather than a question.

"Yes, he picked too green." Even intentionally muted, Conner's laugh was loud in the empty room. "Hyde's always been too cheap to hire an effective manager. He's gone with brutal overseers, as you well know, and these men have pushed the laborers into working incredibly long hours. Tired men make mistakes, or more likely, they don't care. So the whole bloody crop was picked either too green or too wet, and the mold jumped from leaf to leaf to leaf, until his entire yield was destroyed."

"I haven't heard anything and he's one of my near neighbors." Jason tried to damp down his excitement. Experience had taught him that some news was too good to take at face value. "How do you know this is true?"

"I was talking to Marcus Lee a few minutes ago and mentioned that you and Lady Cassandra were going furniture shopping tomorrow. Lee said Shockley's should have a good choice. He saw four big wagons crammed full of interesting items being unloaded there yesterday. He was afraid someone he knew had died and he'd missed the notice, so he asked where the items had come from. It was all from Hyde's plantation. Sir Peyton had to sell his fine furniture because his tobacco crop is worthless."

"This has really happened?"

"Damn right. Marcus Lee is not one to believe in rumor. He always knows his facts."

"Bloody hell, but this is good news." Jason couldn't keep a broad grin from splitting his face.

"And when you defeat him in his re-election attempt next summer…" Conner's voice trailed off and he gave Jason an answering silly grin.

A sliver of concern pierced Jason's euphoria, however. "Do you think Sir Peyton already discovered I now hold his notes? This would explain the mysterious fire in my study two nights ago. He might have hoped to burn the notes. When it was obvious the damage hadn't been that extensive, he carted some of his furniture into town to try to raise cash."

Conner was quiet for a moment. Jason could almost see the invisible quill tapping his teeth. "Yeah, the timing is suspicious. As far as Sir Peyton is concerned, you need to watch your back." His friend's face dropped when he realized what he'd just said. "Shit. I'm sorry, Jason."

"Don't be. Sir Peyton Hyde is about to get paid back for every stripe he put there. And I can tell you, the revenge will be very, very sweet."

The two men left the office buoyed by their shared feeling of victory only to be met by a frowning Mary, who'd been delaying dinner until the host reappeared. She directed Jason to one of the three round tables where, unsurprisingly, he was seated next to Mrs. Lee. Jason counted this as a penance for upsetting Mary's plans. Mrs. Lee was fulsome in her praise of the incomparable Lady Cassandra, however. Since Jason agreed with her assessment, for a change, the woman's conversation was agreeable.

Cassy was seated at the adjacent table. By pretending attention to Mrs. Lee, Jason could watch Cassy's changing expressions. How Cassy sparkled. She wore a shimmering blue gown that showed the soft top of her breasts. Her hair, loosely gathered at her nape, glowed golden in the candlelight. He could not hear her words, but occasionally a tantalizing echo of her laugh reached him.

He wanted to touch her so badly his hands ached. He'd been circumspect in his attentions all evening, conscious of others watching. For now, all he could do was imagine pulling down the neck of Cassy's gown to expose the tight, rosy nipples beneath. He wanted to suckle them as he ran his fingers through the damp curls at the juncture of her thighs. He felt his cock stiffen and was glad the table hid his condition. Good heavens! What if horse-faced Mrs. Lee noticed and believed she was the cause? What a horrible thought!

Jason decided it might be wise to give some attention to his table partner on the other side. He was reacting like a stallion that was ready to mount with just a whiff of a mare in season.

Supper finally drew to a close and the ladies left the men to their port and conversation. Jason took small sips of his wine. As far as he was concerned, port and Madeira might as well come from the same bottle—both were ghastly. The conversation was also not particularly interesting. The seven men in attendance were well acquainted with each other's opinions, but that didn't keep each of them from restating his position on whatever topic came up.

When a second round of drinks was poured, Lemuel Davis introduced a new conversational stream. "I, for one, want to know about the secret goings on at the Bloomery," the florid faced man said. "What can you tell us, Anders?"

Jason froze for two heartbeats. Was gossip circulating about him and Cassy? "Excuse me?" he said.

"Don't be coy, Anders. What's this new furnace I'm hearing about?"

Jason's pulse returned to its normal rhythm. "Ah, the blast furnace. It's built and ready to use as soon as a specialist arrives from Ireland. It will revolutionize iron making in Virginia. We'll no longer have to buy English iron to get the quality we need to make everyday items." Jason took a sip of his wine and decided it was beginning to taste better.

"Does that mean prices for everything from kettles to plow shares will come down?" Marcus Lee asked.

"It should. There will be no transportation costs. We'll be able to go from raw bog iron to the finished product right here in Virginia. We can even ship those products back to England, instead of just the raw materials. The process will be American from beginning to end."

All of the men looked pleased. English restrictions on trade were a constant bone of contention, and if they could be eliminated, it would be a victory for everyone.

"But I thought you already had furnaces," Davis said. "You've been melting down that useless-looking, ruddy sledge into blooms for years."

"This is new and exciting technology," Jason explained. "My old furnaces are really nothing more than expanded forges like you'd see at any blacksmith's. The blast furnace is much bigger. I've put up a chimney that's over twenty-five feet tall."

"You're kidding."

"No, this is a major project. I've had to put in a millrace so I can use a water-powered bellows as well. The iron smelted in a blast furnace will have most of the impurities taken out. It gets its name from the blast of air that's needed. Limestone is used as a flux and the furnace temperatures are much higher." Jason stood and retrieved an unused fork from the sideboard. "Here, I'll show you."

The men crowded around as Jason began to draw on the tablecloth with the handle of the fork. Even though the lines in the linen surface were only indentations, all of the men followed Jason's explanation, asking pertinent questions and joking about looking for Shadrach, Meshach, and Abednego hovering in the furnace's depths.

Jason was surprised when a manservant came to say some of the ladies thought it was time to leave. Conner looked at him and wiggled his brows. "Are we in trouble with Mary again for tardiness?" Jason asked when he came abreast of his friend.

"I'm not," Conner said with a chuckle, "but I don't think Mary's going to have to think too hard to figure out who made indentations in her best tablecloth that may never come out."

"Does this mean every time I put my feet under your table, I'm going to be seated next to Jane Lee?"

"Probably."

Jason moaned as they parted. Conner went to fulfill his duties as host and Jason went to find Cassy, hoping they could finally have a semblance of privacy.

In the drawing room, Cassy was still in conversion with two other ladies. Jason joined their group, much relieved when carriages began to arrive and wraps gathered. When the last of Cassy's newfound friends got up to leave, he shifted seats so he sat with her on the sofa. He stretched his arm across the back of the settee and surreptitiously rubbed the side of one of his fingers along her bare arm. He felt her tremble at his touch.

"Have you enjoyed your introduction to colonial society, Lady Cassandra?" he asked. If anyone were to notice, this would appear to be a harmless conversation. Jason didn't feel particularly harmless, however.

"Very much. You're blessed with good friends." She turned to bring her arm more firmly into contact with his hand, the edges of her mouth curling slightly.

"And your room here with the McAllisters, do you find it comfortable? I assume you're in the guest suite on the first floor."

The quiver at the sides of her mouth turned into a full-fledged smile. "The room is lovely, as you well know, since Mary has said that's where you usually stay when you're in Williamsburg."

He nodded. "Then you will have noticed the French doors. If one goes through them, there's a brick walk leading to the back of the garden where there's a white painted gate. And if one goes through that gate, one would find herself in a small lane that leads to the mews."

"What would one find there?" Laughter accompanied her words.

"Oh, if one were to wait about a half hour after I leave, there might be a small, anonymous carriage from the livery standing there. And the carriage would be very, very lonely if you were not to come."

"Then I think it best that I arrive on time. With this in mind, I will wish you a good night."

206 • Hannah Meredith

They both stood and Cassy extended her hand. He bowed over it, brushing her knuckles with his mouth. "You do not have to wish me a good night, my lady, for I am sure I shall have one."

Jason walked with Cassy to the door, where he thanked Mary and Conner for the lovely evening. Cassy turned toward her quarters at the rear of the house as he departed for his short walk to Christina Campbell's Tavern. Or, more specifically, the livery stables at the rear.

The rain had stopped. It was now cold and blustery, the errant autumn wind sending eddies of damp leaves swirling around his feet as he walked. Jason didn't feel the chill, however. To him, it was a glorious night. The downfall of Sir Peyton was imminent. In the process of explaining his new furnace, he'd realized he was capable of making his first pour from the blast furnace on his own. And he was about to have the most fascinating woman in the world in his bed.

Chapter Seventeen

*C*assy entered her bedroom to find Ellie staring glumly into the fire. She was sorry her friend and lady's maid was finding her first night in Williamsburg to be less than she'd expected. But Ellie's dejected attitude could in no way diminish the thread of excitement that wove through Cassy.

When Jason had arrived this evening, Cassy had thought he'd behaved oddly. He'd seemed to ignore her, but every time she'd looked in his direction, his eyes had been on her. She'd worried he was having another attack of conscience that, in the past, had caused him to keep his distance. Her concerns had been assuaged in the last few minutes, however. What she'd initially perceived as withdrawal, she now saw as his attempt to behave circumspectly.

He wanted her alone, tonight. And that was something she, too, longed for. Watching him across a roomful of people had been sheer torture. He was by far the most irresistible man in the room. Conner might have been slightly taller, but he looked inconsequential next to Jason, who appeared to be the primal male.

She had no idea now why she'd thought he needed to wear brighter colors. The grays and browns he favored were perfect for him. The only thing that could make him more attractive would be if he had on nothing at all.

She smiled at her thought. All of the ladies present would have been shocked. But she was sure they would have looked.

"You can go on to bed, Ellie," she said. "I think I may take a stroll in the garden before retiring."

A smile formed on Ellie's angular face. "At least yer gettin' to stroll."

Oddly enough, Cassy wasn't embarrassed by Ellie's quick assessment of the situation. Like most of the women at the Bloomery, Ellie was well acquainted with lust. She could even accept Cassy's being with Jason while supposedly planning to marry someone else. Cassy's admission that she wanted to be with no one else, however, would have confused her.

"We'll see if we can't find something exciting for you tomorrow," Cassy said. "In the meantime, see if you can find me my cloak. Oh, and don't lock the garden door."

Ellie snorted. "Lockin' doors is for England. Here," she shrugged, "I guess ev'ry thing is wide open." Then she went to the dressing room to get Cassy's brushed wool cloak.

Cassy had made the cloak from material Mavis had stored away. The fabric had been intended for bed hangings, but Mavis decided it was too drab. Cassy found the dark olive color soothing. When she slipped it on, she realized it would also blend into the shadows.

Closing the door softly behind her, Cassy walked out into the garden. She suspected that neither Mary nor Conner would be as understanding of her night's activities as Ellie. She hoped their bedroom didn't overlook the garden, or if it did, that they would be otherwise occupied.

She wandered down the walk to the back of the garden, the night alive with the rustling of the wind in the trees and shrubs. As Jason had said, a white gate bisected the back wall. She heard nothing beyond the gate, however. She was early. She leaned against the brick wall, trying to make herself as inconspicuous as possible. Her pulse accelerated when she thought about the hours to come. She craved him and the feelings he engendered. Was her desire bordering on obsession? It was an uncomfortable thought.

Then she heard the measured steps of a horse and the creak of a carriage in the lane and decided not to think at all. Instead she acted, slipping through the gate and watching the carriage approach. This was a small, two-wheeled vehicle similar to the gig they'd taken into York, but this one was enclosed. Not only would the hood protect them from the weather, at night it made them nearly invisible to anyone they might pass. Cassy smiled.

A large, familiar hand extended down and hoisted her into the carriage. To her surprise, Jason immediately lowered his lips to hers. He held her head as he ravaged her mouth. When he pulled back, he was breathing heavily. "You have no idea how long I've wanted to do that," he said, putting the horse into motion.

"Where are we going?" she asked, equally breathless.

"Campbell's Tavern. I told the innkeeper I was a light sleeper and wanted to stay away from the traffic noise at the front. So I now have a room conveniently located near the rear stairs."

"It sounds like you were confident I'd accompany you." Cassy wanted to be nowhere else, but she couldn't resist teasing him.

Jason chuckled. "Let's just say that I was hopeful."

In almost no time, Jason swung down from the carriage and tied the horse to a hitching post in the large rear courtyard of an inn. "My heavens," Cassy whispered, "we could have walked."

"Not if we wanted to remain unrecognizable," Jason whispered back. He lifted her down and they entered the building. There was the rumble of masculine conversation and the clink of glasses further up the hall. "Taproom," Jason said, his mouth near her ear.

He ushered her into a narrow stairwell lit intermittently by rush lights on the wall. Obviously intended for servants, the area was clean but without decoration. One flight up, they entered a much wider hallway. At the first door on the right, Jason paused, unlocked the door, and guided her inside.

The room was simply furnished. It would have reminded Cassy of a room designated for an upper servant in one of the great houses of England had it not been for the size of the bed, which was enormous. Jason turned and relocked the door. He moved behind Cassy, pulling her back against him as he nuzzled her neck and reached around her to untie the laces at the neck of her cloak.

"I've never been in an inn before," she said, unaccountably nervous. Their previous encounters could be seen as unpremeditated—well, perhaps by stretching credulity a bit—but there was no doubt she had come here for only one purpose. That she had become as morally lacking as Ellie crossed her mind, but with Jason's lips tickling the fine hairs on the back of her neck, she suddenly didn't care.

"If you traveled any in England and didn't stay in a post house, where did you stay?" Jason asked, as he took the cloak from her shoulders and draped it over a chair.

"We always stayed at the estates of friends or acquaintances."

"Then this will be a new experience for you."

He left her and went to a small table set near the hearth. His movements were less smooth and confident than normal. Cassy wondered if this were the first time Jason had been to an inn, at least for an assignation. She knew he visited the whores at The Blue Heron, but did he also bring slightly more respectable women to this type of accommodations?

"I ordered some wine, if you'd like to have some," he said, pouring an amber liquid into a glass from a pitcher.

"Are you having wine?"

"No. Ale."

"Then I think I'd like to try some of that. I'd never had ale either."

He poured a glass for her and brought it to where she stood. "Then this will be a night of firsts," he said, handing her the glass.

Taking a sip of the ale, she found it bitter but not unpleasant. "And is this the first time you've been to an inn?" She wanted to add "with a woman," but lacked the courage to do so. She wasn't sure if she wanted to know the answer or not.

"No. I use them when traveling. When I'm in Williamsburg, I sometimes stay here at Christina Campbell's, at least when the House of Burgesses is not in session. During the legislative period, the whole town is filled to bursting, and I don't relish sharing a bed with two or three other men, so I stay with the McAllisters."

He shifted his weight. "Maybe we should sit down." He nodded toward the chairs on either side of the small table.

"Yes," she said, although her eyes slipped to the big bed instead of the chairs. At least its size had been explained. But three or four men in it? Heavens! A smile flicked over the edges of her mouth as she imagined the complaints Jason's shoulders would elicit from the other occupants.

When Jason had taken his seat, he placed his glass on the table and leaned forward with his hands on his knees. "I think I'm doing this wrong." He gave her a chagrinned smile. "I thought an inn would be good place. It's anonymous. There are no servants who give you knowing smiles even if they say nothing." Cassy thought of Ellie, who always had something to say, but decided not to point out the error in his thinking.

"I imagined when you came here, there would be a slow seduction. I know in the past I've almost attacked you, and I wanted to prove I had self-control. I didn't want you to think I'm an undisciplined beast. But I now realize I don't know how to seduce someone."

He sat upright, as if trying to put more distance between them. "This seems so artificial and contrived. All those years when I'd meet women in the woods, it was planned. But it was just a way of finding release, a way of forgetting. Those meetings didn't mean anything. And now that I want our being together to count for something, I don't know where to start."

Cassy wondered if Jason knew he'd just seduced her with his words. He wanted their time together to be significant. This sentiment chimed like a bell in her heart. "I'm a bit new at seduction myself," she said with a soft smile. "But is what you said the other night about men liking the same thing as women true?"

"As far as I can tell." His eyes flashed with mischief. "I may not be practiced in seduction, but I think I'm good at satisfaction."

Of that, Cassy had no doubt. Satisfaction *was* the seduction. She was sure he'd never lacked for willing partners during his years of indenture. She was equally positive that many of those women had hoped that what they did together would mean something to him, but it obviously never had. And as for the women who worked at the Heron—she suspected many of them wanted their time with Jason to be more than a job. But he seemed to be saying that none of his past encounters had meant anything.

Oddly, his uncertainty and insecurity gave her confidence. She stood, but motioned him back to his chair when he also began to rise. "No, just sit there and watch. If we both like the same things, then I must admit I like to watch you take off your clothes."

"I didn't know you watched," he said.

Cassy laughed. "Oh, I most definitely did. I enjoy seeing pieces of you revealed. It's like watching a package being unwrapped, and I know that particular package is something I very much want. So you sit there, and I'll get rid of some of these clothes."

She walked over toward the bed on watery knees. This had seemed like a good idea when she'd said it, but now she wasn't so sure. The shadows were deeper by the bed, but the two candles on the table and the fire in the hearth seemed to make everything noontime bright. She took the pins from her stomacher and carefully laid it on the bed. Her fingers trembled as she unlaced the tapes of her dress and then the binding of her hooped petticoat. Sliding the dress off her shoulders, she pushed the dress and petticoat to the floor. She now stood in her stays and shift.

Only then did she look at Jason. He was leaning forward again, an avid look on his face. She saw him lick his lips and felt herself make an answering gesture. He made a quiet groan. A secret smile curled her mouth. Jason, too, liked to watch the package being unwrapped.

It dawned on her that removing her clothes had never before been a consideration. She'd always arrived in her night shift. She unconsciously licked her lips again, not wanting to examine what this said about her previous intentions. She picked up the discarded dress and small hoop and placed them on the bed.

She boldly faced Jason as she began to unlace her stays. Watching Jason watch her, she slowly pulled the tapes through the holes. He had the look of a starving dog chained just a few feet from his food. Cassy liked that she could so attract him.

She removed her stays and dropped them on the accumulating pile. She stepped out of her shoes and tucked them under the dust ruffle. Then she pulled her shift to mid-thigh and swung her leg up so her heel rested on the high bed. She unfastened the ribbon holding one of her hose and began to roll it down.

The sound of Jason abruptly standing brought her head around. "Bloody hell, Cass," he said, taking a step toward her, "I can't stand this."

She dropped her foot to the floor and pointed a finger at him. "Sit down," she ordered. "I've decided to take over this seduction, and what's required of you right now is that you not move from that chair."

Somewhat to her surprise, he settled back into the chair. She continued to roll down one stocking and then the other, until finally she wore only her shift. When she turned to face Jason, he was almost quivering. A heady feeling of power washed over her. She untied the tapes at the neck of her shift, opening the neck as wide as it would go. She slid first one shoulder and then the other through the opening. Pulling the garment at the waist, she inched the sleeves down her arms, the neckline following and slowly exposing her breasts.

"Dear God, woman. Can I move now? You're killing me."

"No, you have to stay in the chair. I'll come to you." As she walked toward him, she noticed her hips rolled a bit more than usual. She wanted him to want her with every fiber of his being. She was surprised to feel the warm wetness between her legs as she approached him. She was as aroused as she hoped Jason was.

When she stood in front of him, he reached forward, pulling her body between his legs as he pulled her head down. He kissed her, hungrily and open-mouthed. His tongue plunged into her as one hand came up to rub her breasts. Dear Lord, he felt and tasted marvelous. It would be so easy to become a viscous puddle in his arms and let him do as he willed.

But she hadn't come so far to relinquish the delight of control. She took a step back and pushed on his chest. His face registered his confusion. "Cassy?"

"Don't distract me," she said. "It's time for me to unwrap my present." As if to emphasize her intent, she ran a hand along the edge of his coat and thrust it back.

"I can do that in a thrice." Jason started to his feet.

"Don't get up," she said sternly. "I mean to be the one to do the unwrapping. You are to sit there like a good little present and let me have my way."

He looked bemused, but he slumped back into the chair. She folded his jacket back on both sides and forced the two sides toward his shoulders. "A little help here would be nice," she said.

"Now I'm supposed to help? I thought you wanted to do this all by yourself." As he grinned up at her, one of his arms snaked out and he trailed a finger over her left nipple.

Cassy grabbed the questing hand. "I admit I need your help, but until I get this done, there will be no touching."

"If you say so." He helped her strip off his jacket. She went to work on the buttons and his waistcoat soon followed. She unfurled his neckcloth and opened the neck of his shirt.

Pulling the tails of his shirt from his breeches she said, "Lean forward with your arms up." For a heartbeat, he hesitated. "I want to feel your skin. I enjoy it when you touch me, and I want to return the favor." He raised his arms and she lifted the shirt over his head.

Since he was sitting in a chair she couldn't see the horrible scars, but they both knew what hovered beyond her sight. She hated that he was so sensitive about his back. She knew he didn't want her pity. But what she felt was an abiding tenderness.

"Are you done now, Cass?" he groaned. "If this is a seduction, believe me when I say I'm already seduced. I was hard as a rock when you got into the carriage. The rest of this has been pure torture. I've a pikestaff in my breeches and I'm about to die."

"You won't die," she said with confidence. No one could die of a prolonged cock stand, could they? She quickly shifted through the wisdom she'd heard from the women at the Bloomery, but could think of nothing that addressed this particular problem.

She ran a hand across his now naked chest, following the line of springy hair that crossed it in a T. The sensation made her fingers tingle. He reached to do the same to her. "Fair is fair," he said.

She leaned back and placed both of his forearms on the arms of the chair. "Fair has never been fair, a fact to which we can both attest. Now leave your arms there as I check out my new present for any damage in shipping."

She continued to stroke his chest, marveling at the array of muscles that crossed it in heavy striations. She was amazed that such leashed power trembled under her hand. She could feel the thunder of his heart beneath her palm. Jason had said men liked what women did, but their bodies were very different. Only the flat nipples, surrounded by wispy whorls of hair, had any similarity. She brushed the area with her fingers and was surprised to see Jason's nipples pucker in a manner like her own. On impulse, she slipped to her knees so she could kiss them.

She leaned forward, bracing her forearms on his thick thighs. When she lowered her mouth to lick and then suck his tight nubs, Jason muttered, "Sweet Jesus" in the tone of a prayer. His hands gripped the chair arms, the knuckles showing white.

She left a trail of kisses as she followed the line of hair down the center of his taut belly. He tasted of salt and some exotic spice. His pelvis jerked up from the seat as her mouth lowered. His chest moved like a bellows.

Her hands began to work at the buttons on his breeches. "No," he said, his hands grasping hers painfully. "It's time to end this play."

"But you said I could touch and lick and suck." She tried to inject an innocence into her words that she definitely didn't feel.

"I said it could be done, not that you should do it." He tried to urge her up. "Cass, I don't think this is something ladies do."

"And you know this from your vast experience with ladies?"

"Well, no," he said, sounding amusingly grumpy, "but—"

"But this is obviously something men enjoy," she continued his thought, although she knew this was not what he meant to say. She twisted her wrists and his hands fell away. She pushed the fabric aside and his cock sprang free, dark and heavily veined. She ran her fingers up and down his shaft. He made incoherent growling sounds. When she looked up at him, he was pressed back in the chair, watching her. His eyes were bright with a kind of desperation.

She kissed the broad head. Acting on instinct and imagining what his cock was doing when he moved within her, she sucked him into her mouth, mimicking the motion. She felt his hands on either side of her head, holding her steady as he began to move within her mouth. He exhaled unintelligible words on each stroke, his pelvis flexing and relaxing.

Abruptly he stood, pulling her to her feet in the process, and pressed his mouth to hers as his arousal rubbed against her stomach. She felt the warm gush of his seed hit her belly and slide down her thighs. He held her tightly against him, rubbing a hand up and down her back, cupping and massaging her buttocks.

Both of them were sweat soaked. Cassy rubbed her breasts over Jason's chest. The feeling of him against her, around her, left her as breathless as he was. She felt she was about to tumble from the peak and had only ministered to his needs. As if he knew, he dropped a hand to fondle her between her legs, pulling his finger once, twice into her cleft, and she fell from the heights, calling his name.

He scooped her into his arms and carried her to the bed. With one hand, he threw back the bedcovers, tumbling her carefully folded clothes to the floor where they were instantly forgotten. He stretched her out on the cool sheets. "I judge we're even," he said. "And now it's my turn."

As if he'd memorized the pattern, he began stroking a hand down her body and then suckled her breasts. She arched into him, a part of her mind amazed he'd been able to stay so still. His hot, wet mouth worked its way down her torso, stopping to lave her navel. And then lower still. He lifted her legs onto his shoulders.

When he slipped his tongue between her cleft and licked her, Cassy was beyond coherent. Only feelings flooded through her. When he sucked her nub, working his teeth lightly over her, she came again in a blinding flash of color.

She had no time to rest, however, as he entered her, his cock pumping into her relentlessly. He took her higher and higher, her hands like talons along his scarred back, fingers wildly gripping his flexing buttocks. The headboard of the bed banged against the wall in time to his thrusts. She realized she was crying out in counterpoint to the pounding of the bed. And then they both came together in a crescendo of sound.

They lay spent, both of them trying to get their breath and their bearings. A different pounding came through the wall. "Pay her well," shouted an aggrieved voice. "She earned it."

Jason began to laugh, which pulled Cassy into a fit of hilarity. "Inns are indeed anonymous," he said near her ear, "but I see now they're not necessarily private."

Chapter Eighteen

$\mathcal{S}$ hopping with Cassy was an educational experience. One moment she was as excited as a child in a toy store, the next she was every inch the demanding and decisive English aristocrat. She, by turns, charmed and terrified the clerks at Shockley's.

Jason had originally planned to look at the sketches of the furniture available for order from England and choose appropriate pieces. They could then fill in missing pieces from what was offered at Shockley's. Cassy had vetoed this idea even before they'd left the McAllisters.

"It makes more sense to see what is locally available and can be delivered quickly," she said. "Then you can order pieces you can't get here—but in the meantime, you'll still have enough furniture to make your house usable." She was resplendent in a teal walking dress and looked none the worse for her night's exertions. Jason wasn't sure the same could be said for him.

"My bedroom is usable," he laughingly whispered, bending down until his lips touched the top of the perfect shell of her ear. She smelled of a sweeter, floral scent today. He was more accustomed to the slightly astringent fragrance of lavender. But whatever this new scent was, he liked it.

She swatted at him. "You can't entertain *there* when people come to visit."

"I beg to differ with you." With difficulty, he tried to appear stern.

She swatted him harder but gave him a devastating smile. "You need furniture now, not a year from now."

"I can afford new, so why not get new? Everything at Shockley's has been in and out of other houses, sometimes multiple times."

"New isn't always better." She settled her rather drab cloak around her. "It all depends on the original quality. Anything that needs reupholstering can easily be taken care of and it will look new. No one will think you were forced to buy used for lack of money."

He escorted her down the walk and into the carriage. "Take us to Shockley's," he said to Hats in the driver's box. Jason was willing to graciously admit defeat.

He sat opposite her, drinking in her appearance. He had plans for this evening. Cassy was going to get her chance to remain stoic as he worked her to a fever pitch. He smiled at the thought. Perhaps all he had to offer her was passion, but she was a willing participant. He didn't think any woman had ever brought him to such roaring climaxes, and he knew damned well no other man had ever done the same to her.

How would she remember him when she was back with her own kind? Would he be easily forgotten, or would she awaken in the dark of night with her pulse pounding and recall his lips on her breasts? He knew he would never lose the image of Cassy wantonly sprawled across the bed at Campbell's Tavern. He'd wanted to gather her to him and shout, "Mine!" and defend her against the rest of the world. He wanted her now, in this carriage in the middle of an autumn morning. His major problem, however, was that he wanted her for forever.

The carriage slowed. They'd arrived. For the next few hours he could pretend they were furnishing *their* house instead of the one he would live in alone. A much tamer fantasy than rolling with her naked, but just as satisfying.

Shockley's, located on the outskirts of Williamsburg, wasn't what he'd anticipated. The merchandise spilled from one large barn to another to another. At some time in the past, an effort had been made to organize the pieces, with chairs in one place, tables in another, beds at one end of a barn, and smaller outbuildings bursting with odd bits and pieces that included everything from impressive paintings to chamber pots.

But from either a lack of care or an uncontrollable influx of furniture, this system had broken down. Dining chairs sat upended atop sofas, their legs punctuating the air. The mates to the set were dispersed throughout the barns, no one knowing exactly where the scattered pieces could be located. A portrait of someone's grandfather leaned between a horse collar and a bird cage. It was as if the contents of a dozen large homes had been dumped here and then stirred.

"Oh, my heavens," Cassy exclaimed when they walked into the first of the barns, "I think we've come to the right place."

A short, rotund man suddenly appeared as if he'd popped from the earth. His hair had escaped from its queue and his neckcloth was askew. He introduced himself as Leonard Peel, Mr. Shockley's associate. Jason introduced himself and Cassy, her title causing the little man to twitch as if stung by a bee and apologize—the first of many times—that Mr. Shockley was delivering goods out of town and was not available.

"We've come to begin decorating Mr. Anders' new home near York," Cassy said, delving into one of the pockets hanging inside her dress. She pulled out two closely written pages. "I've made a list of the basics required." Upon seeing the length of this list, Mr. Peel became obsequious.

"Any particular style?" he asked. "We recently acquired some chairs made by Chippendale that are outstanding."

"No particular style." Cassy looked at Jason as if for clarification. He had no idea furniture even had different styles, so he just nodded and smiled. "Nothing too light or spindly, however. I would hate for a chair to collapse under Mr. Anders or one of his guests."

"But for milady's boudoir, I'm sure light and airy would be desirable."

"Lady Cassandra and her companion are currently staying at a guest house on my property," Jason interjected, "and it is fully furnished. She does not reside in the house." He glowered at Peel, who flushed, mumbling something about misconceptions, and then began leading them through the serpentine pathways between the piles of furniture.

"Where in the world does all of this come from?" Cassy asked.

"People come and go all the time," Peel said. "They arrive with their furniture, but if they decide to return to England, the furniture is most often left behind. And then, of course, older people die and their children don't want everything.

Mr. Shockley has been in business on this very spot for over forty years, so he's accumulated a large inventory."

Cassy looked around the dark, dusty interior. "So large that it would be impossible to choose things from this jumble. I'll need men to take pieces under consideration outside where they can be inspected."

"Of course." Peel raised his voice, calling out names, and various minions appeared from among the stacks.

"Let me know what appeals to you," Cassy said, moving to stand next to Jason.

"Imagine you're choosing items for your own house and I'm sure I'll be satisfied." Jason indeed wished Cassy were choosing furniture for herself and that both the woman and her choices would always reside in his house.

He followed in her wake, amazed at how quickly she chose items to be removed to the front yard. Fortunately, it was a clear, crisp autumn day. Jason had no idea what they would have done if it had been raining. Cassy was like a general commanding his troops. She would point, then Peel, her second in command, would issue orders, and a team of men would make the piece in question disappear out the door.

If Jason stopped to look at anything, Cassy would circle back to see what had taken his interest. He paused to consider how the shape of a specific chair leg could be forged and Cassy was at his side.

"Do you like that chair?" Her tone of voice indicated the piece had not caught her fancy.

"I thought the legs interesting," he said.

"Mr. Anders admires cabriole legs," she called to Mr. Peel, who immediately sent men scurrying to other areas. Jason grinned. It was nice to know what he liked. The shape had attracted him because it looked like a man beginning to squat with knees thrust forward and ankles locked back. If there were a Mr. Cabriole, he would certainly look humorous walking about with his legs at such an angle.

In the second barn, two matching portraits caught his eye. One was of a stern-faced gentleman wearing the ruff of an earlier generation. The companion painting featured a starkly beautiful woman, also wearing an antique costume, who reminded him a bit of Cassy. The living woman appeared at his arm.

"Do you know them?" she asked. "The man has a bit of the look of you."

He laughed. "I thought the woman looked like you."

She frowned as if trying to see a resemblance. "Altogether, these are quite lovely paintings. They need to be cleaned and re-stretched, but they'd look good in the dining room." Her eyes sparkled up into his. "Think of them as instant ancestors."

"It might be hard to explain why I have someone else's great-uncle hanging on my wall. It's possible a guest will recognize these people."

She leaned forward, running her finger across the gritty frame. "No. These are well executed and quite old. And if their descendants were still here, the paintings would not be." She straightened and pointed and the portraits were whisked away.

Somewhere in the midst of the third barn, Jason realized he was hungry. He raised a finger as if he were about to point at something and a young negro man immediately appeared. "Can you go to the nearest decent tavern and get some meat pies and ale for the lady and myself?"

"Yessir." Teeth flashed very white in the man's dark face.

"Then do so, please." Jason handed over some coins and then added an extra, saying, "This is for your trouble."

Jason saw the war going on within the man. He was a slave, and slaves were not supposed to earn money that wasn't paid to their masters. "I'm sure no one need ever know," Jason said. The white teeth appeared again and the man was gone.

Cassy was poking at a settee from which stuffing was escaping. "It will have to be reupholstered, of course, but the lines are very nice," she said when Jason approached. At his nod, she said, "Outside," and the piece was carried away.

"You also need to go outside," he said. "You've been at this for most of the day and I'm having some food brought here. I thought we could eat under the trees. I don't want my expert decorator fainting from hunger."

"I could stand to eat." Cassy looked surprised at the pronouncement. "I've been having such fun I didn't noticed how much time had passed." She placed her hand on his arm and let her lead her into the light.

She stopped as if thunderstruck. Furniture littered the lawn in front of them. "Good heavens, I had no idea how much I'd chosen. I'm so sorry, Jason. To buy even part of this will cost a great deal of money. I'll begin eliminating pieces as soon as we've eaten."

"Cass, has it yet to dawn on you that I *have* a great deal of money? I hope you didn't think you had to buy used furniture to protect my purse."

"Oh, these pieces are wonderful, not used. They'll give grace to your house." But he knew what would give the most grace to his house was the woman standing next to him. She'd said she was having fun, however, and she did seem to be in her element. When the furniture was chosen, fabrics would have to be selected, walls painted, and then specific small objects assembled. Decorating his house could take a *very* long time, and if Cassy were enjoying herself, perhaps she would stay. He was confident he could make the nights as interesting as the days.

"Then don't worry about the cost. I do need to warn you, however, that I believe in getting value for money and will certainly not pay the initial price asked. If my haggling like a fishmonger will embarrass you, then you can return to McAllister's before we begin our negotiations."

"I've already seen you dickering to get the best price. On the ship." She gave him a broad smile, so the memory must have been pleasant.

"Well sometimes I can make a shrewd bargain. I recall paying four pounds for something that is priceless."

"Flatterer," she said. But Jason knew he'd spoken the truth. There was no flattery involved.

They sat in the shade to eat. A light breeze brought golden leaves, nearly the color of Cassy's hair, drifting down. She told him they were dining *al fresco* and that it had become all the rage in London. Jason wondered if the poor bastards who dropped with exhaustion at the end of a tobacco row and pulled a wormy apple from their pocket knew they were being fashionable. It was one of the many thoughts he'd never express to Cassy.

When they'd finished, they strolled among the items in the yard. Cassy's eyes flashed with enthusiasm, and her hands shaped pictures in the air as she described how this piece and that piece would look in a particular place.

"I thought celadon for the grand salon," she said.

"A what?" He looked around, trying to remember if Cassy had mentioned a celadon. He wasn't sure what one looked like. Was it an upholstered piece? Of course, he also wasn't sure if he had a grand salon. He'd always thought of the largest space in the house as the drawing room.

"Celadon is a color, a gray-green similar to your bed hangings. I thought it would be a nice, restful, background color. You know, for the woodwork, drapes and the like." She reached over and gave his arm a quick squeeze, as if she thought he might be offended by her using a word he didn't know. He smiled reassurance. They each had their own areas of expertise. At least he knew a bloomery had nothing to do with flowers.

"Restful sounds better than what Mavis has done," he said.

"Everything won't be the same color. We'll use accent colors picked jup from the rugs. Oh, rugs. What was I thinking?" She raised her voice so it carried to where the omnipresent Mr. Peel hovered. "Do you have any Turkish rugs, Mr. Peel, or will we need to look elsewhere?"

The portly man came over as fast as he could, his short legs churning. "We have a wonderful selection in the far shed. Carpets I've at least been able to keep separate." The last was said with a put-upon expression. "Actually, we've just recently received a shipment of some excellent rugs. Lovely hues. Would you like to view them?"

"Most definitely," Cassy said as she snagged Jason's arm and they followed in the small man's wake.

"Did any of these rugs come from the home of Sir Peyton Hyde?" Jason asked.

Mr. Peel stopped his headlong rush to the shed. "Why, yes. We don't usually disclose the property from which items arrived, but you obviously already know we have had shipments from Sir Peyton's estate. You've already picked out some of the furniture that arrived in that shipment."

Cassy stopped their movement with a tug on Jason's arm. "We'll need to have those removed," she said quietly to Jason. "I doubt you'll want Sir Peyton's castoffs."

He appreciated her concern for his feelings, but it was completely unnecessary. If he were honest, he'd admit that the idea of sitting in a chair that Sir Peyton no longer could sit in was appealing. That seemed a little too vindictive to voice, however. "I'm fine with what you've chosen. I don't care who the former owner was. Needless to say, I was never in Sir Peyton's house. And the items he's sent here are hardly castoffs. It seems his finances have become perilous and he's trying to raise cash."

The smile that broke over Cassy's face was as beautiful as a sunrise. "Then, by all means, you should have some of his rugs. I suspect it would be satisfying for you to have him underfoot, so to speak."

Lord, how the woman knew him. Jason threw back his head and laughed. They proceeded on to the shed, and soon carpets of all shapes, sizes, and colors were being spread on the grass.

Cassy again took command, nodding her head for those she approved and flicking her wrist for those to be taken back to the shed. "I think that is all for today," she finally said. "If you could cart all of this to Mr. Anders' home, I can see how it will look in the rooms. We may need to add some pieces, but that can wait until the rooms start to come together. Of course, I will need to get many of the pieces reupholstered. Do you have someone you could suggest?"

Of course Mr. Peel had craftsmen he could recommend, and he did so with such enthusiasm Jason was sure he'd receive a commission from the person chosen to do the work. Jason couldn't fault a man for trying to make money wherever he could, however. He was pleased at least one of the suggestions was located in York. Using local craftsmen would make the process go more smoothly.

And then, all that was left was the reckoning and giving Peel his direction. Cassy decided to wait in the carriage during these negotiations. But when he joined her, she raised an eyebrow and asked, "Well?"

"I should have asked you what you thought all this stuff is worth. I suspect I overpaid. Peel named a price and I halved it as a way to get the bartering started—and the damned fool took my price."

She laughed. "So you'd have been happier to pay more if it was the product of hard bargaining, is that it?"

He joined her in laughing at his own ridiculousness. They chatted about their purchases all the way back to McAllisters. Or more specifically, Cassy talked and Jason sat quietly, absorbing the play of happy emotions crossing her face. "I can hardly wait to describe everything to Mary. She's going to think we've been so clever."

"I hope you won't keep her up late talking," he said, as he helped her from the carriage and up the walk. "I've made arrangements to use the livery's small carriage again."

"Then I'll be sure exhaustion strikes me quite early," she said.

Upon entering, Jason was surprised to see one of the younger boys from the Bloomery waiting in the hall. Luke— the boy's name came to him as apprehension slivered through his gut. Any message from the Bloomery sent with a runner could not be good news.

"There's not been another fire?" he asked. He'd left extra men on guard, but that didn't mean a fire would be impossible.

"Na, sir," said the boy. "Miz Mavis sent to ass ya to come home since the man yer've been spectin' is there an Miz Mavis don't know what ta do wid him."

Jason relaxed. Not a disaster, then. But Hanrahan had arrived and Cassy was still in the little house. He could see Mavis's dilemma.

"Who's come?" Cassy squeezed his arm in a death grip.

"Hanrahan. My blast furnace specialist. I'm glad he's finally arrived, since I've been ready to start the furnace up and pour for some time. But where we're going to put him is a bit of a problem. I think he's arriving with a wife and at least one child. They were expecting a second in the last letter I got from him."

"Oh, heavens. I hope some poor woman who's great with child didn't have to make that voyage." Cassy looked a little green just thinking about it.

"Not all women are bad sailors," Jason suddenly realized he was fortunate that Cassy did not do well on a ship. Had she not looked so bedraggled standing on the deck, someone else would have bought her contract well before he got there. The thought was chilling.

"How'd you get here, Luke?" he asked.

"I rode Thunder, fast." The boy looked proud of his accomplishment.

Thunder was one of the big draft horses they used to haul iron, and Jason didn't think the gelding would go anywhere particularly fast. "You've undoubtedly tired the old boy out, then." He ruffled Luke's hair. "You can tie him to the back of the carriage tomorrow when Lady Cassandra returns and ride up with Hats."

He turned to Cassy. "I'm going to have to go directly home and see if I can find a place to install the Hanrahan family. So this means..."

"I can spend the night in a long conversation with Mary." She smiled, but he hoped he saw disappointment in her eyes.

Jason quickly walked back to Campbell's Tavern, Luke dogging his every step. The boy was as excited about riding with Hats in the driver's box as he was proud of his earlier adventure. Jason left Luke and instructions with his coachman. He arranged for a horse from the stables and was soon on the post road toward York. It would be dark before he arrived home again.

As he rode, he mulled over possible living arrangements. That the Hanrahans couldn't take possession of the little house until Cassy vacated it went without question. And Jason hoped that didn't happen for a good, long time.

He finally decided they would have to stay in Mavis's room in the basement of the big house. The room was spacious, although it might be a little crowded for an entire family. Since Mrs. Hanrahan needn't do any cooking, this would be only sleeping and living space. He thought it was workable.

Mavis's anger was not something so easily remedied. To say his housekeeper would be livid at her removal was putting it mildly. The girls who stayed over the kitchen could double up. With Cassy and Ellie in the old house, there should be plenty of room. And then Mavis could have the privacy of her own room there. Of course, this complicated Hats' visiting her. Well, she'd have to go to his rooms or take to the woods. But neither was a good solution since the nights were getting colder.

He prodded every possible sleeping arrangement this way and that. The ideal solution was for Cassy to move into the big house. After all, he'd just bought three new beds. There would shortly be a choice of locations for the evening meetings he desperately hoped would continue.

But he'd been trying so damned hard to protect Cassy's reputation. While she was adamant about not returning to England, it seemed likely she would settle in one of the other colonies, and an aristocratic lady did not bed down with a former convict with impunity. He'd cut off a leg before he'd injure Cassy's future, even if the thought of her eventually leaving throbbed like a strike from a forge hammer.

But Cassy wasn't gone yet, and with luck, she might stay on at the Bloomery for some time. She was his decorating specialist, after all, and he had a hell of a lot to decorate. His mind happily turned from sleeping arrangements to the arrangements that had allowed him little sleep last night.

Cassy had played with him and had a good time doing so. Jason had often been on the giving end of such play, but this was the first time he'd been the recipient. He didn't think he'd ever had his lust stoked so hot, but he'd been proud of his control. It had taken incredible willpower to leave his arms on the chair as Cassy wanted.

He'd wanted her before she'd managed to teasingly undress. But when she'd touched him, dear God, he'd nearly shot off in his breeches like a green boy.

To his credit, he'd gotten even by bringing her to pleasure again and again. He should have kept count, but at the time, the number hadn't seemed important. He realized that on one occasion, he'd again not withdrawn. Something about Cassy made this standard procedure impossibly difficult.

Did he want her to catch a child? This would force their relationship into a direction he secretly wanted it to go. Or would she immediate apply to the cook for some tansy? The thought of an almost-child curdled his gut with an unimaginable loss. He'd never considered having children before, had thought of it as something that would come when he was ready to start a dynasty. With Cassy, though, the thought was never that far from his mind. The idea of Cassy with his child at her breast filled him with a never-before-imagined longing.

He smiled ruefully and put his heels to his horse. He was turning into a sentimental fool. He needed to think of Cassy leaving him as she would surely do. But his mind would not turn to that eventuality. He might not be good enough to have her for a lifetime, but he could at least have her for now. He would take what he could get.

It was very late by the time he turned on to the lane between the gateposts. He was stiff and tired and glad to be home. Because of the hour, Mavis should have already figured out a temporary solution and the Hanrahans should have been taken care of for the night. Jason hoped so. Right now, nothing sounded better than his own bed.

When he rode in, the main house was dark except for a candle glow from his room on the second floor and a glimmer of light from Mavis's quarters in the basement. Mavis had evidently anticipated his arrival. As tired as he was, he still needed to check with Mavis to see what had been done.

He sleepily followed the stairs to the basement hallway. Mavis's room lay to the left. Had he not had other things on his mind, had he not known Hats was in Williamsburg, he might have recognized the sounds coming from Mavis' room. As it was, he knocked on the door softly and immediately entered. The buttocks flexing on top of Mavis looked black in the firelight. Mavis's hands, wrapped around the dark flanks, were startlingly white.

Titus must have heard the door. He started to withdraw, but Mavis held him in place. "I put the bastard in your room," she said, continuing to undulate her hips.

Jason said, "Shit," and closed the door behind him.

Hanrahan must have come without his family and Jason's room had been empty. But then, Hats' room had been vacant as well. Maybe Mavis felt guilty and didn't want Hats to return to discover someone in his private space. As if that hadn't already happened.

Jason made his way up to the second floor via the interior staircase. He felt unaccountably sad. He'd thought Hats and Mavis were in a committed relationship. It had given him hope that such a thing could happen. This hope was now crushed. Everything seemed to boil down to just a fumble in the dark, and it didn't make a bit of difference who was on the other side of the equation.

He walked into his room with the intention of telling Hanrahan he could stay the night and they'd make changes in the morning. He froze in the doorway.

The man sitting in Jason's chair in Jason's room in Jason's house in front of Jason's own damned fire rose to his feet. The candlelight glared off the shiny brass buttons and the brilliant red jacket. He was all Jason had imagined. Tall, rapier thin, with blond hair only one shade lighter than Cassy's. Elegance oozed from his pores. "Where in the bloody hell is Lady Cassandra?" the intruder asked.

Lieutenant Michaels had arrived.

Chapter Nineteen

$\mathscr{E}$ very time the carriage hit a rut, Ellie's head would bounce back against the rear of the seat and then fall forward again so her chin rested on her chest. And the woman didn't wake up. Didn't even stir.

Cassy found it amazing. She'd been watching her friend's head bob back and forth for the last hour. She was sure Ellie would arrive back at the Bloomery with a stiff neck. She thought of waking her and then decided to let her sleep. Ellie was exhausted.

While Cassy had been choosing furniture, Ellie had been exploring Williamsburg. Cassy had left her a short shopping list and a little money she'd gotten from Jason. Ellie's tour of the town may not have followed the pattern of a normal visitor, but it had been successful. Before noon, Ellie had discovered the company of soldiers stationed there and had made the acquaintance of Corporal Flagg.

It was her nighttime tour of Williamsburg with Corporal Flagg that had left Ellie so exhausted. "He's a brawn un, milady. Comes from Yorkshire. Has these big feets an that generly means big, eh, elsewhere. A course, I won't leave till after ya do."

What could Cassy say? She'd been the one who'd sneaked off to be with a lover the night before. She could hardly now become a moralist.

But somehow, Ellie's assignation with this man didn't seem right. She'd just met him, for heaven's sake. She knew nothing about him except he had the potential of having a big cock. Was this all that existed between men and women?

Ellie had arrived back at McAllister's shortly before dawn and had yawned her way through the packing and the departing. When Cassy had asked her if she planned to see Corporal Flagg again, Ellie had looked honestly perplexed.

"Why wud I wanna do that? It were nothin' but a bit a good fun." And then Ellie had promptly fallen asleep, leaving Cassy to fret about the condition of her own "bit of good fun."

Was that all her relationship with Jason boiled down to? Did he see her as nothing more than someone good for a few hours of sweaty pleasure in whatever secluded place they could find? Was this all there ever really was?

Lord, the conclusions were depressing. Lust and casual couplings were prevalent at the Bloomery. Back in England, the motivations may have been different, but the results were equally unsatisfactory. Her now-forgotten mother had married a ne'er-do-well, presumably to have official sanction for whatever they did between the sheets. Her Aunt Amelia loathed her husband, but had dutifully had four children. Relationships seemed to have nothing to do with liking or caring or loving.

Mary and Conner McAllister appeared to be a loving couple, but they were the exception, and how was one to really know what went on between them? The women at the Bloomery might just be more honest than most. Like Ellie, they didn't pretend affection when they were only looking for a bit of fun.

Which brought her back to Jason. She certainly wanted there to be more. There was no doubt he heated her blood, but she also wanted him happy. She wanted to satisfy him in ways other than sexual. A smile, the brief caress of his hand, all meant something to her. But did they for him? Was he kind, attentive, and concerned only to get her naked at the appointed time?

She squirmed in her seat. Had she given the impression that passion was all she was after? Good Lord, the games she'd played with him at the inn in Williamsburg. She'd knowingly tormented the man, had tightened his strings until he had no option but to fly apart. And she'd enjoyed doing it. She was no better than the bawdiest of the serving women.

But she couldn't feel guilty when she remembered the feeling of his chest under her hands, the way he'd moaned when she'd licked his tight nipples. And when she'd taken him into her mouth, she'd thought she controlled him. And she had, hadn't she? But this control was not what she sought. She wanted all of Jason Anders—body, soul, and mind.

Jason seemed only to want the body part of this equation, however. He talked in terms of when she left, accepting that what was between them was ephemeral. She couldn't fault him. Her behavior didn't indicate she felt any different. She obviously reveled in their nights together. She was the one who'd insisted she should go to Boston.

But she did these things because she knew any permanent relationship with her would doom the goals Jason sought so diligently. She couldn't do that to him. She wouldn't spoil his dream. And so she'd held her feelings deep inside. As far as he knew, Cassy only wanted him for his body as well.

And, dear Lord, that body was worth wanting. Yet Jason seemed oblivious to his effect on her, on women in general, for that matter. He thought his scarred back made him less desirable. He doubted any woman would want him just for himself. Building his big house was like a bird constructing an elaborate nest to attract a mate. Once he'd established himself, he would begin looking to establishing a dynasty.

Had Cassy just carefully chosen furniture to be enjoyed by some other woman, some planter's daughter who would fit into colonial society in a way she never would? What a depressing thought. But she could see nothing to do about it but to continue as she had begun.

The carriage turned between the gateposts and entered the Bloomery. It felt like coming home. There really hadn't been a place she'd thought of as home until now. So, why did she have to continue on the same track? She could speak honestly to Jason, explain that she was willing to stay in the old house indefinitely in whatever capacity he wanted. There really wasn't anything in Boston. Anders' Bloomery was the place she wanted to be.

A weight seemed to lift from her shoulders. She found herself anxiously looking out of the window, hoping to catch sight of Jason. It was early afternoon and he would probably be down at the furnace or forge area. With the arrival of Mr.

Hanrahan, they might be planning to start up the blast furnace. But hope still beat in her heart that she would see the very recognizable shape of Jason Anders. The big house and all its outbuildings appeared. No one was evident. "We're home," she said, nudging Ellie in the knee.

Hats drove the carriage straight to the old house. It looked snug and welcoming in the middle of its small grove of towering pines. The dogwoods near the front door blushed a deep autumn red, contrasting with the white of the clapboard. Cassy should have felt bad about appropriating a house designated for the Irish family, but she didn't. Instead, a feeling of ownership flooded through her.

Luke, the young boy who had brought the message to Jason, hurried down from the box, lowered the steps, and opened the door. He extended a slightly grubby hand in his best imitation of a footman. Cassy smiled at him. Everyone had his secret fantasies that were fulfilled in small bits and pieces. She started up the walk, knowing her luggage would follow.

Then she stopped dead, her hand going to her mouth in surprise. A man stood from where he'd been sitting on the porch, hidden by the dogwoods. A slender man with blond hair and a red-jacketed uniform. He descended the steps, holding out both his hands to take hers.

"Lady Cassandra, I've been so concerned for you. I came as quickly as I could find a ship coming here. It's good to see you're in health."

Cassy took his extended hands. "My heavens. Lieutenant Michaels. I didn't expect to see you here." She'd expected him to send her passage money. She was totally unprepared for him to appear in person. With blinding clarity, she realized she didn't want him at the Bloomery. His presence thrust decisions upon her that she didn't yet want to make.

Michaels was as handsome as she remembered. His features were finely molded, his figure taut and trim. An errant lock of pale hair fell forward on his broad forehead. His mouth was mobile and relaxed. His eyes were hazel, a mossy green rimmed with golden brown. Cassy recalled the impression of wiry strength when she'd danced with him. He was a perfect example of the English aristocracy.

And standing there in the pale sunshine of an autumn day, Cassy found him lacking.

He was an officer, a warrior, yet she would have rather followed Jason into battle than this man. The conflict must have been written on her face. He squeezed her hands. "Lady Cassandra, you're all right, aren't you?"

"Of course," she said, good manners taking over. "I'm just so surprised to see you. Please come in and I'll have my maid get us some refreshments." Cassy was very conscience of Ellie just behind her, mouth agape.

"Then allow me to escort you in. The man who runs this ramshackle place said this was where you were living. I must admit I peeped in the windows while I was waiting for you and was shocked he would think this was proper accommodations, but I guess it was the best he could do."

Through Michaels' eyes, perhaps the little house didn't look like much, but his comment was irritating. The entry hall was narrow and dark, and the large, central room tried to cram the needed living space for an entire house into one location. The furniture was old and worn. She sat in one of the two chairs at the front near the window and he sat in the other.

"When you go to the kitchen to get tea, would you please get one of the boys to lay a fire in the hearth?" she asked the hovering Ellie. "It's a bit chilly in here."

"Yes, milady." Ellie gave a deep curtsy. She was laying it on a bit thick, Cassy thought, but Lieutenant Michaels didn't seem to notice.

When Ellie left, he leaned forward in his chair as if to take her hands again, but Cassy kept them folded in her lap. "I can't describe to you what I feared when I arrived to find you gone. Especially when I met the Philistine with whom you've had to live. Do you know he kicked me out of the bedroom where I'd been installed by the housekeeper and sent me to the stables? The stables! Well, actually a room over the stables where the coachman usually stays. You have no idea how small the bed there is. My feet actually hung off."

Cassy was well acquainted with the size of Hats' bed. It was amazing what one could do in so small a space. Her mouth wanted to twist into a smile at the thought, but she schooled it. She doubted Lieutenant Michaels would be thrilled to hear she had intimate knowledge about the room in which he'd been placed.

"Of course, what could the barbarian do? Do you realize there is no furniture in his house? Appalling! But you know about the lack of furniture, don't you? That man said you'd been in town trying to get some furnishings. I'm shocked he thinks you still work for him now that he knows who you are."

His diatribe blessedly stalled when Ellie entered with three of the boys in tow. One went immediately to the hearth in the kitchen area and began getting a fire going. Another carried an elaborate silver service, and a third toted a lacquered tray with various small dishes on it. Ellie unfurled a small tablecloth like a conjurer doing a trick and ordered the placement of the dishes. It was reminiscent of the tea she'd shared with Jason when he was trying to learn if he was doing things correctly, the main difference being that the cupid tray had been replaced with a slightly more subdued black-and-gold one.

At the time, ensconced in Jason's study, Cassy had been unaware the rest of the house was vacant. Now she wondered why he had a silver service.

Ellie, having placed everything to her satisfaction, curtsied again and asked, "Will that be all, milady?"

Cassy refrained from rolling her eyes and said, "Fine. That will be all." Ellie and two of the boys departed. The one at the kitchen hearth was using a small bellows to get the coals he'd brought to light.

Cassy poured the tea and noticed Michaels eyeing the small sandwiches. "Do you think these are safe to eat?" he asked.

"Of course." Cassy considered cramming the whole plate into his face. Instead, she reached out and popped one straight into her mouth without using one of the small plates. "They're quite good." And they were. Cook was being as fancy as she knew how to be in an obvious effort to impress the lieutenant.

"I wasn't sure after what I was offered for breakfast. It was an odd-tasting, gritty oatmeal."

"Oh, that was grits. It's obvious where the dish got its name, since even you thought it gritty. It's a very popular dish here, made from corn. I think it's a delicacy one learns to enjoy, however." She gave a gentle laugh, refusing to mention that she'd yet to find this enjoyment.

Lieutenant Michaels placed his cup back on the table and was able to snare the one of Cassy's hands she'd not kept busy holding something. "Lady Cassandra, I hope I'm not presumptuous when I say I know you've had a trying time here. I couldn't believe the tragedy you'd suffered when I got your letter. To have been attacked and then to have lost your memory must have been horrifying. I consoled myself with the idea that you'd been rescued, and then I got here and met that rude colonial who said he'd bought you. Bought you! Well, then I realized your experience was even more appalling than I'd imagined.

"The man was a convict. I'm sure of it. He has shackle scars on his wrists. You've probably noticed them, but may not have known what they were. And to think a gently reared lady would have to associate with that type, much less be under his power. I can now see how dire your circumstances have been."

Cassy had the uncomfortable feeling she knew where this discussion was going and hoped to stop it before Lieutenant Michaels got too far. But the man was impossible to interrupt. She didn't think he even took a breath. She didn't remember him talking so incessantly. She only remembered dancing with him and then kissing him in the garden. Good Lord. She couldn't imagine doing so now. What she most wanted to do was throw him out of her house. She refrained from the action by reminding herself that he believed he was helping.

"But I hope to indeed be your rescuer. I'm here to marry you and take you back to Boston, where, if we're lucky, none of this unfortunate indentured business will ever be known. By the time my regiment returns home, it will long be forgotten and you can resume your normal place in society."

He finally paused. Too late. "I'm very sorry, Lieutenant, but I'm unable to accept your kind offer. I understand it was prompted by your desire to protect my reputation, but a marriage should be built on more than that and we really don't know each other." The irony that she'd initially thought to persuade Michaels to marry her was not lost on Cassy. But she now saw that such a plan would be terribly wrong and would only further complicate her life. The thought of having to listen to such a volume of words from morn to night was daunting.

For his part, Lieutenant Michaels looked poleaxed by her refusal. "But I've come to rescue you, don't you see? It's what I should do as an officer and a gentleman. And, of course, I find you very appealing. I agree we don't know each other well, but familiarity can come over time. I know I didn't show well in London. Your beauty and inaccessibility left me tongue tied. But now I know you have need of me, I can be all and more than you want."

"I'm sorry, Lieutenant. Marrying you would be impossible." Especially now his tongue has gotten *untied*. But she didn't say that.

"Then why did you ask me to send you the funds to get to Boston? I thought you wanted a safe haven to recover from your trauma. You didn't ask me for money to see you to England, after all, so I assumed you wanted or, eh, needed, a husband before returning home."

His face suddenly cleared as if a puzzle had been explained to him. "If something brutish has happened to you, you needn't be concerned. I would never throw the fact you were ruined when we married in your face."

Cassy didn't know whether to laugh or cry. She was undoubtedly ruined, but the process had most definitely not been brutish. Instead, she reveled in it. Poor Michaels was trying, he really was. He thought he was her rescuer, so he was going to do the right thing. The problem was she didn't want him. She didn't want him at all. But how to explain this to him without hurting his feelings?

There was a quick knock on the door, followed by Jason's coming in from the hallway without being asked. He looked stricken for a brief second and then his face became impassive. Cassy wouldn't have noticed the odd, lost look that preceded the harshness if she'd not been directly facing him. "Excuse me. I keep entering before I'm bidden and intruding on personal affairs." He turned as if to leave.

"No, Jason. Stay," Cassy cried. She then realized that sometime during Michaels' impassioned plea, he'd dropped to one knee before her while he still held her hand. The tableau Jason had witnessed could only suggest one thing. It hardly seemed proper to explain she'd rejected the lieutenant's suit.

She immediately stood, forcing Lieutenant Michaels to flounder a bit before he, too, came to his feet, scowling. "Was there something you wanted?" she asked in the most normal voice she could muster.

"I just wanted to tell you that Cook will send supper down here for you and your guest." The last two words were said in the same tone she'd heard Jason use when uttering a filthy oath. "Needless to say, I can't offer you a formal invitation to my table, since it isn't here yet. And even if it had been delivered, I seem to have a housekeeper who is staying at a distance and a butler who has completely disappeared, so you'll have to make do with irregular service, but the food should be good. Cook has gone into a frenzy of preparation."

"It would be most acceptable. And I'd enjoy your company also, if you would join us." When she said the words, she was unsure if they were a monumental mistake or if they exactly expressed what she wanted. The two men were some distance from each other, but both had taken the stiff-legged stance most often seen in dogs contesting territory. It was all she could do not to throw her hands in the air and utter her own string of curses.

For better or worse, Jason stood silent for a moment, then said, "I'd be delighted to join you."

Chapter Twenty

*F*ury rose in waves to pound against Jason's temples, but he maintained strict control as he walked across the lawn. *I'd enjoy your company also, if you'd care to join us.* Who did too-good-for-you Lady Cassandra think she was talking to? As far as he could tell, she and that red-coated asshole would be eating his food, in his house, on his land. How nice of them to ask him to partake as well.

They probably wanted him to drink a toast to their upcoming nuptials. He could hardly have missed the earnest Lieutenant down on one knee. The army bastard would be shocked to learn his charming intended had been in quite a similar position the night before. Jason had a flash of an image of Cassy doing the same thing to that effete, blond son of a bitch. Something akin to a hot poker stabbed him in the gut.

Well, that was not going to happen. It sure as hell was not. He regretted now that he'd allowed Conner to give him the money and to mark Cassy's articles as satisfied. He really wanted to hold her to the whole four-year commitment, and then she could satisfy him over and over.

He stopped and supported himself against the trunk of one of the big pines. He leaned over, trying to relieve the pain in his head and the nausea churning in his gut. Who the hell was he fooling? It didn't make any difference what he did or thought. He would never be good enough for Lady Cassandra Spathe. Even with all the money he could ever make, he'd still be nothing more than a transported convict, a thief who had made good as a glorified blacksmith. He'd always be big and uncouth and have the smell of the forge about him.

He straightened, sucking in deep breaths. The bark on the tree was rough under his hands, anchoring him to the here and now. At least he'd bruised the bastard's overinflated dignity by having him sleep over the stables, even if it did mean that Hats had to bunk with some of the men. But poor Hats was as screwed as he was; the little man just didn't know it yet.

He needed to find that damned, unfaithful Mavis and kick her ass to make sure the fanciest supper with the classiest service arrived at the little house at the appointed time. He'd get himself togged out in his best clothes and, by God, he'd have dinner with Cassy and her adoring lieutenant and he'd look down his nose at them and see if he could make them squirm.

He walked into the entry hall and bellowed, "Titus. Mavis." Only silence answered. He'd seen Mavis hiding out over by the dairy, so he knew she was around, but Titus, who should have been in the house, seemed to have completely disappeared. If the stupid son of a bitch had run on him, he'd have him hunted down.

Jason was familiar with all the time that could be added to the period of servitude of an indentured servant who'd run away. He'd run away himself, twice, stupid ass that he'd been, and ended up with four more years of hell than he should have had. He'd been young and rebellious and idiotically thought he was proving something, but he'd learned from his mistakes and Titus would do so as well. If the man reverted back to his shiftless ways, he'd end up bonded for years more than the seven-year indenture Jason had offered instead of enslavement.

Jason walked to the stairway and yelled into the basement. "Mavis. Titus." Still nothing. He ran his hand through his hair, pulling strands from the ribbon that bound his queue. God, his head hurt. He could feel his pulse pounding in his temples and his teeth.

He started for the front door again and, through a side window, saw Mavis coming slowly up the walk from the kitchen. He crossed to the window and jerked up the sash. "Mavis, get your fat ass into my study, now!" He slammed the window shut and turned, not bothering to see if she complied.

He made his way to his study to see a mostly empty room that still smelled faintly of ashes. Would nothing work out today? Was he to be thwarted at every turn? He heard a noise behind him. Mavis came panting in. She must have run. Her gray hair fell in wild corkscrews from her cap.

"Where in the hell is my furniture?"

"I had it moved to the parlor."

"In there, then," he said, pushing past her. When he entered the room Cassy called the grand salon, he stomped over to one of the darkened, flame-stitched wing chairs and threw himself into the seat. "Sit," he said, pointing to its equally soiled mate.

Mavis sat. Jason pulled in some calming breaths. They didn't help. He was not feeling calm. Somewhere during this hideous day, he'd gone beyond anger into fury, and fury didn't respond to deep breaths. "Where in the hell have you been all day? I've had need of you."

Mavis just sat there, twisting her fingers around each other. "I, eh, I..."

"Have been hiding from me?" he supplied.

The portly woman sat straighter. "Well, not exactly."

"Then you might be able to tell me *exactly* where Titus has gone, since he also seems to be missing."

She sat there in silence, looking at her hands. For the first time since he'd known her, the spark that made her Mavis was missing. She looked old and tired.

"If he's run, Mavis, you know it will go hard on him. I've paid for his labor and now I expect him to work off that commitment. If he doesn't, you know I can be a mean son of a bitch. So if he's just hiding, you need to tell him to get back here and we'll go from there."

"He's hiding, Jase. He's scared."

"Scared? What does he have to be scared of me about? Yeah, it was pretty obvious it was him tupping you last night. It was definitely a black ass pumping away and his is the only one around here that matches that description. But that's nothing for me to be angry about. Disappointed, I'll admit to that, but not angry."

The housekeeper looked at him with skepticism. "If you ain't angry, Jase, you're sure doing a good impersonation."

He nearly laughed. "I guess I am angry, but not at you and not about what I saw last night. That's something for Hats to be angry about, not me."

Jason tried to relax his muscles so he didn't appear furious. "Mavis, you're a free agent. I just hire you and pay you a salary. A damned good salary, at that. So you can fornicate with whomever you want, as long as it's on your own time. Neither you nor Titus has anything to worry about as far as I'm concerned, as long as you do your god-damned work. And in Titus's case, that isn't getting done."

Mavis just sat for a moment, looking at the floor. "You haven't told Hats yet, have you?" she asked softly.

"No, I haven't said anything to Hats and don't plan to. Whatever either of you does is up to you. I can hardly pretend to be morally superior."

"Then let me explain about Titus."

Jason sighed and leaned back in his chair. "Do I need to hear this?"

"Yes, Jase, I think you do."

"Then tell me whatever it is you have to say, but be quick about it."

"What happened with Titus was, well, I guess it was sympathy." Mavis made a graceful movement with her hands. "It was just past dark, and I was heading for my room after checking that the doors were locked, like you said to do while you were gone. I heard an odd noise in the dining room and I admit it scared me. I didn't want anyone trying to light any fires again. I figured that before I hollered for one of the men you'd set to watch the house, I'd better see if we actually had an intruder. There was a dark figure looking out of the window and I realized it was Titus. God, that was a relief. But he was staring so intently, I thought maybe there was something going on, so I walked up to see.

"Out on the lawn, one of the women was being held by one of the men. I'd guess it was Ruth and that rusty haired fellow, but it doesn't make any difference except he was holding her real tender-like. And then I heard that noise again and I realized Titus was crying. That big, strapping man just leaning on the window frame with tears running out of his eyes.

"So I touched him on the shoulder. I may have said his name. I don't know. But he turns to me and says, 'I am so lonely.'

"Now, Jase, we both pretty up the past, but in the end, I'm just an old whore. I can only think of one way to comfort a man who is hurting so much. So I put my arms around him and held him and well, you walked in a little later when I was giving him comfort the only way I know how."

She sat in silence. Then said, her voice very soft, "I'll say something to Hats in my own time, so I'd appreciate it if you kept this to yourself."

"So you do care some for Hats?" The answer had become important to Jason. He had to think that people cared for each other. That the world didn't just revolve around one happy hump after another.

"Hats is the best man I've ever known," Mavis said. "Oh, I know when he was jockeying, he threw some races to make some extra money and that's what got him transported. But inside, he's good. And I care for him a lot. He'll understand about Titus and probably won't much care. This field has been plowed so many times no one could notice a new furrow. But I want to tell him in my own time and in my own way."

"That's up to you, Mavis. But I need to know where Titus is, and he needs to get back to his duties. I will set the magistrate on his trail if he's gone."

"He's holed up in the little shed behind the dairy."

Jason nodded. "Good. Now walk with me part of the way and let me tell you what I need you to do for tonight. I'll see Titus and then I'll say no more about this."

The sun was making long shadows across the yard and as he walked with Mavis, Jason was surprised to discover his fury had left him. In its place was a dull sadness. *I am so lonely*, Titus had said. The echo of those words lived in Jason.

When he got to the shed, Jason knocked and called out his butler's name. Only a fool startled a frightened man. When people were scared, their behavior became erratic. A muffled, "Yes," came from inside.

"I'm coming in to talk with you." Jason opened the door and stepped into the storage building.

The slanting sunlight came through places where the boards didn't fit tightly, striping the interior. Titus stood near the rear wall, his eyes wide and white in his dark face. He held a milk bucket in front of him like a shield. The small area reeked with the sharp tang of fear.

"You can kill me where I stand, Mr. Anders, but I ain't going to be made into no gelding. If it's just a whipping I'll get, I'll take my punishment."

Jason kept his voice calm, as if he were speaking to a spooked horse. "My only concern is that none of the women get a child from what goes on in the night. The Bloomery isn't a charity to take care of other men's bastards. But since I don't think that's going to happen in Mavis' case, what would I punish you for?"

"You caught me with a white woman, and I know what that means. You can lash my back until I'm dead, that might be your right, but you can't chop off my prick and whirligigs and let me live. I think you're a fairer man than that." With a rustling sound, Titus stood up straighter and lowered the bucket.

Realization arrowed through Jason, making his own stones hurt. Did owners castrate slaves who had bedded a consenting white woman? Jason had no idea. The scars across his own back seemed to tighten in remembered pain and dread. But there were some things he'd never feared, and couldn't imagine doing so. A shudder ran across his skin.

"I've talked to Mavis and I know she was agreeable. Rape would have been a different matter. But what I inadvertently saw was private business and I'm not punishing anyone for that."

"It weren't Mavis's fault. I was just weak. It seemed like I'd been cold for so long and when she put her arms around me, I was suddenly warm, and things just kinda happened from there. I ain't had no pleasuring except with what hangs at the end of my arms since I came here, and I made a mistake."

Jason became aware of the acute isolation Titus must feel. He and Cook were the only Negroes at the Bloomery, and Cook was white-haired and made Mavis look young. Jason had bought Cook cheaply, since her former mistress was sure she was trying to poison the family. Evidently, the entire household had been felled after a dinner party, and Cook had had to go. Jason had put her on a four-year contract, but she'd stay on for wages. He liked her food, and no one had ever sickened.

But Cook couldn't provide the comfort a man needed. "Did you have a special friend, where you were before?" he asked.

"No one special," Titus replied.

Jason could see he was going to have to do something about this, but the idea of buying a slave woman specifically to service Titus seemed somehow wrong. What could he do? Take Titus with him to the slave market and tell him to pick out some woman he wanted to tup? Dear God, that wasn't the way these things were supposed to happen.

Of course, if he were honest, his going to The Blue Heron wasn't all that different. At this point, he knew all the girls there, and unless he was looking for something particular, any of them would do. They were just willing bodies who could take the edge off. He'd pay and leave and that would be the end of it. Even when he'd been indentured, looking for a quick tumble in a shed or dark woods, it had all been about the release, that brief moment in time when sensation overwhelmed the world. The partner hadn't mattered.

But somehow, since he'd met Cassy, it did. Bloody hell, he was not letting that red-coated asshole take her away. If he did, he'd be lonelier than Titus had ever been. "I'll see what I can do about your problem," he said. "But until then, I need you for certain things—one of which I need now. I want you to make me look like a bloody earl, and do so in less than an hour."

Titus looked uncertain, as if he couldn't believe what Jason was saying. And then a smile flashed across his lips and he said, "I'll have you looking like a duke at the least."

Chapter Twenty - One

C assy would have dressed for dinner had she known their meal was going to be a formal affair. As it was, she wore the same clothes she'd donned in Williamsburg for the journey back to the Bloomery. Instead of resting and dressing again, she'd spent her early evening talking with Lieutenant Michaels, or Gilbert, as he'd become.

Once she'd convinced him she would not marry him, she'd discovered she rather liked the man. When Gilbert relaxed and no longer thought it was his duty to rescue the fair maiden, Cassy again found the appeal she'd sensed in London

Released from the burden some misguided sense of chivalry had placed on him, Gilbert became capable of carrying on a conversation instead of a droning monologue. He offered some intelligent suggestions. He was affable and kind, and she thought he could be a friend. But she felt not the slightest sexual attraction. Gilbert was certainly handsome enough to turn heads; he just seemed painfully young and naive, even though Cassy knew she was at least three years his junior.

She'd managed to redirect his compulsion to be a knight-errant into helping her find gainful employment if she decided to relocate to Boston. While he was appalled by the idea of her working, he understood why she would not want to again place herself under her father's control. He was incensed with Baron Tilton's behavior, which she explained in a much-edited version. As it was, he would have challenged the man to a duel had Tilton been available.

Gilbert's dignity continued to be offended at having to stay in a room over the stables, and he was quite sure Jason was a jumped-up blacksmith at the best, but Cassy still hoped the meal she'd impulsively asked Jason to share would pass in harmony. She was unprepared for his entrance, however. Jason arrived in his best clothes, which she'd last seen at the party in Williamsburg, but this time he'd added lace at his neck and wrists.

When she'd imagined the dressing of Jason Anders, she'd never imagined lace. He was too elementally male. But he somehow pulled the look off. Compared to Gilbert in his bright uniform, Jason was still the most obvious warrior in the room. He was as polished and buffed as she had ever seen him. He filled the room with masculine energy, making poor Gilbert seem like a boy by comparison.

The train that followed him was equally astonishing. Mavis marshaled in four women carrying trays of food, and they were all wearing something that looked suspiciously like a uniform. At least they all had on matching white aprons and mobcaps. Bess, one of the number, gave her a broad wink. Titus was also dressed formally, wearing gloves she didn't even know he possessed. He took the position of footman, ready to serve drinks and food whenever they were desired.

And the food—well, it definitely wasn't normal dinner fare for the Bloomery, which tended to be light and often cold. The meal began with fish soup, and then sliced, salty ham appeared along with a roasted chicken, corn pudding, and boiled peas. Titus seemed determined to keep everyone's wine glasses filled with a decent claret. The final course was a selection of fruit tarts that Gilbert exclaimed over.

The meal actually went quite well. Jason was the epitome of a gracious host and Gilbert ate with such enthusiasm, he had no time to make critical remarks. Cassy was bemused that such elegant dining was going on at the same table where she and Ellie enjoyed their normally casual repasts.

As the desserts course was being cleared, Jason said, "In these surroundings, it would be ridiculous to expect Lady Cassandra to retire, so if you would, Titus, please bring both tea and port. And then we will take care of ourselves."

Cassy had to hide her smile behind a napkin. Jason sounded exactly like Conner McAllister when he said similar words. It was obvious who the model for Jason's dinner behavior was. Her later laugh came out disguised as a cough when Jason took a sip of his port and had to carefully school his face to hide his negative reaction.

"Would you prefer tea?" she asked.

"No, thank you." But he looked longingly at the pot.

As soon as Titus quit the house, leaving the three of them alone, Gilbert gestured to where the butler had earlier stood and asked, "Do you find slaves efficient servants? We see so few in Massachusetts, it's hard to form an opinion."

"I have no slaves here," Jason said, his voice edgy as if he'd perceived an affront. "I think it a poor way to form a labor force. Enslaved people have no expectation of a better life, and so have no motivation to improve themselves and excel at their jobs."

"So you rely on indentured servants?"

"Primarily. We haven't enough people locally to hire for all of the work that needs to be done, so people have to be brought in from elsewhere. It would be nice if there were enough regular immigration to fill these needs, but so far, that's not been the case. If articles of indenture are strictly adhered to by all parties, the system can work for the benefit of all. Unfortunately, many of those who purchase these articles erroneously believe they've bought short-term slaves and treat their servants accordingly."

"Oh, come now," Gilbert said, his smile edging toward superiority. "As someone who employs indentured servants, you must admit most of them are the useless refuse of England, made up of people of the lowest orders, if not transported convicts. We often have similar trash foisted upon us in the Army and I can assure you, it takes a heavy hand, often wielding a lash, to meld those people into any type of a fighting group."

Cassy saw anger spark in Jason's eyes. She wasn't sure if Gilbert was oblivious to his offensive words or if he'd intended them to goad Jason. If the latter, this was foolish on Gilbert's part. In an effort to defuse the situation, she lightly touched Gilbert's sleeve and smiled up at him. "Since I've been in the ranks of those servants, I'd say your assessment is generally wrong."

Gilbert covered her hand with his own. "That's hardly relevant, Lady Cassandra. Anyone looking at you would know you are quality, and your being in such a situation a horrible mistake. I have a number of friends who employ indentured servants in Boston and hear constant complaints that they're nothing but thieves and doxies who are too lazy to be worth the price of their transportation."

"Ah, now we're talking about the strata of society into which I fit." Jason's voice was deceptively calm, but his look was decidedly dangerous. He glared at where Michaels' hand covered Cassy's and she resisted the urge to jerk it away. "It's hard for the lord on the horse to notice the peasants milling around at his feet. And one of the things he doesn't notice is that there are so damned many of them."

Gilbert straightened and said, "Your language, sir, is offensive with a lady present."

Jason laughed, but it was not a happy sound. "That language is mild to what I'm sure Lady Cassandra has been subjected to here. It simply shows I'm what you think I am. A crude, rude, common colonial. My butler insisted I wear these lace cuffs, undoubtedly appropriated from his former master. He thought they would cover up the scars on my wrists, which I'm sure you've already noticed. And you may even have guessed that I have matching scars on my back, since I was one of those shiftless, rebellious servants your friends complain about. The important point is that I'm no longer any man's servant."

Cassy opened her mouth to say something placating, and he glared her into silence. What could she say, anyway? What Jason said was only the truth.

Jason stood, bringing Gilbert across the table to his feet. Suppressed violence hovered in the air. "You, sir, are no gentleman," Gilbert said in his most dismissive tone.

"You are absolutely right," Jason growled. "And there's not a damned thing you can do about it. You and your kind are stuck with me. I can match you acre for acre and guinea for guinea. In your case, since I assume you're a younger son sent off to carve a brilliant swath through the military, I'd guess I can do better than match you. In the colonies, wealth is the great leveler."

"Which is why you would still be nothing in England," Michaels said. Cassy marveled that Gilbert thought this was an argument in his favor. Not that Jason was necessarily right. After her time at the Bloomery, she'd come to see that people should be judged by their character. Birth and wealth were secondary to that.

The sad realization was that it had taken her so long to arrive at this conclusion, and she was sure she never would have, if she'd not ended up in Virginia. She'd just dined with an aristocrat and an ex-convict, and there was no question that the ex-convict was the better man. For now, however, there was nothing she could add to the argument. She sat silently and watched the carriage wreck that was about to take place.

"Again, you're correct," Jason said, bracing his arms on the table and leaning forward. "I have no intention of ever returning to England. I'm making a new place for myself, here in a new land. A land you are only visiting. And with this in mind, I'd appreciate your ending your visit. You've made it clear the accommodations are not up to your standards, so tomorrow you can take yourself to an inn in York to await a ship that will take you back to wherever you came from. Your sojourn here is over."

Gilbert's face flushed red to match his jacket. Cassy suspected this was the first time he'd been summarily dismissed from anyone's estate. "I will gladly depart," he said, pulling his tattered dignity around him. "But I will not leave Lady Cassandra here without a protector."

"She's been doing just fine without you as a protector, and she will continue to do so. You leave. She stays. I'll do whatever protecting that needs to be done. It's simple."

"It is not simple. After all her travail, you have no doubt manipulated and browbeat Lady Cassandra into thinking she has no other choice but to stay here. I offer a different choice. She wants to go to Boston with me and the two of us will be leaving on the first ship bound for there. But until that happens, she will come with me to town."

The two men glared at each other. The air vibrated with intense emotions. Jason's hands flexed into fists. Cassy knew he wanted to put one of his massive hands through Gilbert's face. Dear Lord, what was she to do? She rose from her seat at the table. "Gentlemen," she said, her voice as cold as winter, "I believe you're both suffering from a misconception. I don't need either of you to protect me. I'm free to make my own decisions. And what I've decided is that you will both leave this house. If you wish to take your ridiculous quarrel elsewhere, that will be fine. The bone you seem to be arguing over, namely me, wants nothing to do with either of you. So, be gone!"

Gilbert's cry of, "Cassy, you don't mean that," overlapped Jason's roar of, "Now listen here."

She overrode both with a quiet, "Leave. Now."

Both men stuttered into silence, still glaring at each other. Then Jason waved his hand in the direction of the door, a mocking gesture indicating that Gilbert should precede him. Gilbert chose not to respond to the mockery. Instead, he pulled his jacket down and marched to the door. "I think we should go out together," he said. "And Lady Cassandra, be sure to lock the door after us." The look he gave Jason was almost a challenge. To Cassy's surprise, Jason shrugged and walked to the door and they both did go out together.

"Lock this." This time the command was Jason's. When the door was shut, Cassy dashed to it and turned the lock. She watched the two men from the side light of the door. They walked not quite together, as if they were two strangers heading in the same direction. At some distance, Gilbert put his hand on Jason's shoulder and both men stopped. A conversation ensued, too distant to be heard. Backlit by the lights from the big house, they appeared mostly as shadows, but their gesturing was obvious.

Then Gilbert took swing at Jason. Cassy put her hand to her mouth. Oh, the fool. Gilbert could only guess at the powerful muscles under Jason's sedate clothing, but Cassy was well acquainted with them. If Jason began pounding on Gilbert, she would have to go rescue him, and she really didn't want to be involved with either of the idiots right now.

Instead of hitting Gilbert back, Jason picked the younger man up by his neckcloth and shook him, much like a dog with a rag. He then straightened his arm and Gilbert went flying to land in a heap some distance away. Without checking on the condition of his foe, Jason turned and walked to the house.

Cassy held her breath. Was Gilbert injured? She relaxed with an exhale when the Lieutenant stood, brushed himself off, and made his way toward the stables. She leaned down and unlocked the door. Ellie would undoubtedly be coming in later, and the men seemed to have retired to their own beds. Chaos had been averted. For now.

Almost without thought, she returned to the table, collected the glasses, and placed them on the carrying tray. She smiled at the fat cupids cavorting all over it. When the new things began to arrive, maybe she could hide this particular tray in an out-of-the-way drawer. It really was tasteless and using it would hardly help Jason establish himself socially.

Not that she should care one way or the other, of course. She should stop worrying about smoothing Jason's rough edges. He'd been doing just fine before her arrival and would continue to do so when she left. She folded into one of the chairs at the table and leaned forward to place her head on her arms. That was the trouble. She didn't want to leave. She didn't ever want to leave Jason Anders.

Even when he was acting like a complete idiot, as he had tonight, she wanted to be with him. Both he and Gilbert Michaels had behaved like possessive fools. Both had assumed they had the right to control her future. But a part of her knew Jason had the most right to feel that way. She wanted a future with him. And he'd said he wanted her to stay. Even if he said that simply to perturb Gilbert, he'd said it, and it reflected the deepest desire of her heart.

She jerked her head from her arms and looked blindly at the opposite wall. Bloody hell, she was in love with the big blockhead. She wanted him to fit into Virginia society and she wanted him to win election to the House of Burgesses, because this was what *he* wanted. His desires had become hers. She would do whatever she could to make his dreams come true.

This emotion ran much deeper than her constant ache for his physical presence, although she couldn't imagine never again being held in his arms. She needed to feel him around her, in her, with an abiding hunger. But somewhere, lust had turned into love. What had been a game had become an essential part of her life.

She heard the latch click and turned toward the door, expecting to see Ellie. Instead, Jason stood there. His hair had loosened from his queue as it did when he ran his fingers through it. The lace jabot at his neck was slightly askew and what would be a bruise was forming on his left cheek. The swing she'd seen Gilbert make must have connected.

"You can't go with him," he said in a strangled voice. "And you certainly can't marry him. Lieutenant Michaels isn't worthy of you. I know I'm not good enough for you, but neither is he, no matter who his father is. He's simply not man enough to care for you for a lifetime."

He walked further into the room without his normal grace. She rose to meet him. "Cassy, I'll die if you leave me." She felt herself being enfolded into his strong arms. She leaned her head on his broad chest, inhaling the spicy scent he carried with him, and listened to the solid beat of his heart. And she knew she too would die if she went away.

"I'm not leaving," she said into his waistcoat.

She felt him stiffen. He moved back slightly and turned her face up to look at him. "Say that again."

"I'm not leaving."

His mouth came down on hers in an act of pure possession. His lips slanted over hers almost savagely, his tongue delving deeply. He pulled her flush to his body, one hand cupping her buttocks to fit her against his already apparent erection. She matched him in his frenzy, her own desire to assert ownership as powerful as his.

When he finally broke the kiss, they were both breathing heavily. She expected him to pick her up and carry her into the bedroom, but instead he held her face in his hands, his fingers gently tracing her temples and brows as he looked deeply into her eyes. "Michaels said you'd agreed to marry him, and all sorts of desperate ideas came to my mind. My first thought was to beat him to death; then, of course, there could be no marriage. But this would have proved what he and many others think of me was true, and I'd end up with a rope around my neck."

He gave her a brief smile. "That didn't seem like a good solution. So I came here with the idea of demanding you stay until you were sure my child wasn't growing in you. You make me so crazy I've ignored the habit of a lifetime and not withdrawn in time to assure you didn't catch a child. I thought to use this to my advantage and if possible, keep making the same mistake until you were wide with child and had to stay with me. The thought of losing you brought out my worst traits."

"Getting me with child doesn't qualify as one of your worst traits," she whispered, the idea suddenly appealing. "As a matter of fact, I think I might quite like it. But I think it would be best if we married first. A Burgess shouldn't have bastard children running about."

At this, he did swing her off her feet and cradle her to his chest. She could feel laughter running through him. "Oh, Cass, if having bastards disqualified a man from being a Burgess, we'd have many fewer Burgesses than we now do. But I believe you just said you'd marry me, and I can't imagine anything sweeter. I love you, woman. You're in my heart and in my soul. Together we can brazen out any gossip of our unsuitability. And if it means some think I'm not worthy of election, so be it."

"I don't want you to give up your dreams for me," she said, nuzzling his neck as he walked into the bedroom. "I think we can have it all." Cassy hoped what she said was true. It was possible this relationship would cost both of them. She knew many would think she was marrying a man much beneath her, but she saw his intrinsic value and knew they would be wrong.

When he laid her across the bed and slowly began removing her clothes, kissing each bit of exposed flesh as it appeared, she was sure she would give up anything for this quickening of the blood, the sound of his voice whispering endearments.

She became impatient with his leisurely approach and began snatching off pieces of his clothing with vigor. When one particularly powerful tug on his waistcoat sent buttons flying, Jason scooted away from her and hopped off the bed. "Have a care with the clothes," he said, "I'm afraid my seamstress is about to take another position."

"And what position would that be?" She let her legs sprawl and opened her arms to him. The speed with which he managed to become completely naked was amazing. Within two heartbeats, his warm body was covering hers, chasing away the cold of the room. As if Jason knew there was no need for further preliminaries, he immediately knelt between her legs. With a quick flex of his hips, he had filled her to the hilt.

She met him movement for movement, wrapping her legs around his hips to pull him deeper. The feel of the hairs on his chest teasing her breasts and his cock moving within her spiraled her desire to a fever pitch. Her hands roamed his body mindlessly, seeking for even greater contact. Her climax came so suddenly and violently she screamed and bucked against him like a wild thing.

He slowed his strokes and held her as, shuddering, she slowly returned to herself. She realized he was still hard. She had snatched her satisfaction but had left Jason wanting. She began to undulate beneath him, but he abruptly withdrew. She felt a moment of panic. She wanted this incredible glory for Jason as well as herself. She made a weak, mewing sound at his departure.

He chuckled softly, scattering kisses across her face, running his tongue along the side of her neck. "I mentioned my seamstress would soon have a new position," he murmured against the sensitive place where her neck joined her collarbone. "Could I show you one?"

"What are you talking about?"

"Ah, Cassy, love, there are infinite varieties of ways we can pleasure one another. Here, turn over on your stomach."

He rolled to one side and gave her room to do so. Once she was facedown on the bed, he pushed her legs wide and again knelt between them. She felt his strong hands stroking down her damp back, relaxing muscles she had not known were tight. He worked his hands up and down her back, pausing to knead her upturned buttocks. After the tensions of the evening, the sensation was wonderful.

Just when Cassy felt she was going to completely melt into the mattress, Jason nudged her thighs forward and lifted her at her midsection. "Get on your elbows and knees, Cass," he said. She complied, trembling when he ran a finger through her cleft, circling her nub at the front. He then bent over her back and slowly entered her from the rear. The feeling was totally different and sent shockwaves quaking through her.

And then he began to move, slowly picking up speed. She arched back against him, pressing her rear against his groin, reveling in the tingling sensations. It felt odd that she could only feel him in the area where they were joined and in the roughness of his thighs rubbing against hers. Her fingers unconsciously gripped wrinkles in the sheet. She laid her forehead on the mattress.

Jason held her steady against his thrusts with his hands wrapped around the top of her thighs. Then his right forearm supported her as he moved his hand to the front, rubbing her nub in time with his strokes. His other hand came up to play with her breasts, rubbing each in turn, rhythmically squeezing them. The only sounds in the room were their labored breathing, the creak of the bedstead, and the wet sounds of their mating.

"Come for me," he panted, his head riding just above her shoulder. "Come for me now." He pinched the nub between her legs and she came, waves of pleasure rolling though her, taking the breath from her laboring lungs. He held her thighs again as he spent himself within her, his hot seed filling her.

They both collapsed to the bed like a chair with a broken leg. His weight crushed her against the mattress until he rolled to one side, keeping her trapped with a heavy leg draped across both of hers. They lay, completely spent.

"That was marvelous," she said, managing to turn to one side enough to free a hand to stoke his face.

He smiled and gave a nibbling kiss to her fingers. "Yes, it was," he laughed. "You were marvelous. You have no idea how long I've imagined doing that. Your ass has always made me hard, and I really enjoyed watching it."

"You're very naughty." She gave him a quick tap on his nose. "Have you always misbehaved? What were you like as a boy?" As she asked the question, Cassy realized there were entire volumes of Jason's life she knew nothing about.

"As a young boy, no. My mother kept me tightly controlled. She worked in a tavern kitchen and one of my most vivid memories is of sitting under a worktable, making whole ranks of soldiers out of turnip peels. Once she died, I probably ran wild. I made coins wherever I could—holding horses, carrying messages, sweeping crossings. But they were never enough. I stole food when I was hungry and couldn't pay. I slept rough in abandoned buildings. I managed to stay alive."

Cassy had difficulty imagining such an existence. She had thought her life hard, crushed under the scorn of her Aunt Amelia. What an idiot she'd been. She had never worried where she would sleep. She had never been hungry. She could see now a whole other world existed that she'd been unaware of.

"And then I stole a watch. That's what got me transported. It was a stupid thing to do. I had no training as a pickpocket. I had no skills in that line. But this slightly built man checked the time on his watch near where I was standing with a broom, hoping to make a few pence by keeping rich people from having to wade through horse shit when they crossed the street. And that damned watch called to me. I swear it did. The gold cover sparkled in the sun like the greatest treasure I'd ever seen. Without thought, my hand reached out and grabbed that treasure. I dropped my broom and ran.

"I could have outdistanced the watch's owner—he was small and weak looking—but there was nothing weak about his voice. His calls and the promise of a reward attracted some larger laborers and I soon found myself facedown on the street." He chuckled. "One of the first things I bought when I started making money as a blacksmith was a gold watch. Sometimes I take it out just to watch the light flicker on the case, thinking about how far I've come."

"But the time in between, when you were indentured?" She thought of his scarred back. Regardless of how evil Sir Peyton Hyde was, he had to have some reason for whipping Jason so mercilessly.

"Oddly enough, when I first came here, I always followed orders. It's hard to admit now, but I was probably too scared to do otherwise. I was eleven when I was arrested and transported. Tall for my age, but still a boy. I'd spent enough time in an English prison to learn how to be agreeable and invisible. It was the best way of protecting my ass, eh, myself. So when Hyde bought my contract, I figured I could do the same for the next seven years. Oh, I slacked off whenever I thought I could get away with it, like most people do, but I really caused no trouble.

"But there was this girl, Kate…" his voice trailed off.

"Was this someone you cared for?" Cassy needed to know this. At the same time, she really didn't want to hear the answer.

He pushed her damp hair off her forehead and gently kissed the uncovered spot. "Oh, I cared for Kate, but not in the way you're imagining. She was a funny little thing, I'd guess about thirteen, all long, bony legs and teeth that seemed too big for her mouth. I liked her. She was my friend. And one afternoon I caught Sir Peyton raping her. Of course, he would tell you she wanted it, that he had the right, but I saw him, and all his excuses were lies.

"I attacked him. I was nearly fifteen then. Still growing, so I was lanky with oversized hands and feet. God, I wanted to kill him. But like the man with the watch, Sir Peyton wasn't the only person I had to contend with. He had a lot of men in his hire who were much more afraid of him than they were of me. So that was the first time he lashed me. I was lying facedown on a bunk with a poultice on my back, unable to move, when I heard Kate had hanged herself."

He stopped speaking, his eyes focused somewhere in the middle distance as his fingers idly ruffled her hair. Cassy could see the boy with clumsy hands and feet he'd yet to grow into, and her heart ached for that boy who had long disappeared.

"After that," he continued, "it became a contest of wills. That I knew I'd lose made no difference, I just kept pushing him and pushing him, until the last time he about beat me to death.

"And then Hyde thought to finish me by putting me to work with Hiram, the plantation blacksmith. Hiram had a reputation for violent fits of temper and everyone gave him room. He was big and black, much darker than Titus, and he turned out to be the best friend I ever had."

"And you've taken the knowledge he gave you and made a success," Cassy said, knowing Hiram had given Jason information on bog iron and its smelting.

"Almost a success. I still have things to accomplish. I still have to make Sir Peyton crawl. And that's about to happen. God, yes, that's about to happen. But let's not spoil the night with thoughts of Sir Peyton. Tell me about when you were a girl. Were you good?"

"Not as good as I should have been. Aunt Amelia called me wicked more than once." She went on to tell him of dares and silly escapades that were part of what she now saw was a rather normal life. But he laughed at her tale of getting stuck on the barn roof and teased her about being afraid to learn to swim.

And then he sat in a chair and showed her another way they could be naughty together, which she found was very good indeed.

Chapter Twenty-Two

November 1755

*J*ason walked through the silent house, pleased he was no longer startled by the appearance of furniture in places he'd long been accustomed to being empty. Of course, the upholstered pieces were still draped with a wide variety of patterns and fabrics, but Cassy was taking care of that. For weeks now, he'd pretended to care about swatches of material, had nodded at color choices, and had rubbed his finger over samples to appreciate the nap. What he'd really enjoyed was watching the intense look of concentration on Cassy's face. He joined in her delight when she found patterns that harmonized. In the end, of course, all of the choices would be Cassy's, and that was how it should be.

She was soon to be mistress of this house, just as she'd become the mistress of his heart. They'd finally be married in two weeks. Jason found the wait impossible, but Cassy had insisted everything be done right and proper. No one could ever accuse them of sneaking around or question the legality of their union.

They were to be married in Grace Church in York with all the pomp Cassy could devise. Along with their close neighbors, friends would be coming from Williamsburg, some of whom would stay in the furnished but undecorated rooms here at the Bloomery. Others would be housed with various nearby planters and merchants. It seemed the entire county was involved in his nuptials.

The parish priest's insistence that they become members of his flock had delayed their arrival at the altar. Jason had seen blackmailers before, although never one who wore a clerical collar. But he'd acquiesced and, to convince the man of their sincerity, had dutifully driven them into York every Sunday to hear incredibly boring sermons.

Into the early morning stillness, shuffling sounds and other noises indicated the house was beginning to awaken. As if practicing for all the houseguests to come, they were currently hosting Conner and Mary McAllister. His friends had arrived yesterday to watch the first pour from the blast furnace today. It was excitement and concern for this endeavor that had chased Jason from his bed well before dawn.

He'd heard from Mr. Hanrahan at last, but the message had informed him that the expert would not be arriving. According to his note, Hanrahan's wife had developed complications with her pregnancy, and he felt they could not leave Ireland at this time. Since he'd not given Jason another date, Jason assumed he'd had a better offer from a furnace in either England or Ireland, since he'd initially expressed reservations about bringing his family to this "raw, new land."

So Jason would make his first pour in this raw, new land on his own. He'd read all the material he could find—he'd tested and retested the furnace and the bellows. He was as ready as he would ever be, but this did not keep his guts from drawing into knots at the thought of all that could go wrong.

He needed to eat, he thought. That would settle his stomach.

He walked into the dining room to find breakfast already laid out on the sideboard. The expanded staff had undoubtedly anticipated an early start to the day. A cold veal pie looked most appealing, and he helped himself to that as well as one of Cook's fresh corn muffins. He bypassed the tea and chose instead to pour a glass of small beer. Brewed with a low alcohol content, the beverage was refreshing without being inebriating.

He sat at the long table and looked at the portraits gazing at him from the wall. Cassy had christened the man his Great-Uncle Frederick Anders. The man's wife had yet to be given a first name and currently was known only as Mrs. Anders. He smiled at this small example of silliness that Cassy had brought to his life.

"What are you smiling at so early?" asked Conner from the doorway.

"Just a bit of whimsy," Jason replied.

"No, I think that's the look of a contented man, and I'm willing to admit, it's an expression I wasn't sure I'd ever see on your face." Conner was surveying the breakfast offerings. "Is this Cook's raspberry jam?"

"As far as I know."

"God, Jason, you really are a Philistine. Your cook makes the best raspberry jam I've ever eaten and you don't even notice when it's served." As if to prove his point, Conner placed two pieces of freshly baked bread and a huge mound of the jam on his plate. He poured a cup of tea and moved to join Jason at the table.

Titus dashed in, somewhat out of breath. "Miz Cassy said I'm sposed to serve," he said indignantly.

"Anyone in this house is perfectly capable of getting his own food once it's on the sideboard," Jason said. Then, getting a good look at his butler, he blurted, "Bloody hell, man, what do you have on your head?"

"It's a wig."

Jason could tell that, almost. The white confusion of hair looked more like an animal lying in an untidy nest on top of Titus's head. "Why in the world are you wearing a wig?" Jason asked. Conner made a choking sound but said nothing.

"When I was at Mista Dickens' house, all the house servants wore wigs. I figured now we're gettin' fancy, I should get this out."

"We're not getting that fancy. I'm sure Cassy didn't suggest you wear such a thing." Titus's nod affirmed this statement. "Then go get rid of it. Put it back in its cage or kill it, whichever is appropriate, but I don't want to see it again."

Titus huffed with affront, but he departed, at which point Conner convulsed in laughter. "Wherever did he find that frightful thing?" Conner choked out.

"I'm sure it came from the Dickens' property. I have no idea how Titus got so much stuffed into the small kit he had when he was sold, but occasionally the oddest things appear." He immediately thought of the lace collar and cuffs he'd worn to supper at Cassy's little house.

"Well, when he leaves your employ at the end of his indenture period, I'd suggest you check what all he's taking with him."

"If it's one of those wigs, he's welcome to it." Then the two men dissolved into laughter again.

"On a more serious note," Jason said, trying to remove the memory of the white glob sitting on Titus's head, "do you know of any free Negresses we could hire to work in the house?"

"Not right off the top of my head, but I'm sure there may be a few. Why do you specifically want Africans?"

"Well, I think Titus is lonely, and I thought if he had a few women to choose from, he might find someone to care for. He's free and eventually he'll have his fifty acres and be paid regular wages, so he'd not be a bad match for some free Negro woman. I doubt they have much to choose from themselves."

Conner unsuccessfully hid a grin. "My God, Jason, you've got it bad. You think since you've found your beloved, the rest of the world should follow suit. You sound like one of those matchmaking grandmas you see around town."

Jason stopped his rebuttal as Mary entered. Her actual arrival was preceded by a decided protrusion in her midsection that held the first of the next generation of McAllisters. Hard on her heels was Cassy, who had been staying at the little house during the McAllister' visit. Cassy had warned Jason away from any nightly visits there and told him she wouldn't appear in his bed at the big house. Propriety seemed the order of the day. Damn propriety. Jason missed Cassy's warm body wrapped around his.

"Where's Titus?" Cassy immediately asked.

"I sent him away," Jason replied.

"Why did you do that? I told him to serve." Cassy gave him a frown reserved for those times he flouted her orders.

"He was wearing this..." Jason's hands went to his head and tried to shape Titus's head covering, "wig." Then both he and Conner began again to laugh. This, of course, required an explanation, and the meal passed in joyful amusement.

"Well," Jason said, pushing back from the table, "I guess I'd better go get the process started. I'll expect to see you all down at the furnace shortly after noon."

"Aren't some others coming?" Conner asked. "At least I thought poor, stranded Lieutenant Michaels was supposed to be in attendance."

Indeed, Gilbert Michaels was still waiting in York for a ship to Boston. All of those that had docked recently had been bound for England with the tobacco crop. He and Jason had made a semblance of peace. At least sabers hadn't been drawn, and there had been no dawn meeting.

It had been a close thing, however, when the morning after their dinner together, Michaels had come to Cassy's house to say goodbye and found Jason there in his wilted finery from the previous night. Cassy had talked and soothed and taken the Lieutenant for a long walk. She wouldn't tell Jason what she said, but when they returned, Michaels had wished him joy in his marriage and departed for York.

"Everyone else is coming tomorrow," Jason said. "I thought I should make a trial pour before I have too big an audience. This way, if all doesn't go well, I'll only make a minor fool of myself."

"Oh good, then just the four of us can be burned to cinders if something goes amiss," Conner commented. "I'm filled with confidence."

"As you should be." Jason clapped his friend on the shoulder and quit the room.

He was soon on his way. His gelding slopped through mud on the way to the furnace area. Some places looked deep enough to bog down a carriage. It was possible that the most dangerous part of the day for Conner and the ladies would be getting to the furnace site.

The day was overcast, but at least the rain had stayed away. It had been cold enough the night before to leave a hint of frost on all the vegetation. The season had definitely turned. He wished he'd worn his heavy cape, but knew he'd soon be very warm.

He stopped when the expanse of the furnace area came into view. The big house and all its dependencies were for show. Here was the heart of the Bloomery. Buildings and forges lay scattered across a large, cleared area leading down to the river. A slight pall of smoke hovered over the scene. The glow of fires flickered from the forges. Men moved purposely about, darker gray figures in the gray light.

And rising from the midst like a crusader's watchtower of old was the blast furnace. Clad in stone brought overland from the mountains, the massive structure was lined with imported refractory brick. Cassy worried about the amount she spent on fixing up the house, but that was a pittance compared to the coin eaten by the construction of the furnace. But it was his future, and the future was without price.

In his mind, Jason saw a rolling mill and a steel operation added in areas purposely now vacant. Both of these were prohibited by the Iron Act recently passed by Parliament. But the Virginia Colony was far away from these legislators, and most local officials would look the other way. He knew of two illegal operations in Pennsylvania and suspected there were more. He just hadn't corresponded with more than those two.

He rode into the chaos and left his horse with one of the omnipresent boys. He really should stop buying the indentures of young boys—they weren't a good investment—but he recognized himself in them and couldn't leave them standing on a deck to possibly be purchased by someone cruel. The bulk of his indentured servants were big, strapping men, mostly convicts.

These were the workers he most needed. Soon he was surrounded by these huge men, all of them intent on making the blast furnace a success. The furnace workers wore leather aprons or vests over shirtsleeves, and in some cases, over nothing. Being around forges and furnaces was hot, sweaty work, no matter the weather. Jason was soon down to shirtsleeves and had donned a leather vest. The process of starting the blast furnace was complicated, but once it was going, the furnace would be worked twenty-four hours a day for every day of the year. Jason hoped for at least four years of continuous production.

Carefully measured amounts of charcoal, limestone, and iron ore were added at the top of the tall furnace. The water-powered bellows started up, its loud whoosh and clank becoming a continual background noise. It would take six to eight hours for the molten iron to be ready. But when it was, this iron would be of much higher quality than anything he'd previously produced. The additional heat induced by the bellows and the use of limestone as flux would cause the impurities to form slag, which would float on top of the molten iron. This slag would be pulled off first from a valve on the upper part of the furnace, leaving high quality iron behind.

Unable to continue to stand and point and shout, Jason joined in with the working men. Few gave him a glance, accustomed to this peculiarity in their employer. At one point, he found himself working next to long-armed Tom, who had caught him with a solid blow when he'd first arrived. The man had gained weight. His shoulders were more powerful. He grinned at Jason and said, "Thank you, Mr. Anders, for making me an iron man."

A warm tendril of pride swirled through Jason. He had made many here into iron men. When their indenture period was over, some would stay for wages. Others would farm the land Jason had received on their indenture and passed on to them. And a few would drift away to be lost in a land that was hard on rootless men. But Jason had given them all a start. He had built more than an iron works here.

The morning passed almost without his notice, and he was surprised when the carriage arrived. The dresses of the two women were bright spots in a landscape of browns and grays. He walked over to where they alighted, registering Cassy's frown at his untidy appearance. He grinned at her disapproval.

"There's a good spot to watch at the edge of the pouring shed," he said, offering Cassy his arm. He escorted the small group to one side of a long, open shed, trying unsuccessfully to ignore the tension he felt.

"What am I looking at?" Conner asked.

Jason supposed the shed area wasn't particularly impressive, but it was as necessary as the massive furnace itself. "The pour area is covered, to keep rain off the iron as it cools," he said. "The floor is thick sand. We've dug a long channel in it to accept the pour. You can see that ingot-sized protrusions jut off the channel at right angles. When the pour is complete, the resulting shape will look like a row of piglets sucking on a sow. Hence the name 'pig iron.'"

"Will we then live on a piggery rather than a bloomery?" Cassy gave him a teasing smile. He recognized her levity as a response to her own nerves. He gave her a quick kiss for luck, for the future.

"Do it," he yelled to the man situated at the upper valve. The man opened the valve and molten material ran out. This was waste material that had previously been part of his blooms, material he'd had to ship to England to have removed. But no longer. Taking a deep breath, he again waved his hand and the main spigot was opened.

The liquid iron rolled forth, glowing red, steaming. It filled the channel and its attendant ingots with the molten material that seemed a foretaste of hell. Waves of heat blasted where he stood and the air was filled with the pungent odor of hot metal. And it was beautiful. All their tomorrows arriving in a bright and fiery birth. Jason found his eyes filling with tears. He felt like a fool until Cassy's hand came to nestle in his, tightly gripping his fingers in her excitement, and he saw the answering moisture in her eyes.

Chapter Twenty-Three

C assy watched as three carriages and an assortment of riders left the house, everyone laughing and waving. Their guests were in good spirits as they made their way to see Jason make his second pour from the new blast furnace. All were treating the event as a great celebration, which, of course, it was. That friends and neighbors could understand the importance of this day was particularly heartening.

Every person employed at the Bloomery was equally excited. The men who had worked the first pour had obviously embroidered on what took place when the blast furnace disgorged its molten prize. Cassy had heard from at least three women now helping in the house that flames had shot as high into the air as the barn and that the smell of brimstone had been overpowering. Most of the servants were convinced the pour was extremely dangerous, and so, naturally, none wanted to miss it.

Cook had assembled a nice collation of cold meats and breads for their guests, all of which had been washed down by a wide selection of spirits. Many toasts had been offered for the success of Jason's operation. The visitors were no sooner out the door, however, than the staff had rapidly dashed about, cleaning and straightening. Then they, too, had disappeared like fog in the sun. No one wanted to miss the excitement.

But Cassy was stuck here at the house awaiting the arrival of a long case clock they'd ordered from Pennsylvania. The carter had sent a message that he would be arriving this morning and someone needed to be there to receive the piece. Cassy volunteered for this duty since she'd experienced the first pour and was anxious to see the clock.

It had been ordered from a sketch that had shown intricate carving and a whimsically painted face. Cassy hoped it met her expectations. There were two possible places for such a piece, but she felt she needed to know exactly what it looked like before deciding where it should rest.

Jason had seemed disappointed she would not be there again, but she doubted he would really miss her in the mob of people that would ring the pouring shed. Anyway, this was his victory, and he really didn't need his still-mysterious betrothed standing next to him to deflect some of the interest. Until today, she hadn't met many of their neighbors, and she could tell they still found her a curiosity. Cassy suspected that over the course of her life, she would see more pours than any one person had need to.

The only other people who would miss the exciting event were Titus and young Luke. Titus had been adamant in his belief that Cassy would need his help to place the clock. Luke stayed for purportedly the same reason, but more likely he was motivated by pique for not being chosen to help the arriving guests with their horses. The boy was certainly horse mad. He'd taken to shadowing Hats, much to the ex-jockey's irritation.

Cassy would have felt guilty had she not been sure that both the man and the boy would see the blast furnace in action sometime during this week. At that time, their view would be unobstructed, a situation none of the servants attending today would enjoy.

She walked through the silent house, her heels clicking on the polished wood floors, her heart filling as she envisioned everything completed. In her mind, walls were painted, draperies hung, and furniture reupholstered. It was going to be a nice house, a gracious home, and most importantly, it was going to be hers.

She could still not believe the serendipitous route that had brought her to this place. In only thirteen more days, she'd be Mrs. Jason Anders. She'd never in her life imagined she'd feel such joy. She'd initially felt regret when her monthly course had arrived a few days ago, but then she'd decided this was actually a continuation of her incredible luck. Now, when she gave Jason his first child, all of the gossips who could count to nine would be satisfied.

She caught herself humming. Tonight they'd have the house all to themselves. The McAllisters had departed this morning. As much as she loved Mary and Conner's company, she was anxious to enjoy nightly activities with Jason again. She wondered what other things he had to teach her. As it was, she wasn't sure she could ever look at a dining room chair in the same way again.

Her reverie was broken by the sound of wagon wheels coming down the long drive. "The clock's here," she called to Titus, who was somewhere at the back of the house.

The approaching wagon was more decrepit than she'd expected. Two large men sat on the wagon seat, however, so there would be no need for Titus to help lift and carry. She wondered briefly if he could still have time to get to the furnace area.

The men stopped the wagon at a distance from the house. What idiots. Didn't they know such a fine clock was destined for the principal residence and not one of the outbuildings? She hurried down the steps. "The clock goes in here," she called, irritated to see the men ignore her and swing down from the wagon where it stood.

She picked up her skirts and quickly walked to where the two men stood at the back of the wagon. One of the men dropped the rear hatch and rustled a tarp lying in the bed. "The clock goes in the main house," she said, slightly out of breath. "There's no need to carry it such a long distance when you could simply drive closer."

"We hit a bad rut an' thought there were damage." The man kept playing with the tarp.

For heaven's sake. The earlier rain had left the roads muddy, and some mud might have formed a rut, but Cassy could have sworn someone had smoothed the drive before their guests arrived. But she couldn't fault the carters' caution. She'd hate it if the clock were broken in any way. She hastened to have a look, wrinkling her nose at the acidic smell of old sweat coming from the driver and his helper. The two men were as disreputable looking as the wagon. When she next got into York, she'd give the shopkeeper a piece of her mind for employing such ramshackle deliverymen.

"Thar," said one of the men, pointing.

Cassy leaned over to peer into the wagon bed—and a number of things happened all at once. The larger of the men grabbed the back of her hair and pulled her backward. When she opened her mouth to scream, someone jammed a foul-tasting cloth deep into her mouth. Her mind flashed back to Lord Tilton and panic shot through her. Not again. No, never again.

She brought both of her elbows back sharply into the gut of the large man holding her from behind. Simultaneously, she jerked her head forward, the pain in her scalp so sharp it momentarily obscured her vision. She twisted and writhed, kicking back, knowing her foot had connected but feeling she'd done little damage through the heaviness of her skirts.

She saw the other man approaching from the corner of her eye and struck at him, her hand balled into a fist, her elbow straight. She caught him on the side of the head and knocked him back. "Jesus Christ, Ben, cain't ya control the bitch?"

The larger man still held her hair, and instead of pulling back as he'd been doing, he suddenly pushed her forward, grabbing her around the waist as he did so. Her forehead bounced against the back of the wagon with a sound that seemed to echo in her head. The edges of her vision darkened and all the strength left her arms and legs. She tried to make her limbs move, but they refused to answer her desperate call. She slumped between the man and the wagon.

"Git 'er tied while ya can, ya ass."

She felt some sort of cloth cording being wrapped around and around her body, pulling her arms flush against her torso. She tried to flop away, but even that seemed beyond her capacity. A whirlwind suddenly hit the man tying her. There were windmilling arms and legs and loud, high-pitched curses. Luke.

She wanted to tell the boy to run away, to get help, but could do nothing as the man pushed her into the wagon bed and turned to bring Luke to the ground with two powerful punches. He then gave the fallen boy a hard kick with his booted foot. Luke made a mewing sound but didn't move. The man fished in his pocket and came out with a crumpled piece of paper, which he placed in Luke's limp hand.

"Tie 'er bloody legs and let's go," he said, straightening.

She now had limited control of her legs and she kicked out ineffectually. Her legs were quickly wrapped, and she was stuffed further into the wagon bed, cocooned in place by the crumpled tarp. Lying on her back, all she could now see was the bright sky overhead. The men leaped onto the wagon seat and started the horse into motion. Above the clomp of the hooves, she heard running footsteps, coming fast.

"Miz Cassy!" Titus's voice pierced the air.

The long, dark barrel of a musket appeared over her head, aiming back. The sound of the shot hit her like a blow. "My god, didya see that. I took that bastard right offen his feet."

"We warn't sposed ta kill nobody," the driver groused.

"It were jess a darky," the other replied, the musket barrel disappearing from her view.

Realization stopped the breath in her throat. Dear Lord, Titus had been shot. Funny, do-anything-for-you Titus, who wanted to make Jason proud. White teeth flashing in his dark face as he pulled on the white gloves he thought looked fancy. Tears leaked from her eyes, filling her nose and threatening to suffocate her. What was happening? What was the cause of this nightmare? The only person she could think of who might hate her enough to do this was Lord Tilton, and he should have been an ocean away.

The wagon picked up speed, bouncing all over the road. If she'd been a clock, it was likely something would have broken. Her bound body flew up from the hard wagon bed and back down again with disgusting regularity. She hurt all over, but the throbbing in her head was debilitating.

Her eyes stung and she closed them against the brightness of the sky. She wanted to be out of this wagon but feared what she would find when they stopped. Shadows covered her and she opened her eyes to see pine trees leaning out over the road. They proceeded further into the woods and finally came to a halt.

The driver dropped to the ground from his place on the wagon seat and came around to the rear, laughing and grabbing Cassy's legs when she tried to kick at him. He pulled her along the wagon bed, slivers from the rough wood abrading her flesh wherever it wasn't covered with cloth. The man briefly set her on her feet, then bent down and flipped her over his shoulder. The move knocked the air from her lungs. The world passed by, upside down, and they entered a dim shed. He unceremoniously dumped her to the ground and left without a word.

Cassy lay there, breathing hard through her nose. She attempted to take stock of the situation by rolling from side to side. She was on a dirt floor in a good-sized storage shed. Large barrels were stacked haphazardly. Rakes and other garden implements leaned against the wall. The men seemed to have departed and she was alone.

She tried to force her legs apart and move her arms away from where they were imprisoned against her body. The bindings, some sort of thin, prickly, fiber rope, gave slightly but held. If she could get rid of the nauseating rag in her mouth, however, she could call for help. She doubted anyone would come to her aid, but it would be wonderful to be able to take a full breath.

She wiggled and rolled until she was looking at the dusty floor. She then pushed at the rag with her tongue while rubbing her face back and forth in the dirt. The grit stung her cheeks, but it would be worth any pain to dislodge the gag. The material seemed to be sliding forward. She beat her tongue against the obstruction and was finally able to rub it free. She lay there, panting, dust and some pungent, sweet odor filling her nose.

A sound intruded into her jumbled thoughts. Hands clapping? She shifted until she could look in the direction of the sound. A man sat on an overturned barrel, indolently leaning back against the shed wall, applauding.

Cassy had seen the man only from a distance, but she knew instinctively who he was. Sir Peyton Hyde. He was a big man, probably in his fifties, but fit. He was either bald or had shaved his head to accommodate a wig. He grinned as he brought his hands together.

"Oh, my dear. I can't tell you how much I enjoyed your little performance. All of that writhing around was positively arousing."

"Untie me." Cassy tried for her frostiest tone, but sounding as if she were in command was difficult while lying prone on the floor.

"All in good time." He chuckled. "But excuse my manners. This is no way to treat a great lady. Let me help you sit up."

He pushed himself to his feet and walked toward her. She tried hard not to shrink away, not wanting to give him the satisfaction, but she was sure her fear was palpable. He grabbed the topmost cord and pulled her back until she rested against one of the barrels in a sitting position.

"Untie me," she said again.

"I'm not willing to untie you completely, but I will retie you. Ted has you trussed up like a chicken ready for the spit. Only your hands and feet need to be restrained, and I'll gladly see to that. I'm sure you'll be more comfortable. Now sit very still and let me change these bindings. If you fight me, girl, I promise I'll leave you just as you are."

She sat without moving. "There's no reason to tie me up at all. I don't know where I am. I won't try to get away."

He laughed. "Of course you'll try." He cut through the bindings on the upper part of her body. When the rope was loosened enough that she could move her arms, she considered hitting at him and then thought better of it. With her legs still hobbled she was going nowhere, and her defiance might push Sir Peyton to violence. She allowed him to pull her arms forward and tie her wrists in her lap. He cut the cords on the upper part of her legs and left only her ankles bound. He hummed off-key as he did so.

He stood back as if to view his handiwork. "Now, isn't that more comfortable. You can say 'thank you.'"

"I'd hardly thank you for kidnapping me. I don't know what you're about, Sir Peyton, but it isn't going to work."

"Oh, but it will," he said with a smile. "It's a wonderful plan that will take care of all my problems." He reached down and took her chin in his hand, turning her face one way and then the other. She tried to shake him off. "You are a fine-looking woman, Lady Cassandra. Or is it Cassy Spade, the indentured servant, I'm talking to? You seem to have a number of different personas, and I think it's up to the one in charge to decide who you really are. And since I'm in charge," he laughed, "I think you'll be Cassy for now."

"I'm Lady Cassandra Spathe, the daughter of the Earl of Chelle, and you would be wise to release me."

He wandered back over to the far wall and took his seat on the barrel. "I don't see any earl around here, do you? So I guess elevated connections aren't going to do much good. And I've told you, I'm in charge, and I've decided you're Cassy. Ah, yes, Cassy. The servant girl who is leading Jason Anders around by his prick. The one who made him forget all his grand pronouncements about not tupping the help."

Sir Peyton laughed and rubbed his hands together. "Your hot little body has been a real help to me. I've left Jason a note telling him where he can find you—and we both know he'll come. And when he does, I'll be forced to kill him. You see, you fled here for my help this afternoon. You confessed your story of being a lady was a hoax. You'd hoped it would gain you a place in society here, but instead all you attracted was a jumped-up convict, and that wasn't what you wanted. You asked me to help you, but Jason found you and I had to protect you."

"No one will ever believe such lies."

"Of course they will. Everybody loves a good story. Look how they sucked up your tale of amnesia."

Cassy looked up quickly and he chortled. "I didn't say everyone was gullible, only most. And my story is as good as yours, filled with angst and misunderstandings. Poor Jason cut down in a possessive rage, you throwing yourself into my arms in appreciation for what I've done. And I have notes of hand secured by all Jason owns, did you know that? The forger was expensive, but he was a good one. Yes, this is an exciting tale that gets me his woman and his property and allows me to ride over this nasty financial downturn with my name intact."

"That's insane," Cassy said, realizing the truth of the words as they left her mouth. The man was indeed insane. "Too many people know the truth."

"The truth!" His voice rose to a shout. "I'll tell you the truth. I plucked a convict lad off a ship and gave him gainful employment. And he repaid me by defying me at every turn. No amount of chastisement could break his stubborn rebelliousness. He even took me to court. Twice! Can you imagine? Me! A baronet in court because some scum complains of his treatment. And then, when he finally got out of his contract, he started making iron. Iron, of all things! And he now ships so much of the bloody stuff back to England it's forcing the crops of substantial planters like myself off the bills of lading."

Sir Peyton moved around the small building, running his hands over the articles strewn about as if claiming his mastership of this diminished domain. "And now he wants to get elected to the House of Burgesses so he can pass laws that will restrict how planters can use indentured laborers. He even advocates freedom for Negroes. He wants to financially destroy his betters."

Cassy looked at the man in fascinated horror, as one might watch a wagon pulled by runaway horses. A collision was imminent, but she was powerless to stop it. The man was raving. Sweat rolled from his distorted face. What she saw was unreasoning hate.

"But he'll come now and I'll stop his meddling forever." Sir Peyton collapsed back on the barrel. "And you'll sit there without saying a word until your ill-born lover arrives. If you make a peep, I'll beat you senseless. But I see no need to do so when all we have to do is wait."

He again began his tuneless humming. His head lolled back and he beat it against the shed wall in time with some rhythm in his head. To her horror, Cassy noticed his hand also moved to the same beat as it rubbed back and forth over his engorged crotch.

But at least he wasn't paying attention to her. She'd noticed Sir Peyton had cut the cord wrapped around her thighs and left the bindings on her ankles, but he hadn't actually retied them. She should be able to work the cords loose. She wiggled her feet a little further apart, felt the ties slip, and kept widening her legs by increments.

She looked back at her captor to see if he'd noted her movement. But Sir Peyton was oblivious to her. He'd unbuttoned the front of his breeches and his hand was actively pumping up and down while he hummed and beat his head. Cassy bent double until her questing fingers found the cord around her ankles. Then, as if she'd found her embroidery floss tangled, her fingers began to sort through the various loops of cording.

Chapter Twenty-Four

*J*ason couldn't stop grinning. He wondered if seeing so much molten metal could ever become commonplace. The crowd that had gathered around the edges of the pouring shed had dispersed into the gathering twilight. Even though some of his neighbors wouldn't make it home before dark, they'd all stayed to slap him on the back and shake his hand.

After years of servitude and despair, followed by years of dreams and hard work, this accomplishment was very sweet. He felt he had the right to enjoy others' congratulations.

He rolled his stiff shoulders. This time he'd stood with the crowd, watching as the process took place, but he'd mentally done each of the required tasks, muscles bunching as if they had done the actual work. He felt comfortably tired and looked forward to a relaxed evening alone with Cassy. He smiled. Well, maybe not too relaxed.

He walked to where his horse was tethered, well away from the heat and the fire. He was about to swing into the saddle when Hats came running up. The little man's face was so twisted it was nearly unrecognizable. "Trouble, up at the house," he panted, nodding to where a knot of men half-dragged and half-carried Luke.

Heart in his throat, Jason hurried toward the staggering group. At his approach, the men let Luke slide to the ground, supporting his shoulders to keep him in a sitting position. Jason hunkered down next to the boy.

"Clockmen stole Miz Cassy," Luke forced out between bloody lips. The boy's face ran with blood and tears and snot. He breathed like a winded horse.

The clock men stole Cassy? Jason's blood froze as he tried to make sense of what Luke was saying.

"Tha' boy run all the way from the house, beat up like 'e is," Hats said. "'e had this in 'is hand." Hats reverently handed Jason a crumpled piece of paper. Like many who were unable to read, Hats believed all written messages held significance.

Jason stood, smoothing the wrinkled paper, turning the words up to the waning light. *If you want to see your ladybird again, come alone to the place of chastisement at first dark.* There was no signature. There didn't need to be.

Jason became numb all over. His legs were locked in place. His eyes became unfocused. He was well acquainted with Hyde's place of chastisement. The thought of Cassy's pale loveliness stretched over one of the hogshead barrels, of the whip coming down, momentarily stole his breath. Dear God, how had this happened?

Feeling returned in a flood of pain. His first impulse was leap on his horse and ride to Hyde's, screaming like a banshee. But he needed to think. He needed a plan. Whatever else happened, he had to get Cassy away from Sir Peyton. He was well aware of the man's sick proclivities.

He must have gazed off into the gathering dark for a few seconds. He felt Hats' hand on his arm. "Luke says Titus is dead." Hats' face worked again, as if he were holding back tears. The words struck Jason like a blow and reinforced his opinion that Sir Peyton had gone mad.

"Okay, Hats, you have to listen to me and do exactly as I say. Sir Peyton has kidnapped Cassy and he'll hurt her if I don't follow his instructions." He waved the piece of paper. "I want you to send your best rider for the magistrate in York. Tell him there's been murder done and probably more to follow. He'll come. The man is solid. While you're waiting for the magistrate to get here, assemble the men. Explain there will probably be a fight and someone could even get killed, so anyone who wants to be excused can be. This is not part of their job.

"When the magistrate arrives, bring him and our men to the sheds near the river where the tobacco that's ready to ship is stored on Sir Peyton Hyde's estate. Do you know where that is?"

Hats nodded.

"Good. Come to the second shed from the river. I think that's where Cassy is being held. I'm going there directly. You should be less than an hour behind me. Now, whatever happens, you must make sure that Cassy is safe and that Sir Peyton is charged with her kidnapping at the least."

"The least?" Hats questioned.

Jason had neither the time nor the inclination to explain that a more serious charge of murder, specifically his murder, might easily be lodged. He was sure Hyde had taken Cassy only to get Jason to come to the isolated spot by the river and that the man's plan was to kill him in some way that might appear accidental. "Just make sure you get there with the magistrate in tow. I want the power of the law behind whatever happens."

"I think this is a bad plan, Jase. Ya should take our men with ya right now. Every man jack of 'em will fight for ya like a berserker, ya can count on that."

"No. If a virtual army comes riding up, Sir Peyton will harm Cassy. I have to appear to do as he says. I hope to get her away from the son of a bitch before you get there. And the presence of the law is essential to make sure the slimy worm doesn't wriggle out of the situation. Do you understand me, Hats?"

"Yessir. But I doon like it."

"Just get it done."

Jason swung around and mounted his horse. Hats was already working his way among those still assembled. He saw him stop and speak to a wiry boy, who streaked off in the direction of the barn that held the horses used in the forge area. That must be Hats' fast rider. Jason couldn't worry about the rest of his orders being followed. He needed to get to Hyde's estate with all speed.

He turned his horse and rode into the night. He had to travel carefully now that darkness had fallen. The quickest way to Sir Peyton's landing from the furnace area was to follow the river, and the way was treacherous. Since the two men had always been antagonistic, no path had been established as a shortcut between the two holdings.

Jason eased the gelding into the undergrowth, always keeping the river or its sound on his right. He initially wished there were a moon but then was glad there was none tonight. Sir Peyton had undoubtedly set men to capture him as he approached, and he'd soon need to travel on foot to avoid detection. Hyde was a bully and a coward and he'd not want to face Jason unless Jason was being restrained by others.

As much as he needed to concentrate, Jason's mind kept returning to Cassy. Dear God, she must be afraid. The thought of a whip cutting into her soft skin nearly crippled him. Even if Sir Peyton intended to kill him, he hoped Cassy wasn't included in this insanity. He tried to force the thoughts of her away. The time to worry about Cass was after he'd gotten her free, assuming there was an after.

His horse slowed, shook his head, and stopped in front of a deep cut that was full of water at high tide, but was currently a muddy bog. Jason was now sure of his location. He dismounted and secured the reins to a branch. There was no need for the horse to wander and announce his presence before he was ready to do so. From here on, he'd proceed on foot.

Jason moved cautiously though the dark woods. Even if men were waiting to ambush him, he had the advantage of being as familiar with the area as they were. For the ten years of his indenture, only stealth and the knowledge of hidden paths had given him brief moments of freedom. Now, this ability should get him to where Cassy was being held without alerting any watchers.

Jason ghosted from tree to tree, his feet silent on the thick mat of fallen pine needles that covered the forest floor. He passed two huddled groups of men, but they were more intent on grumbling about the damp cold rising from the river than on keeping a careful watch. Fear did not inspire loyalty, and as always, Sir Peyton was poorly served.

Hugging the tree line, Jason approached the storage shed from the rear. Lantern light, filtered through cracks in the small building's poorly maintained siding, winked like fireflies on a summer's night. He was correct in Sir Peyton's choice of venue.

He tried to blank from his mind the number of times he'd been hauled to this particular shed, tied over one of the hogsheads, and whipped until he could no longer keep his screams from rending the night. A memory of fear and pain curled through him. He shook it off. He was no longer that helpless boy.

He crept closer to the shed, slithering on his stomach for the last few yards. No men seemed to be closely surrounding the building, but he couldn't be sure. After trying four different places, he found a slit in the siding that gave him a full view of the shed's interior. Cassy sat with her hands tied in front of her, leaning on a barrel, seemingly unharmed, although her face was dirty and her hair was in disarray. Holding a pistol in his right hand, Sir Peyton paced near the door.

To enter through the door was an invitation to be shot, but there was no other way in. The closest group of men was too distant to stop his approach, and with luck he could take Sir Peyton by surprise. The man would only have one shot and then they'd be on equal footing.

Jason eased around the building until he faced the door. Taking a deep breath, he steadied himself. He depressed the latch and pushed the door in one swift movement. Bending his knees, he dashed through the opening low and parallel to the ground. He heard the sharp bark of the gun, thought Sir Peyton had missed him, then felt a burning in his left thigh.

Jason rolled and tried to come to his feet, but found his left leg unresponsive. Warm blood coursed down his calf. Sir Peyton leaped for him, swinging the now useless gun at his head. Jason managed to roll again and the gun missed its target.

Cassy screamed and launched herself at Sir Peyton. She flailed at his shoulders with a loose barrel stave awkwardly gripped in her bound hands. The man pivoted, swung his arm wide, and caught her across the chest with the gun. Cassy was knocked backwards, making a strange whooshing sound and crumpling to the dusty floor.

White hot fury propelled Jason to his feet, but before he could go for Sir Peyton, the shed filled with men. Two of them grabbed Jason's arms and pulled him from his unsteady feet onto the ground.

There was a moment of frozen silence broken only by heavy breathing, then Cassy moaned and Sir Peyton laughed.

"I'm glad you arrived for your final chastisement," he said. "I'd planned to just shoot you and be done with it, but I think it will be more interesting to see just how many lashes it will take to kill you. I always wondered, you know, but stayed my hand since you'd hauled me into court with your complaints, and others would think I'd purposely gone too far."

Jason tensed his muscles and threw himself away from the men holding him, trying to get to his feet. But his traitorous leg would not follow his dictates and he was unable to get free.

"The support barrel and the wrist and leg straps are where you remember them," Sir Peyton said almost conversationally. He then looked at the men restraining Jason. "Strip his back and get him tied down over the barrel and leave." Then as an afterthought, "Pull his breeches down too. We want to give his sweet little whore the best show we can."

Jason fought against the men and even in his weakened condition, it took four of them to fasten him over the barrel. In the end, one simply cut his shirt along the back with a knife and ripped it open, the loose pieces of material floating from his shoulders like wings. When they jerked his breeches down, they were sodden with blood. Open to the air, the wound stung and quickly made a stream flowing down his leg.

In the meantime, Hyde had pulled Cassy into a sitting position, leaning her back against a wall for support. He gently tapped on her face. "Pay attention now, dear Cassy. I think you'll enjoy this. Did Jason tell you how loudly he can scream? And when the pain gets bad enough, his prick grows marvelously big and hard. It's really most amusing. Of course, I imagine you've already seen him looking like a rampant stallion."

He turned to the men still shuffling near the door. "You can get out or you'll be the next ones lashed. And don't come back regardless of what you hear." They rapidly departed, closing the door behind them.

Sir Peyton walked to where Jason was tied. He ran a hand up and down Jason's back in an obscene caress. "Do you like to pet all these pretty ridges I've left here, Cassy girl? I find the texture rather stimulating. And be sure to watch his nice hard ass." The man reached down and grabbed Jason's buttocks in a firm grip. "I love watching how his muscles here flex and strain as he pumps himself into the barrel with every stroke of the lash. No doubt he does a better job pumping into you, but you've never been in a position to actually watch before, have you?"

"You bastard," Jason forced out between his clenched teeth. "Let Lady Cassandra go and just kill me if that's what you want." Jason could see Cassy where she sat. Sir Peyton had undoubtedly positioned her there so he could watch her view his humiliation. She slumped forward, boneless, but he caught the movement of her eyes under her fall of hair.

"Oh, I will kill you," Hyde said almost happily. "But I don't think I'll be letting sweet Cassy girl go anytime soon. I'm going to use her for the purposes she was built for. Whipping you always makes me hard. I bet it will make her wet as well. So it would be stupid to let all that preparation go for nothing. I think I'll enjoy mounting her while I look at your dead body draped over that barrel. Maybe I'll drape her over one as well and take her from the rear. Yes, I think that would be very satisfying."

"You'll not get away with this." Jason jerked against his bounds, although he knew it was useless.

"Of course I will. I'm Sir Peyton Hyde, Baronet. I own a goodly portion of this county. I've served in the House of Burgesses for nearly twenty years. No one would dare question my version of what happened here."

Then Hyde began to hum off-key, a sound Jason well remembered. He felt his gorge rise and choked back the acid taste. He was afraid. Damn it to hell, he was afraid. Just as he'd been as a boy. It wasn't the anticipated pain that devastated him. It was the helplessness. And Cassy was here to watch.

He heard the slither of the long whip being dragged across the dirt, the singing of the lash in the air, and then the white-hot slash of pain across his back. He saw Cassy move from the corner of his eye and he want to shout, "run," but his throat had so tightened, he couldn't get the word out.

Cassy did go toward the door, but she whirled, clumsily holding a pitchfork mid-handle in her tethered hands. With a keening, feral sound humans seldom make, she rushed at where Sir Peyton stood behind him, the sharp tines of the fork held out before her. He heard the sound of collision and a ghastly scream, followed by a thud.

Jason strained against the thongs that held him in place, trying to turn his head to see what had happened. Was Cassy safe? Dear God, was she safe?

"I think I killed him." Cassy's voice was thready. Then she gave a dry chuckle. "But then, I've thought that before. How do I know?"

"Release me, Cass, and I'll check." Jason tried to keep his tone calm, although he didn't feel it. Had she killed the madman or would he rise up and attack her? He needed to get her away from his vicinity. He would send her running, except Hyde's men were undoubtedly hanging around the front of the shed, probably waiting for more screams.

Cassy appeared in his line of vision. Her face was pale and she looked as if she were about to swoon. But her hands were steady when she knelt and released his wrists. As he painfully pushed himself into a standing position, he felt her working on the straps that held his ankles.

"Dear Lord, your leg is bleeding badly," Cassy said from behind him. He felt a stinging pressure as Cassy pressed her hand firmly against the wound. It crossed his mind that loss of blood could account for his weird lightheadedness. He could brace himself upright with his hands, but he didn't feel confident to take a step. The need to protect her from Sir Peyton, should he rise from the floor, overwhelmed him.

"Help me turn around," he said. At least he could face the bastard.

Cassy offered her shoulder, and using it and the hogshead to support himself, he managed to turn and settle his rear back against the barrel. Sir Peyton lay like a broken doll, arms and legs in improbable positions. The pitchfork had caught him just below the ribcage but was angled up. It still protruded from his body. From Jason's vantage point, the man looked very dead.

He pulled Cassy into his shaking arms. It was difficult to tell which of them trembled more, but there was comfort in contact.

A loud noise outside brought both of their heads around to face the door. There were hoof beats and loud shouts. Then, what sounded like a brawl ensued. Over the chaos he heard Hats' deep voice ring out: "This is Magistrate Chilton. Give way before the power of the law."

Jason felt he should go to the door and see what was happening, but it didn't seem all that important. He wanted to stay here with his arms wrapped about Cassy. He really didn't care what happened outside of the circle of their embrace.

The door burst open, letting in a flood of men armed with staves and branches and farm implements. In the midst was the magistrate, looking remarkably unruffled. All came to a silent halt when they surveyed the scene.

Jason tried to stand. "Help Cassy," he said, and then the world seemed to be formed of objects with soft edges that slowly melted together. As from a distance, he saw Lieutenant Michaels pull Cassy away from him. *Good*, he thought, *she'll be safe now*. Everything around him became viscous, he felt himself slipping to his knees, and the world went dark.

❖ ❖ ❖

A glass was pressed hard against his mouth and an angry voice said, "Drink this, damn you." With difficulty he opened gummy eyes and looked into Cassy's stern face. When she realized he gazed back at her, she relaxed her hold on his back and let him recline against a stack of pillows.

"Oh, thank God, Jason." She looked as if she wanted to throw her arms around him but was impeded by the glass she gripped in her hand. "If you're awake you can help me get some of this water into you. The doctor was quite adamant we do so, but it's certainly been difficult without your cooperation."

She pulled him more upright again and tilted the glass against his lips. He hungrily gulped some of the liquid. Nothing had ever tasted so good. Slowly he realized he was lying in his own bed. Cassy took the glass away and let him settle back into the pillows. She put her arms gently around him and laid her head on his chest.

"You scared me so badly, I could kill you." A weak smile flickered over her face as if she realized the ridiculousness of her words. "Or maybe it was the doctor who frightened me with all his talk of blood loss and the suggestion that you might never again regain consciousness. At any rate, I've been in a panic, and seeing you awake is wonderful."

"How long?" he croaked, surprised by the rusty sound of his voice.

"Three days." Cassy sat up and smoothed his hair back from his face. "Three impossibly long days. But the doctor said if you woke, you would probably mend, so your attempt at getting out of marrying me hasn't worked."

He attempted to smile at her weak joke. "Cass, I'd marry you if I had to come back from the grave. Woman, you have no idea how much I love you." He pulled her head toward his with a shaky arm.

She gave him a quick kiss and then pulled back. "I love you, too, but without putting too fine a point on it, you taste just a bit like you *have* come back from the grave." And then she laughed—the husky, carefree sound he so loved.

"Maybe I'm not quite ready to be amorous," he said, unoffended. "But I will be in what, a little over a week? Unless I'm still unable to meet you at the altar. How bad was the damage?" He ached all over, and there was a burning spot on his left thigh, but he didn't feel incapacitated.

"Primarily blood loss. Sir Peyton shot you in the upper leg, but the bullet went straight through. The doctor had trouble getting the blood to stop. But he did and you're here. Oh, Jason..." She carefully wrapped her arms around him and held him.

She may not want to kiss him right now, but it was heaven to have her snuggled firmly against him. It was lucky the bullet hadn't lodged in his thigh. Since he'd ben shot three days ago and he didn't feel flushed, he had to assume he'd avoided an infection and the fever that accompanied it. He would get well. He would marry Cassy and their life together would be one of joy. He was content with that.

"You know Titus was killed, don't you?" she asked softly.

"Yes." The word held so much regret.

"We had his funeral two days ago. Everyone attended. There were a lot of tears, mine included. He was trying to help me, as he always did, when he was shot. Even Hats cried, but he was leading the service, so being emotional seemed normal." She sat up abruptly. "And that's why we're getting married here at the house."

"Because you felt a big celebration wouldn't be appropriate. That's fine with me."

"No, it's because I refuse to be married by the rector of the church in York. Do you know that man refused to let us bury Titus in the church cemetery? He said no Negroes allowed. So we buried him at the end of the orchard and one of the men from the forge is going to make a fancy iron fence to go around it. I would have ordered him a headstone, but I don't know what to put on it. 'Titus' hardly seems to be enough."

Jason was quiet a moment. Cassy pulled a handkerchief from her pocket and wiped her eyes, then she gently did the same for Jason. "If he had any other name, Cassy, I don't know it. And I have no idea when he was born or even where. It probably doesn't make any difference. The important thing is that he's remembered. We can show our children his grave and tell them he died trying to protect their mother. That's not a bad legacy for any man to carry into eternity."

"Yes, we'll do that. I don't want our children to be as narrow-minded as I've been, and as the rector in York still is. I've come to see that people are people and should be judged as individuals, not as a member of some arbitrary group or class."

"And I'm glad you've changed your attitude, or you wouldn't be about to make me the happiest of men." Jason was pleased his hand was much steadier when he raised it to her face and ran his knuckles along her cheek.

"Oh, you," she sighed, rubbing her cheek back against his fingers.

"So the priest from the Bruton Parish Church in Williamsburg will come here and marry us. And while he's here, Hats and Mavis would like to get married, also. Hats said you might not allow it since he still has years of his contract to work off, but I told him it would be fine. He said to tell you he was glad Mavis did what she did, whatever that means. They've been a couple for a long time and it seems right for them to proclaim their love to all the world."

"I agree, just so everyone doesn't get the same idea and we have people marrying all over the place. The Bloomery will end up awash with children."

"Good, then there will be plenty to play with ours."

She snuggled back onto his chest. He could feel her heart beating next to his and he knew he wanted her in his arms for as long as his heart did beat. Cassy was his completion. He couldn't begrudge anyone else from sharing this feeling. Perfect contentment. The two words stayed in his mind as his eyes grew heavy and finally closed.

Epilogue

June 1756

The ballroom at the Governor's Palace in Williamsburg was ablaze with the glow of candles. Cassy gazed around the beautifully proportioned room, enjoying the ebb and flow of all the brightly garbed people. Her attention was most focused on the large man laughing with his fellow Burgesses, however.

Jason looked resplendent in a burgundy coat over a gold brocade waistcoat. He was half a head taller than most of the men present and his shoulders were twice as wide, but he looked every inch a gentleman. A smile creased the corners of her lips. He was also every inch a primal male, and she was sure every lady present felt his draw.

"Och, your husband is a braw man," a soft, Scottish voice said next to her. Cassy turned to see Mrs. Dinwiddie, the lieutenant governor's wife, smiling at her. Cassy felt a blush rise, embarrassed at having been caught ogling her own husband.

"That he is," Cassy agreed. "And I sometimes still have trouble believing that he's mine." She unconsciously dropped a hand to her waist and caressed the small rounded ball no amount of clever tailoring could disguise as anything other than a forthcoming child.

"There's na question of that," the older woman said, looking at Jason's tall form and not Cassy's expanding waistline. "If you're na looking at him, he's looking at you. The two of you make the very air crackle." She patted Cassy on the sleeve. "Ah, to be young."

As if he felt their regard, Jason looked up at Cassy and smiled. He quickly said something to the men he was talking to and walked toward Cassy. Mrs. Dinwiddie was right. Jason Anders was most assuredly a *braw* man.

He greeted the lieutenant governor's wife and effortlessly conversed with her until Mrs. Dinwiddie's hostess duties took her elsewhere. "The dancing will soon begin, and then I can show off all the steps you've taught me." He winked at Cassy and then grinned when he saw her flush.

The last time they had "practiced" before leaving the Bloomery, Jason had untied or unbuttoned something on Cassy's clothing at every pass and did the same to his own when the figure took them apart. They had not gotten to the end of the figure before they'd fallen into bed and done an altogether different dance.

Jason was fascinated with Cassy's pregnancy. He loved to rub his hands over the slight lump of her belly and talk nonsense to the child within. He seemed as proud of Cassy's pregnancy as he was with the output of his blast furnace. He acted as if no other man had ever sired a child and embarrassed her to no end by disclosing the fact to all and sundry.

"Congratulate me," he'd say even to total strangers. "I'll be a father this coming fall."

She had caught him making sled runners at the forge. "A child should have a sled," he said. "I always wanted one." And so a child-sized sled was being made, regardless of the fact that it seldom snowed in tidewater Virginia or that their child was years away from using one. She would have pointed out that the Bloomery didn't have many elevations, let alone sled-worthy hills, but she was afraid she would find him with shovel in hand making one.

Lord, how she loved this man.

"Do you ever wish that you were at some grand ball back in England?" Jason asked, suddenly serious.

"Heavens, no!" Cassy was confident that over time, Jason would come to realize that in this country, with this man, she was truly home and wanted no other. "In England, no one knows the lost-clothing dance, and it's the one we both do best."

"Just so," he said, his mood lightening again. And then he took her arm and they began to walk again around the room. They were universally greeted with pleasure. A few diehards still insisted on calling her Lady Cassandra, but most had come to understand she preferred Mrs. Anders. She was a new woman in a new country who wanted to follow a new way. The blessing of her life was that she'd found perhaps the only man who would let her be herself.

Author's Notes

Usually, the seed that will eventually blossom into a story starts with characters who yammer in my head until I find a plot for them. *Indentured Hearts* began differently. In this case, I became fascinated by a hole in history—specifically the scarcity of information on indentured servants in Colonial America. Indentured servants were mentioned in my history classes, that's true, but this brief mention is all they ever got. I assumed, therefore, that they were few in number and had no lasting effect on the development of the American Colonies.

But historical holes always pique my curiosity, and I decided to do some research. Of course, I will cheerfully admit that any excuse to fill my magpie brain with useless facts is a good one. I love digging around in the past. And, as it turned out, research proved all my assumptions were wrong.

In the 17th century, nearly two-thirds of all European immigrants to America were indentured. Isn't that an amazing number? The importation of indentured servants declined in the 18th century, except in the mid-Atlantic colonies, where records for English immigrants for as late as 1773—1776 indicate over ninety percent arrived with their labor already contracted. Fleeing to the colonies in 1755, Lady Cassandra Spathe/Cassy Spade would not have been alone.

The bulk of the men and women who became indentured did so voluntarily. The cost of passage to the colonies was prohibitive for most who hoped to find a better life on a new continent. Promising their labor, typically for a period of between four and seven years, seemed a fair exchange for a fresh start.

Unfortunately, life in the colonies was often brutal and harsh. People accustomed to England's milder climate did not flourish in the heat and humidity of the American south. Over a quarter of those who came to America's shores as indentured servants did not live until their contracts' completion. Also, many contract owners treated these servants like chattel, whipping and abusing them. My fictional character, Sir Peyton Hyde, would not have been an aberration.

Not all who arrived bound for servitude were volunteers, however. Many were transported convicts. With the passing of the Transportation Act in 1718, England hoped to eliminate the criminal element by sending it elsewhere.

Before the American Revolution, this "elsewhere" was a destination in the American Colonies. Afterward, the dumping ground for undesirables became Australia.

Ascertaining the percentage of transported convicts in the throng of indentured servants is difficult, but it was undoubtedly substantial. In the sixty years between the passing of the Transportation Act and American Revolution, records indicate there were over 50,000 transportations from the courts of the Old Baily in London alone. It is not surprising that in 1769 Dr. Samuel Johnson referred to Americans as "a race of convicts."

Since convicts already existed outside of society's rules, they could be easily exploited, and their term of servitude often ran to fourteen years. Unlike the situation endured by African slaves, however, when a convict's indenture period was completed, he became a free member of society. Whether he then became a productive citizen or was cast adrift to live a life of crime depended on the individual.

Jason Anders' political goals were not beyond the realm of possibility, since former indentured servants did indeed serve in Virginia's House of Burgesses. George Taylor, one of the signers of the Declaration of Independence from Pennsylvania, came to the colonies as an indentured servant and ended up a wealthy ironmaster. Oddly enough, Jason had already assumed this profession before I discovered George Taylor's background. I love it when history walks hand-in-hand with my imagination.

Despite the prevalence of indentured servants as early colonists, family histories seldom mention an indentured ancestor. Unlike out Australian cousins, Americans like to ignore this possibility. But the next time someone tells you their progenitors came over on the Mayflower, you can be legitimately skeptical. These ancestors may have arrived as indentured servants on very different ships.

I hope you enjoyed reading Jason and Cassy's story as much as I enjoyed writing it. I currently have a number of other tales available that are set in the Regency and Victorian periods. It's obvious that I can't get my characters to live in the same century, much less form a series. But recently, Lieutenant Michaels has been yammering in my head, so as soon as I can find his plot, a series might be in the offing.

Please check out my other books at www.hannahmeredith.com or visit me at www.facebook.com/HannahMeredithAuthor. I love hearing from readers.

Thanks,
Hannah

Acknowledgements

In a slightly different form, *Indentured Hearts* was written in a month-long sprint, since I wanted to finish this novel in time to enter it in the RT/Brava Writing with the Stars Contest. To my delight, *Indentured Hearts* was one of the ten stories chosen for the competition.

What followed were months of excitement and, eventually, a second place finish, so I "just missed" getting a publishing contract with Kensington Brava. But the experience was priceless. I would, therefore, like to thank RT Book Reviews and Kensington Brava for sponsoring this contest. I was also lucky enough to be assigned a wonderful mentor, Bronwen Evans, who gave me invaluable suggestions. By chance, I was traveling in Bron's home country, New Zealand, during the contest period and got to spend a lovely day with her.

The real heroine of this decidedly crazed time, however, was my sister, Barbara Scott. Barbara cheerfully critiqued chapter after chapter after chapter, which arrived almost daily in her email inbox. I would not have been able finish the story without her incisive comments nor have done so well in the contest without her constant support. So, thanks B. for always being there for me.